## "ARE YOU ALWAYS SO STUBBORN?" SHE ASKED, WRAPPING HER ARMS AROUND HIS NECK.

"Always."

He carried her into the mud room, forgetting to catch the screen door before it slammed with a repeated *thump, thump, thump.*

"Shhh!" Charity put her finger to her lips, and then whispered, "There's no need to wake everyone up. Do you want Jack and Sam and my brother and sister-in-law, not to mention the kids, to rush into the hallway and see you carrying me up to my bedroom?"

He stopped halfway up the semi-dark stairwell. One black brow rose as he stared at her. "All I plan to do is look at your twisted ankle. Did you have something else in mind, something you think we need to hide?"

"No, but people have a tendency to jump to conclusions."

"Let them."

# PATTI BERG

*Something Wild*

AVON BOOKS

*An Imprint of* HarperCollins*Publishers*

14129506

AVON BOOKS
*An Imprint of* HarperCollins*Publishers*
10 East 53rd Street
New York, New York 10022-5299

To Charlotte Wager and the
lovely ladies at the Book Barn in Folsom—
for friendship, good times,
and yummy goodies on Thursday nights!

And, as always,
for Bob.

## Prologue

*Lead me not into temptation;*
  *I can find the way myself.*

RITA MAE BROWN

CHARITY WILDE STARED AT THE TUMBLER full of amber liquor, giving serious thought to abandoning the oath she'd made long ago, not to drink anything more than a celebratory glass—or maybe two—of champagne. History had proven that one or two sips of anything else would make her tipsy within minutes. Downing a few ounces of the hard stuff in one quick gulp would knock her off her barstool, and would probably kill every worry she'd ever had—for at least ten or twelve hours.

That, of course, was exactly what she wanted— a swift escape from her troubles. She wanted to forget she'd ever come to this afterhours dance club. She wanted to forget everything she'd seen, everything she'd done, but there was no way to forget that Josh Malloy had been shot, that his wife had been handcuffed and hauled off to jail, that the festive crowd had fled this nightspot fearing for their lives, or that she herself had been responsible for every dreadful thing.

"You causing trouble again?"

Charity's gaze stayed fixed on her glass of whiskey, even as strong fingers plucked it from her hand and shoved it halfway down the bar. Slowly her weary eyes trailed from the glass to the detective towering over her. He looked big, bad and annoyed. Logan Wolfe was playing his cop role to the hilt, when right now she wished he could just be her friend.

"Don't give me a hard time, Logan. It's been a bad night."

"Yeah, I can see that."

He turned to the bartender and ordered a cup of coffee, then pulled up a stool and sat beside her. "Mind telling me what happened?"

She'd witnessed a shooting, that's what happened. The guy she'd been with had nearly been murdered.

Still dazed, she stared at the flecks of dried blood still on her knuckles. How had she missed wiping those away? She grabbed a handful of cocktail napkins and scrubbed at the bloodstains, then sighed when they wouldn't disappear. How could an innocent evening out have turned into such a mess?

Hours earlier she'd been on stage, and Josh had been in the wings watching her and the cast of Sheer Ecstasy, making sure they didn't miss a step, that his exacting choreography was followed to a tee. It was the show's premier night, launching the grand reopening of a legendary Vegas hotel and night spot. They'd all been anxious and on edge, but the extravaganza went without a hitch.

Two hours ago she and Josh had come downtown to celebrate their success, then all hell broke loose.

"Charity?"

Logan's voice drew her back to the present. "Hmmm . . . ?"

"Are you going to tell me what happened?"

"I didn't do it."

"I already know that much."

He'd known no such thing five years ago, when they'd first bumped heads. He'd pegged her as a woman who looked and acted guilty—of something, anything—simply because she didn't want to talk about the armed robbery she'd witnessed. Logan had been in no mood to put up with a difficult woman, so he carted her off to the station and fired one question after another at her, before he realized she'd merely been an innocent bystander who wanted to mind her own business—for a change.

How they had become friendly after that was anyone's guess. Logan was a nice guy, but definitely not her type, not that her type existed in Vegas. She wasn't on the prowl for a boyfriend, or any man for that matter. She simply wanted to do her job and have fun occasionally with someone like Josh Malloy, a man she'd worked with off and on, a guy who'd suggested they party after the show. Some party this had turned out to be.

"Is Josh going to live?" she asked, clutching her hands around her black beaded purse, to keep her fingers from trembling.

Logan chuckled cynically, a pretty typical laugh for the detective. "He took a bullet in the arm and another grazed his temple. He could have walked out of here if he hadn't passed out."

"What about his wife?" Charity couldn't forget the anger in the woman's eyes, fury mixed with heartache, when she'd pulled the gun and fired. But she also felt an ounce of sympathy for the spurned spouse. "What's going to happen to her?"

"That's for the courts to decide."

The bartender slid a mug of coffee toward Logan. He shoveled in four heaps of sugar and clanked the spoon around the insides so violently Charity thought the cheap cup would shatter and he'd cut his hand. Hadn't she already seen enough blood to last a lifetime?

Logan pushed the cup in front of Charity. "Drink this. It'll warm you up."

She wrapped her hands around the mug, hoping some of the heat would seep into her body. She'd never been so cold. So troubled.

Logan took a notebook and pen out of his pocket. "All right, tell me what happened."

She sipped the coffee, concentrating on the scribbles Logan was making on the paper instead of looking at the blood on her hands. "I fixed Josh up with a blind date—"

"You always play matchmaker with married men?"

"I didn't know he was married. The guy's a choreographer and all he talked about was work. For heaven's sake, Logan, until he asked me to set him up, I thought he was gay."

Logan's impassive expression was hard to miss when he tore his gaze from the paper. She wanted to murder him for being so composed while she was a wreck. "Drink some more coffee," he said. "It'll calm you down."

"It's too sweet. Besides, I wanted whiskey, and you took it away from me."

A familiar grin touched his usually serious face. "That was rum, not whiskey. Either one would have killed a teetotaler like you."

"Las Vegas is trying to kill me. We've got this love-hate relationship going on, but right now hate's winning."

Logan shrugged, the sign of a burned-out man who didn't want to listen to the ravings of an on-the-verge-of-being-burned-out woman. He took the coffee from her hands and gulped down the sickly sweet brew himself.

"How do you stand it?" she asked. "Don't you get tired of seeing stuff like this every day of your life?"

"I tune it out." He jabbed the point of his pen into the paper. "So what happened after you fixed Malloy up with the blind date?"

"We came here after the show. Sheila—the lady who does my hair—said she'd meet us. How was

I to know she'd tell her clients she had a hot date with a choreographer, or that one of her clients was Josh's wife? This is a big town. Things like that just don't happen."

"Yeah, well, this is Vegas. Things that shouldn't happen usually do. You should know that better than anyone."

She should, but one bit of trouble kept bumping into the next. She should be used to it by now, but she wasn't.

Logan scratched a few notes on his pad. "So what happened next?"

"Sheila walked into the club. It was crowded, but you can't miss Sheila. She's got spiked orange hair, towers over everyone, and her smile lights up a room. Josh looked smitten the second he saw her waving at us, but he went pale when he saw the platinum blonde who walked in right behind her."

"His wife?"

Charity nodded.

"Did he say anything to her? Did he walk toward her?"

"I heard him say something like, 'I'm screwed,' but he didn't move, not even when she pulled the gun from her purse. He just stood there. Stunned."

"Did anyone try to stop her?"

"It happened so fast that I don't think anyone saw the gun but me and Josh. There was so much noise in here I'm surprised I could hear the shots, but they were loud, one after the other." Charity took a deep breath, wishing all the horror would go away as she described it to Logan.

"All I remember after that is Josh lying on the

floor. Sheila was screaming. People were running out the doors, trying to get away. And then I saw the blonde—Josh's wife—drop the gun and run toward him, saying she was sorry. So sorry."

"Is that it?"

Charity nodded. "The paramedics were here in minutes. Then the cops came and asked me all sorts of questions until you showed up."

Logan closed his notebook and stuck it back in the inside pocket of his coat. At last, the interrogation was over. He slugged down the last dregs of coffee, then tossed a few dollar bills on top of the bar. "You want a ride home?"

"No, thanks. My car's outside."

"Come on, then. I'll walk you to it."

Logan slipped off his coat and hung it over her shoulders as they made their way through the emptying club. Passersby gawked at them as they walked under the shimmering neon lights on Las Vegas Boulevard. They made quite a pair, her in stilettos, clicking on the concrete, and Logan, a shoulder harness and menacing gun hanging out for all to see.

Thank goodness he'd given her his coat, or her body would have been hanging out for all to see, too. She'd worn black lycra tonight. A tiny, shiny sheath that was too short, too low cut, and far too tight. It had been perfect for her festive mood; now she felt tired and cold and underdressed as they headed for the parking lot.

"Mind if I make a suggestion?" Logan said, taking the keys from her hand when they reached her well-used and under-loved Mustang.

"Go right ahead."

He unlocked and opened the door for her as she shrugged out of his coat and slid onto the chilled leather seat. Logan braced his hands on the top of the car and leaned toward her, hitting her with a brotherly half-smile as she put on her seat belt.

"Get out of Vegas. You don't fit in here, Charity. You never have and you never will."

She laughed. "The anxiety I'm feeling at the moment's only temporary, you know that. Besides, I've landed the best role of my life . . . so far. I've got a solo singing number, which is a first for me. And I'm the lead dancer. This is what I've dreamed of, Logan. This is why I came to Vegas."

"Yeah, you wanna be a star. You wanna be rich and famous like every other showgirl in this town. But you've got no life, and when you do try to have one, this kind of crap happens."

"Do you have a life?"

"I work and sleep. What more could a man want?"

"A wife? Kids?"

"You know me better than that."

"How about a vacation?" Charity plucked an engraved invitation to her sister-in-law's week-long family get-together from the passenger seat. "You like the great outdoors. Want an all-expenses-paid trip to the middle of nowhere?"

Logan tugged the fancy white stationery from her fingers and scrutinized the winter-wonderland photo of the Remington ranch on the front. He couldn't seriously be thinking about going, could he? To Wyoming? Where there would be nothing to do all day but count cows on the range and stare at endless miles of snow? A place that had no slot machines clanking all night, no traffic, no high-rises, no neon lights?

"If it was an all-expenses-paid fishing trip," Logan said, "I'd jump at the offer. Since family reunions aren't my thing . . . I'll pass." He handed back the card. "You plan on going?"

Charity laughed. "You don't really think I'd ask for time off at the start of a new show, do you?"

"What I think is that you work too hard and that you need a break."

"In my next life, maybe. Right now I need the money, and this is the best job I've ever had. I can't risk getting canned."

"Then I suppose you'll just stay here and become cynical like me." Logan leaned down and planted a friendly kiss on her brow. "Stay out of trouble, okay?"

Staying out of trouble was easier said than done. Still, Charity nodded as Logan pressed the automatic lock button and closed her door. It wasn't until she backed out of the parking spot and started to drive off, that she saw him shove his hands in his pockets and walk toward his car.

Logan was far too protective—a lot like her brother Max. More than once over the years he'd tried to get her to slow down, to take it easy. Logan meant well, but he didn't realize that a dedicated showgirl didn't ask for time off—not for anything—especially when she wanted to be at the top; especially when the dream of a lifetime was close to coming true.

She'd been reaching for the brightest star in the Vegas sky for a very long time, and in spite of a few setbacks, in spite of getting in the middle of trouble far too often, stardom was almost within her grasp.

No, she couldn't leave Las Vegas, not for the Remington's reunion, not for anything.

Charity's star plummeted from the sky the very next day.

She was fired.

Chapter 1

THE MARES WERE GONE. THOUSANDS UPON thousands of dollars in horseflesh had disappeared—trouble Mike Flynn didn't need or want.

He stood in the center of his boss's barn and stared at the stalls. Half a dozen of them were occupied by geldings, two by aging mares. But the stalls, where the black-and-white spotted horses had been stabled when they arrived from Memphis this morning, were empty.

So much for Jack Remington's birthday present to his wife. So much for Sam Remington's plan to breed Tennessee Walkers, at least with those two mares. That Jack would be furious about the missing horses went without saying. When he found out the mares had been spirited away by a renegade stallion, there would be hell to pay.

So much for Mike's good standing as a man who knew horses.

He slammed through the barn door and came to a stop in the corral where he'd left the wild mustang that afternoon. After years of chasing the beast, Mike had finally won, trapping the horse in a narrow box canyon and bringing him back to the ranch, kicking and screaming. But his victory had been short-lived.

Satan had escaped.

He should have known the corral rails weren't high enough to keep the stallion penned up, should have known that the dappled gray devil with the shaggy black mane would find a way to get to the mares. What a fool he'd been to let something wild get so close to something tame.

*Never again!*

Tucking his chin into the collar of his sheepskin coat for protection from the bitter February cold, Mike stared at the ranch house sitting on a gentle rise not more than a long stone's throw from the corral. Through the home's big picture window, he could see the party going on—a family reunion of sorts. No need to march up there now and spoil Jack's evening with bad news about the two prize Tennessee Walkers taking off for parts unknown.

No need to tell Jack that they could forget about inseminating the mares with the pricey sperm in the freezer, because, sure as shooting, Satan had already taken care of that procedure the old-fashioned way.

No need to let his friend and boss see his frustration over Satan's great escape, not to mention the way the blasted animal had flaunted his freedom, parading past Mike's cabin with newfound additions to his harem in tow. The mustang had been Mike's nemesis for years, but if Satan thought he'd won this time around, he had another think coming.

Mike heaved out an irritated sigh, his breath clouding before him as he eavesdropped on the Remington and Wilde get-together. Over the honky-tonk tune plunking away on the piano inside, he heard a woman's laugh, and for one instant he thought he'd see Jessie run out of the house and beckon him to join the fun, as she'd done so often. But his wife wasn't there.

Mike shoved his gloved hands deep inside his coat pockets and watched Jack Remington swing his wife, Samantha, around the living room, while Jack's sister Lauren and her husband, Max Wilde, danced up close and personal, ignoring the brisk rhythm of the music.

He and Jessie had danced that way a long time ago. Her heart had beat against his chest as they whispered about their future together—a future that had ended all too abruptly.

Mike watched Jack let go of his wife and swoop one of his twin babies into his arms, laughing as he raised the tiny bundle high in the air then gently cuddling the infant against his shoulder. Moments like this reminded Mike how much he and Jessie had wanted children, and made him wish he had sons and daughters to fill his home with laughter.

Many times he'd thought about marrying

again, because God knows he wanted to go to sleep at night and wake in the morning with a warm woman in his arms. But his chance for that kind of happiness had come and gone.

What woman in her right mind could be happy with a man who tossed and turned all night, who rarely slept, and when he did, woke in a feverish sweat, haunted by dreams and racked with guilt?

What woman would want to marry a man who'd killed his wife?

Anguish tightened around his throat, a noose that had been his constant companion for six years, one he could loosen at times but couldn't get rid of no matter how hard he tried. It stayed with him now, even though he turned away from the merriment he'd been observing through the window.

He headed for Crosby's cabin on the far side of the corral, just as he did most every night. The old codger had been a hired hand for sixty-some-odd years and could barely get around anymore. He was crotchety and set in his ways and wasn't always the best of company. But spending time with Cros was better than spending time alone with his thoughts.

Knocking his boot heels on the edge of the porch, he left clumps of snow and mud on the redwood steps and walked into the cabin without bothering to knock.

"Thought you were going up to the big house," Crosby hollered at Mike over the blaring noise on the TV.

"Changed my mind."

"Can't blame you. Too damn many people up there making too damn much noise." Cros aimed the remote control at the screen and turned the sound even louder. "There's some kind of fancy dessert on the counter. That chef Lauren married called it Easy Ridin' Mud Pie. Looks like cow dung to me, but you help yourself."

Rufus, the Border collie that had once been Jack's but had lately taken to hanging on Crosby's heels, settled his front paws on Mike's boots and waited patiently for attention, just as he did every night.

Mike shoved his gloves into his pocket then shrugged out of the heavy coat and hung it, along with his hat, on the rack just inside the door. A cool draft wafted past him and while he ruffled Rufus's silky fur he took a quick glance around the room to see if Crosby had opened one or more windows to let in the fresh air. Didn't matter to Cros if the weather was bitterly cold or not. He didn't like being cooped up and was bound and determined to let the outside in.

Mike cranked the thermostat up a couple of degrees, to keep his old friend healthy, then, falling into his usual routine, he headed for the kitchen. Reaching over the sink, he shoved the window closed and latched it before filling Rufus's bowl with dog food and checking out the dark chocolate concoction Max Wilde had cooked up. He wasn't big on chocolate, but he'd long ago tired of his own cooking and figured he might take some home and eat it in the middle of the night, when he woke from one of his dreams and spent the rest of the night prowling the house or immersed in paperwork.

Pulling the glass pot out of the coffee maker, he called out to Crosby, "You want some coffee?"

"That slop's been brewin' all day," Cros answered. "I already got enough stomach problems without dumpin' crap in it."

Mike was more concerned with Crosby's lungs and heart than his stomach, but he pushed his friend's rapid decline to the back of his mind and poured what looked like sludge into a mug, warming his hands on the cup as he headed for the living room.

"Gall darn it! Ain't nothin' worth watchin' no more." Crosby aimed the controller at the television and flipped rapidly from one channel to the next. "No *Gunsmoke*, no *Rawhide*, and I ain't about to watch no do-good angel or one of them game shows."

Mike ignored his cranky old friend. It didn't do much good commenting when Cros got on one of his tirades. At eighty-seven Crosby was deaf in one ear, pretended to be deaf in the other, and didn't much care for feedback anyway.

Considering how much time he spent with Cros, Mike imagined he'd end up just as ornery— not a particularly good state of mind for a man in his profession. Preachers weren't supposed to be ornery, or bitter, or racked with guilt and regret, so he tried not to be any of those things on Sunday or when he ministered to his flock. A ranch manager—his other job—could be all those things and more, and tonight Mike allowed himself to be purebred cowboy.

He took his usual place on the faded brown plaid couch, plopped his boots on the battered oak coffee table, and stared at the worn leather, a pursuit he found to be far more stimulating than the wrestling Crosby had decided to watch.

When monotony set in, he crossed to the big rock hearth and stirred the embers on one lone log until fire leaped about, then added more wood. Inhaling the fresh scent of pine, he rubbed his hands in front of the flames and wiped away what remained of the chill. If only he could wipe away everything else that bothered him so easily.

Heading for the window, he looked out across the yard to see if Satan had reappeared, something he half expected the stallion to do just to grate on his nerves, but Satan was nowhere around. Maybe the horse had given up for the night, just as the occupants of the ranch house were doing. It was well past ten and Mike watched one light after another go out until the house was as still and quiet as the weather outside.

It was a night just like this when his wife had died—bitterly cold with no hint of wind. The skies were clear and the moon and stars had brightened the prairie. But a blizzard threatened. So had Jessie's death.

The grief that had torn him apart six years ago caught hold of his thoughts again, and even though he willed the nightmare away, it stayed with him. He hated it when those memories returned, usually at night, usually in bed when he was alone and lonely. He hated the torment, the guilt.

"Somethin' troublin' you?"

Mike didn't turn from the window to answer his friend. He didn't want Crosby to see his anguish. It was better to let Cros think he was worried about the storm the weatherman had predicted and how many cows would die when the blizzard hit. "I've gotten to where I hate nights like this."

"Then you'd better hightail it out of Wyoming, cuz freezin' your ass off comes with the territory."

After thirty-five years of living on the prairie, Mike knew that full well. He couldn't tell Cros that it wasn't the cold he hated, but the calm before the storm, the way the weather had been while Jessie lay in a hospital bed, so still, so small, kept alive only by a roomful of machines.

A log shifted on the grate, jolting him from painful memories, and from the corner of his eye he saw sparks fly out of the hearth and turn to ash before floating to the hardwood floor. Behind him he heard the heavy thud of Crosby dropping the footrest on his recliner, heard the cheering and catcalls of the wrestling match fade from clamorous to a muffled hum as Cros lowered the volume on the TV.

"Need some help?" Mike asked, as Cros worked his way out of the chair.

"Nope. Don't need help till I'm dead and you

have to plant me in the ground. And I suspect that ain't gonna happen this winter."

"Is that a promise?"

"You know I don't make promises I can't be sure of keepin'."

Crosby hobbled across the room, stopping beside a weathered bookcase filled with ragged paperbacks by Louis L'Amour and Zane Grey. A few bottles of whiskey and an assortment of mix-and-match glasses sat on top. "Want a drink?" He screwed the lid off a bottle of Wild Turkey and poured the liquor into a tumbler.

"No thanks."

"Whiskey cures a lot of ills. Course," Cros said, tilting the glass to his mouth and taking a long swallow, "a good woman's what you really need. Me, I'm long past the days where a woman— good or bad—can get a rise out of me. You hang out with this old guy much longer and your pecker won't work, either."

Mike grinned, glad that Crosby had given him something to laugh about. Of course, he wasn't going to tell Cros that he had no doubts whatsoever that his *pecker* was in perfectly fine working order. He was celibate, not dead.

Cros leaned an arthritic hip on top of a low bookcase and glared at Mike. "I hear Fay Atkinson's got a niece who's lookin' for a husband."

"Yeah, I've heard that, too. Every Sunday morning, as a matter of fact."

"Why don't you go out with her?"

"Since when did you start playing matchmaker?"

"Maybe I want some peace and quiet around here at night."

"Just say the word and I'll stop coming by."

"Then you'd be lonely." Crosby took a gulp of whiskey. "So, what do you think?"

"About what?"

"Fay's niece."

"Not interested."

"I seen her once or twice. Pretty young thing."

"She's nineteen. I'm thirty-five."

"All the more reason for going out with her. I heard stories about things those young fillies do these days. Things that could make a feller blush if he weren't enjoying it so much. Ain't like the old days when a man had to do all the work."

"Still not interested."

Crosby's bushy white brows knit together, deep in thought. "Is it the woman you ain't interested in, or sex? I always assumed a man's a man, even if he *is* a minister. But maybe I been wrong about that all these years."

Mike chuckled. "You aren't wrong."

"Well, that's a relief." Cros swigged down the rest of his drink, his eyes narrowing as a new thought hit him. "What about that Vegas showgirl? Lauren's sister-in-law?" Cros rubbed his fingers over his grizzled beard. "I caught an eyeful of her when she got here this afternoon. Now there's a woman who could get a rise out of a man."

Mike hadn't thought about Charity Wilde in a year. Well, maybe she had crossed his mind a time or two, especially after he'd heard the woman would be staying at the ranch for a week.

Call it blasphemy, but Mike had a feeling the long-legged beauty could raise the dead.

And he was going to stay far, far away from her. It had taken him six years to accept the fact that— no matter what he wanted or needed—he was going to spend the rest of his life alone. He didn't need or want to stare temptation in the face.

"I'm not interested in Charity Wilde."

"Yeah? Well, I seen you ogling her at Lauren's wedding, and you sure as hell looked interested then."

"She's a showgirl and I'm a minister. Ain't no way the two of us could ever fit together, even if I was interested."

Crosby shook his head. "You make too damn many excuses. Plumbing's plumbing, boy. The way I see it, what you got and what she's got could fit together right nicely, given half a chance."

Mike wasn't about to touch that bit of wisdom and thankfully Crosby didn't offer any more. Apparently Cros figured his words were wasted on a minister, so he dumped another healthy inch of whiskey into his glass and limped back to his recliner, ending their conversation by turning the sound up extra loud on the wrestling match.

Again Mike concentrated on the window, watching for Satan, but seeing a vision of Charity Wilde instead.

He hadn't ogled her at Lauren's wedding, he just hadn't been able to take his eyes off the woman's man-killer body. But he hadn't been alone. Every man and most of the women at the reception had watched her. She must have stood six-foot-two or -three in the spiked heels she'd been wearing, and he'd never seen a dress so tight, not to mention so short, so red, or so low-cut, showing off every delectable attribute of her sleek and shapely body.

Charity Wilde was temptation personified, a woman who could easily beguile a man with her sparkling hazel eyes and luscious lips. Oh, yeah, he remembered her lips and her hips and her legs.

And then there were her breasts. More than a handful. Firm. Round. A whole lot of her firm round breasts had been spilling out of her barely-there dress.

He definitely remembered her breasts.

Charity Wilde made him think erotic thoughts no minister in his right mind should be thinking.

For sanity's sake, he had to stay away from her. The woman was far too wild for any man, especially for a man who'd sworn off women and relationships and sex.

Besides, he already had his hands full with one creature that needed to be tamed.

Chapter 2

NOWHERE WASN'T HALF AS BAD AS CHAR-
ity had expected. It was flat, barren, and freeze-
your-fanny-off cold, but at night you could see
the stars. Millions upon millions of stars. They
didn't exist in Las Vegas, not the celestial kind,
anyway. They were obscured by dazzling neon
lights and skyscraping hotels.

Until tonight, Charity had almost forgotten
what real stars looked like; for the longest time,
she'd thought they only appeared on stage—the
place she longed to see her own star shine.

*Someday.*

Wrapping a soft wool scarf tightly about her
neck, she buried her chin into its comforting
warmth and slipped away from the ranch house,
the heavy boots Sam Remington had loaned her

crunching through the slush as she made her way toward the barn and one of the corrals.

Her fingers itched to hold a pair of leather reins, to take a midnight ride on the spirited dappled-gray stallion she'd seen earlier in the day. But the corral was empty now.

As she brushed frost off the top rail and sat atop the paddock, the memory of her first midnight ride came back to her.

The weather at summer camp was so darn hot, that she'd snuck out of her cabin in the middle of the night, saddled a lively mare and rode down to the lake for a quick skinny-dip. But she'd gotten caught.

Her father's face was red with anger when he arrived at the camp the next day. He'd lectured— not for the first time, of course, because Marine Corps Chaplain Jedediah Mattingly loved to lecture—repeatedly telling her that he didn't appreciate having to leave his work or having to drive seventy-two miles through the desert to pick her up. And then came the lecture about her willfulness and her propensity for getting in trouble.

From the all too familiar look on her dad's face, she'd known there would never be another trip to camp.

And there hadn't been.

Chaplain Mattingly had a mission in life. He fully intended to save the sinners of the world. To his dismay, the one sinner he couldn't save was his adopted daughter, no matter how hard he tried.

It wasn't his fault. She hadn't wanted to be saved; she'd just wanted to dance, sing, and exchange her mundane life for a good time in Vegas. In spite of recent events, there had been a lot of good times and there would definitely be more; she refused to dwell on the bad.

The high pitch of a horse's neigh and the pawing of hooves against the frigid earth interrupted her thoughts. She listened intently, her head jerking toward the barn where she thought the sound had come from. Had a coyote gotten inside? Was something else disturbing the horses? She jumped down from the railing, missing a mud puddle by inches, and cautiously peered inside the dimly lit barn.

A tall, broad buckskin with an uncinched saddle on his back looked up at her for a moment, then went back to his peaceful grazing on a pile of hay. There were soft stirrings from the other stalls, but no sign at all of a frightened horse.

Back outside she again climbed the corral and looked out across the snow-dusted prairie but saw nothing. No horses. No coyote. No antelope. Only sagebrush, outbuildings, and endless miles of flat, moonlit land.

But once more she heard the whinny. Heard the crunch of gravel. And then she saw it. The massive stallion she'd seen earlier peered around the corner of the barn. Its dark brown eyes were wary, and as the horse inched out of its hiding place she got a better look at its sleek, dark gray body mottled with white hair and a shaggy black mane that almost shimmered in the moonlight.

She wondered if the horse had escaped from the barn or from one of the outlying pastures. She wondered if something had spooked the creature, because its eyes were wide and panicky as it stared at her.

"Come here, boy." She held her hand out, coaxing the beast toward her. "I won't hurt you." The animal reared up on his hind legs, a vision of overwhelming strength, and when his front hooves hit the ground, she could feel the vibration through the soles of her boots.

*Hmmm, a show of power.* Typical male, wanting her to know he wasn't afraid of her or any woman, that he was merely out for something he thought she could provide.

"I don't have any carrots or apples." She held her gloved palms upright so he could check them out. "Of course, you don't look like the carrot or apple type. What do you prefer? Sugar? A pretty little filly?"

He pawed the ground with one front hoof.

"So"—she laughed—"you like the ladies." Definitely a typical male.

With her hands still stretched before her, the horse took a few cautious steps forward. Something was worrying him, in spite of his burst of bravado.

"What are you afraid of?" She kept her voice low. Calm. "Being fenced in? Someone tossing a rope around your neck?"

His nostrils flared as he studied her, guarded, obviously distrustful of human beings.

Charity leaned casually against the corral, thinking the stallion might come closer if she gave him time to realize she wasn't a threat. Minutes seemed to tick by as she stood silent and still, her only movement the calm rise and fall of her chest. Then, ever so slowly, the animal came within inches of her, his hot breath fogging the air. He was scared, but far too curious to leave.

For the first time, she noticed the scars on his back and sides. Horrendous, jagged scars that slashed every which way across his hide. Had he been beaten by his owner? Were they scars won during battle with other horses?

She wanted to touch him, to show him what gentleness could be. "I won't hurt you," she said, taking a short step away from the corral, moving her hand toward the animal's muzzle. Frightened, the horse jerked its head, but Charity didn't back away. "Easy, boy."

He stilled and at last allowed her to touch him. His coat was cool, shaggy, and thick to keep him warm in the below-freezing winters that were so much a part of this country. He trembled beneath her fingers, but he didn't run, didn't pull away.

"I've got the feeling you don't belong here," she whispered, curving her palm gently over the animal's jaw.

"You're right," came a man's voice from the

darkness, a deep, velvety voice that made the horse lurch. "Take your hand off Satan and back away slowly. He's as wild as they come and if you make the wrong move, there's no telling what he might do."

The man's words didn't frighten her any more than the horse. In spite of his caution, she wasn't about to back away after spending so much time winning Satan's confidence.

"Thanks for the warning, but Satan and I are getting along just fine." She smoothed her hand over Satan's neck and chest, even when he twisted around to glare at the man stepping into the light shining down from the barn.

Charity glared at the man, too. "He's not going to cause any trouble unless *you* get too close."

The cowboy's face was nearly obscured by a black hat tilted low on his brow and the upturned collar of his sheepskin coat, but she could almost feel the iciness of his glare, chilling her in a way the frigid air couldn't. It was obvious he didn't like disobedience; and she was making it clear right off the bat that she didn't like to take orders, especially from strangers. She refused to be controlled ever again.

The cowboy took a slow step toward her. "He could kill you quite easily if he decided to rear again and accidentally clipped you with his hoof."

"That's not going to happen."

The stranger shook his head, but it wasn't his frustration that bothered her, it was the way he fingered the knot on the heavy rope he was holding.

"He's giving you a false sense of security," the man said. "But don't let him fool you. He doesn't like people."

"What he doesn't like is the thought of being tied up."

"You know that after you've been here all of what . . . six hours?"

It was one thing having him keep tabs on the horses, but she didn't like him keeping tabs on her. "I've been here most of the day, not that it's any of your business."

"I run this place. Everything that goes on here is my business. If you get killed, it'll be on my hands not to mention my conscience."

"There's no need for you to worry about me. I've spent a lot of time around horses." No need to tell him it had just been those few days at camp. "I've been on my own a long time, too, and I know perfectly well how to take care of myself."

He laughed cynically. "Okay, so you're tough. Is that supposed to make you an expert on wild horses?"

"He came to me, not you. Obviously there's something about me that he likes and something about you that rubs him the wrong way. I'm no expert," she said, aiming her eyes at the man's gloved hands, "but I'd say it all has to do with that rope you're holding."

"He doesn't like corrals and no he doesn't like ropes, but he took two mares away from here tonight. Two mares I've got to get back, and the only way I'm going to do that is if you move out of the way and let me get this rope around him."

"Why don't you just let him go? See if he leads you to the mares?"

"Because I've been chasing him for more years than I can count. Because he'd lead me straight to Purgatory if he could." The man was getting angry and the loop he was building was getting bigger and bigger by the second. "I've got a perfect shot at Satan right now, so do me a favor—move out of the way."

She really didn't like being ordered around. And she didn't like the thought of the stallion being roped and penned up, especially when it was wild. *Oh, no. Wild things were meant to be free.*

It was probably one of the most insane things she'd ever done—and she'd done a lot of foolish things—but she twisted her fingers through Satan's shaggy mane and with all the grace and agility of a born dancer, threw her long leg over the mustang's back.

The stallion reared, his angry cry ripping through the still night air.

She'd made a mistake. A big one.

The horse started to buck, and she clasped her arms tightly about its neck. Satan twisted and turned and tried like hell to get her off his back, but she wasn't about to get thrown, not into the steel railings of the corral.

"You trying to kill yourself?" She heard the man's angered shout, but she couldn't see his face, couldn't even yell for help, because Satan tore across the prairie as if the hounds of hell were at his back.

"Damn fool woman!" Mike muttered under his breath as he raced for his horse, a golden brown buckskin with black points—his mane, tail, and legs—grazing on the hay he'd tossed on the barn floor hours before. Tightening the cinch, he swung into the saddle and took off after the woman.

A few hours ago he'd told himself that Charity Wilde would be trouble if he got too close to her, and his reasoning had never been more correct. He couldn't remember the last time he'd sworn, but he had the feeling the showgirl was going to be his ruin.

The frigid air bit at his face as he sped across the prairie, but his anger kept him warm. He had ledgers to go over, a sermon to write, and the last thing he wanted to do at midnight was chase an uncontrollable woman. He and Buck had already had a workout when they'd caught Satan earlier in the day. They were both tired, and Mike knew full well that right now his gelding was no match for the stallion.

But if Charity Wilde thought she could outrun him, she was dead wrong.

Buck seemed to have gotten a second wind and was sprinting over the frozen ground, skirting sagebrush, rocks, and prairie dog holes with ease, as if he was on a well-groomed racetrack. They were gaining on Satan and the woman, so close now that Mike could see Charity's heavy braid and her wool scarf flying behind her, could see her legs clenched against the stallion's sides, just as her arms wrapped tightly about his neck.

As much as her arrogance and foolhardiness annoyed him, he couldn't help but appreciate the way she rode. Butt tight against Satan's back. Not much bounce. She looked fine from behind. Real fine. There weren't many women who could race a horse bareback, without means of a bridle or even a lead rein. And never in his life had he seen a woman—or a man for that matter—stay on a wild stallion for more than a handful of seconds.

How much longer could she hold on? The woman was maddening—sexy and beautiful, but infuriating just the same. Still, he didn't want her hurt, and Satan could throw her at any moment.

He'd been right when he'd told Charity the mustang was dangerous. He'd seen Satan in battle, had seen the stallion kick, and bite, and run off other stallions if they got too close to his harem. There was no telling what the devil was capable of doing—and Mike didn't want the beast doing anything that could hurt the first person who'd ever climbed on his back.

They were working their way to the edge of a butte that dropped abruptly into a dried up riverbed. It could be dangerous getting close to Satan, but Mike had no other choice. He had to get Charity off of the stallion's back.

He dug his heels into Buck's flanks and the horse bound forward, moving to Satan's right side, trying to ward the mustang away from the rocky ravine. He was near enough now that he could see fear in Charity's eyes, but even through the veil of fright he saw excitement.

*The crazy woman was enjoying herself!*

Suddenly she disappeared from his line of vision. Buck had raced forward, but Satan had come to a dead stop, trying to outsmart him. Mike spun his mount around just in time to see the stallion rear, its front hooves beating against the air as if he were doing battle with some unseen force.

Mike rode hard toward the mustang, needing to get to Charity, but he was too late. She flew from the stallion's back and in an instant was lying on the hard, icy earth—and Satan disappeared, again.

Mike yanked his gelding to a stop, jumped from Buck's saddle, and ran to Charity's side. She was flat on the ground, her head mere inches from a lethal boulder. She wasn't moving, and a prayer for her safety sped through his mind.

Dropping to his knees, he bent over her, slipping a hand under her scarf and gently touching a finger to the pulse point in her throat. Her skin was cool, her pulse strong.

His own pulse quickened. Every muscle in his body tightened. Charity Wilde wasn't only trouble, she was danger in the worst sense, a temptress who could weave a spell around him or any man, even when she was lying deathly still.

Her eyes opened slowly, and even though he was wary of touching her again, he stroked a damp lock of hair from her cheek, his fingers weaving behind her neck to pillow her head.

It was the right thing to do. The only thing to do.

Then again, it was sheer madness.

A soft smile curved her lips. "I'm not dead, am I?"

She was going to be fine; however, he wasn't sure about his own state of mind or body. Leaving right now would be the safest and sanest thing for him to do. But he couldn't leave. It wouldn't be right.

On top of that and most bothersome of all, he didn't want to leave.

"If you don't answer me," she said, "I'll never know if I'm dead or alive. I'll just think you're some figment of my imagination, like the rocks underneath me."

"You're alive," he muttered.

Alive. And hot. So hot that she made his blood boil.

"Thank goodness." She drew in a deep breath. "My life was flashing by me as Satan was running, and I realized there were a lot of things I still wanted to do before I died."

"Pull another stunt like riding a wild stallion and more than likely you *will* end up dead."

The muscles tightened in her jaws. "I don't need a lecture."

"Obviously you do." He grinned as he lightly stroked away the mud and slush that had splattered her cheeks when she fell.

"Look," she fired back, jerking upright, "I . . . I . . ." Agony swept across her face, stilling her words as her hands slid down the length of her leg and wrapped around her boot-covered ankle.

"You all right?"

"Yesssss." She squeezed out the word through clenched teeth.

"Here, let me look at that."

She cuffed his hand away. "It's fine."

The woman was ornerier than he was!

He sat back on his haunches and glared at her. "All right, since your ankle's fine, get up. It's cold out here and I want to go home."

He thought she'd give in. Figured for sure that she'd tell him she'd never been in so much pain in her life and ask for help. But he should have known that Charity Wilde would do just the opposite of most women.

Putting her weight on her left foot, she pushed up from the ground. She could stand, but could she walk?

She stared at Buck, grazing a good twenty feet away on a few tufts of near frozen prairie grass, then took a tentative step, pain evident in the stiffness of her body. She didn't give into it, though, she just kept on limping toward the horse, stopping only when Buck jerked his head up because she'd gotten too close.

The horse didn't like women. He never had and he never would. Even Mike had disregarded women of late. But he liked this one—too much, he feared, but only because she amazed him. She was strong and willful and obstinate—too much like him. He wouldn't ask for help, either. Never had; never would.

Buck moved a few feet away from Charity, but she didn't give up; she walked those few feet, latched on to Buck's saddle horn, and lifted her left foot toward the stirrup. A big mistake.

Buck decided he wanted to nibble on fresher grass and ambled slowly toward a patch in the distance. Still, Charity clung to the horn and let the horse drag her with him. When the gelding stopped, she again tried to put her foot in the stirrup.

"What do you think you're doing?" Mike rubbed his day-old stubble as he strode toward her.

"I'm getting on your horse so we can head back to the ranch."

"Buck's not crazy about women. I'm the only one he lets on his back."

He was afraid she'd try getting on the gelding just to spite him, but her left foot dropped back down to the ground.

"Then I'll walk."

She limped away from Buck and, as he should have expected, she headed in the wrong direction.

Trouble. The woman was definitely trouble.

He let her go about ten feet, waiting for her to stop, to ask for help, but the fool woman never did. Why she was so mad at him was anybody's guess. That she was going to be even angrier in another moment went without saying.

Trudging toward her and without asking permission—which Mike knew would be flat-out denied—he swept Charity up in his arms. Just as he expected, her eyes narrowed.

"What do you think you're doing?"

"Taking you home."

"I can walk."

Dump her, he told himself. Just drop her right here and now, get on Buck's back and ride away. He gave it serious thought, but he marched toward his horse instead.

Buck glared at Mike. It was late, he'd been ridden too long and too hard all day, and the horse obviously wasn't thrilled about being ridden by two people instead of one, especially when one of those people was a woman.

But Buck stood motionless while Mike sized up the situation, trying to figure out how he was going to get both of them up on the saddle. It wasn't easy—he reckoned nothing was ever easy with this woman—but he hefted her up until she straddled Buck's withers, then he swung into the saddle and tugged the long-legged hellion into his lap.

"Is this necessary?" She unceremoniously moved his gloved hands from her waist and dropped them on the saddle horn. "I could ride behind you."

"It's freezing out here. I'm not dressed as warm as I ought to be on a night like this, and you'll make a good windbreak while we ride back to the ranch."

He expected a retort that never came. Instead, she struggled a bit, wedging her bottom between his crotch and the saddle horn. Riding this way was going to be one of the hardest things he'd ever done, but he gritted his teeth, grabbed hold of the reins, and turned Buck toward home.

"You know," he said, when she wiggled again, "if you'll quit fighting me and just stay good and close, you'll get warm, too."

She twisted around until her narrowed eyes found his. It looked like a slap was coming, but the harshness in her face softened slowly and a sparkle replaced the animosity in her hazel eyes.

"This isn't any more comfortable for you than it is for me, is it?"

"Nope."

"You'd rather be sitting in this saddle all by yourself, right?"

"Right."

"I'm being a pain in the neck. Right?"

The discomfort was centered elsewhere, far south of his neck, but he'd never admit it. "I'll survive."

She smiled. "Thank you."

"You're welcome."

She shifted in the saddle, her bottom nuzzling firmly against him, and with great effort he turned his concentration from her derrière, and the way it rubbed against his zipper, toward the sermon he needed to write.

Maybe he'd preach about celibacy when Sunday morning rolled around. There were one or two teenagers in the congregation who needed a lecture on that topic. Considering his current state of mind and discomfort he needed that lecture, too, but he figured his elder parishioners would dish out their own lecture after the service, chastising him for speaking about such an unspeakable subject in the Lord's house, on Sunday morning to boot.

Charity wiggled again, and he forced his mind from sermons and celibacy to the men who'd applied for the horse trainer job he'd advertised. He'd interviewed four long-time cowboys and none of them had what he'd been looking for—an innate horse sense, a gentleness he himself didn't possess. As usual, he expected a lot, and it frustrated him to think that he'd never find anyone who lived up to his standards.

He shifted in the saddle, looking for a more comfortable position. When that failed, he forced himself to think about the blizzard the weathermen kept predicting. Yeah, a major disaster was just what he needed to keep his mind off Charity. Of course, she was a tempest herself.

And as much as he tried, he couldn't help but think about her sweet curvy bottom or just how good it felt nestled between his legs.

She scooted a little closer, and he bit back a groan when she twisted in the saddle and faced him. "I'm Charity Wilde. I'd shake your hand but a formal introduction seems a little redundant now." A slight smile touched her lips. Luscious lips that matched her luscious body.

"Mike Flynn," he said, aiming his gaze at the

wide-open stretch of prairie in front of them. But even though he was looking straight ahead, he couldn't miss the frown forming on Charity's face, and then her wide-eyed surprise when she realized they'd crossed paths once before.

"The minister?"

"That's right."

Her frown deepened. "We've met, haven't we?"

"I suppose you could call it that." He'd thought about asking her to dance the night of Lauren's wedding, thought about holding a woman close for the first time since Jessie had died. But Charity had walked right past him and latched on to another man.

They were sitting so close right now that he could feel her gulping down her embarrassment, could feel her entire body tense. Without a doubt, everything she'd said and done that night was coming back to her.

"I thought you lived in Florida. I thought you'd been hired to perform Max and Lauren's wedding, that no one would ever see you after that."

"You thought wrong. I live here."

She swallowed again. "You didn't hear what I said to Max and Lauren at their reception, did you?"

Sarcasm wasn't his usual style, but he hit her with it anyway. "You mean about not liking ministers?"

"I don't think those were my exact words."

"Close enough."

"I suppose you're going to hold that against me?"

He wasn't a vindictive man. It went against his nature, but Charity didn't need to know that.

"Maybe." He grinned. "Maybe not."

## Chapter 3

ACTUALLY, IT WASN'T MINISTERS CHARITY
didn't like. It was the *preaching*. The moralizing.
The lecturing. And most of all, the constraints.
Her father's hell-fire-and-brimstone sermons
weren't just for show. He didn't espouse one
thing on Sunday and something else during the
week. Oh, no. Chaplain Mattingly ruled his
household strictly. His word was gospel and
heaven forbid anyone disobey.

Pastor Flynn seemed to see things in the same
light. He felt that wild horses needed to be con-
strained and controlled; so did wild women,
which meant she and the good pastor were
doomed to butt heads. Too bad, because he was
the most devilishly handsome creature she'd ever
encountered.

He didn't look like a preacher, nor did he look like the kind of man who could stand at a pulpit—or anywhere for that matter—and lecture about right and wrong, about righteousness, morality, or the sins of the flesh. He looked and acted like he could break every commandment except "Thou shalt not kill"—but then, there had been a few moments tonight when she thought he might be capable of doing just that.

He had an amazing way of controlling his temper—there was that control factor again—but she could see it seething beneath his surface. There had been no doubt at all that he was hotter than hell when she stood between him and Satan, and ready to explode after Satan got away. She figured Mike could easily strangle her for instigating that fiasco.

But here he was taking care of her, in spite of her waywardness. She supposed that was the ecclesiastical thing to do, but there was no telling what was going through his mind. He probably assumed she was a trollop, a no-account showgirl who'd go to hell for sure. Her father and mother thought that, in spite of their love for her, so why shouldn't he?

She let go of her frustration on a sigh, knowing full well that it didn't do any good to brood over the disdain her parents felt for her profession, a career that meant everything to her.

"Something troubling you?"

For the past ten or fifteen minutes she'd been staring at the moonlit prairie, but now she twisted about and looked at the man whose legs she sat between.

Mike Flynn not only controlled his temper, but he seemed to have extraordinary control over his anatomy as well. She'd danced with men who had no interest in her at all, but let her breast brush over them or her fingers accidentally sweep between their thighs, and they'd pop to attention, hard and ready. Most of the time the reaction didn't last—but it happened.

Not to Mike, of course. The good pastor was too self-restrained for that. Thank goodness. She'd long ago tired of men who put the make on her, thinking she was a tease, that she was easy, when she was anything but. Mike, of course, was above all that, which pleased her to no end. She had enough other sins to contend with without being indirectly responsible for a minister's downfall.

"Are you going to stare at me or answer my question?"

She frowned as she struggled to remember what he'd asked, and slowly it came back to her. "Of course I'm not troubled." It was only a small white lie. Her thoughts about him troubled her, but she didn't think she'd get struck by lightning for fibbing about that, not now, especially when she was riding with a man of God. "I was just wondering how long it would be before we get back to the ranch."

"It's less than a mile from here. Shouldn't take long." He watched her for a moment, a question still in his eyes as if he didn't believe her response, and then his gaze went back to the snowy prairie, all show of concern gone as quickly as it had come.

Somewhere in the distance she could hear a coyote howl and not too far ahead of them she saw a small herd of antelope racing across the prairie, the patches of white on their bodies illuminated in the moonlight. It was peaceful out here. Quiet. And far more comfortable than she ever would have imagined, even though the saddle horn was rubbing her intimately and the icy cold had made her fingers and toes begin to burn.

A brisk breeze blew across them, carrying with it bits of sage, sand, and ice that stung her face. She shivered, and Mike's arms tightened around her, drawing her against the warmth of his chest, his hands and the reins resting just under her breasts. Their bodies melded together and an unfamiliar heat spread through her veins.

If this kept up, it was quite possible the good pastor might contribute to *her* downfall.

"How's the ankle?" he asked, his breath hot against the chilled skin of her ear.

Buck's gait had been so smooth and easy and Mike's hold on her had been so gentle but strong, that she'd forgotten the pain. It hadn't left her completely, but Mike had made sure her feet—not his—were in the stirrups to support her twisted ankle.

She tilted her head to answer him—to thank him—and her lips brushed against his bristled cheek. This time it wasn't warmth that spread through her but a jolt so electrifying that her whole body tingled. "I think it's going to be okay," she said, but she wasn't certain about the rest of her.

"I'll take a look at it when we get back, just to make sure."

That's all she needed. It was one thing for Mike to hold her when she was wearing layer upon layer of clothing, but she had no idea how she could survive the touch of his bare hands on her naked flesh. This man could, quite possibly, batter down her resolve to remain a virgin.

Good heavens! She shouldn't be having such thoughts about a minister, especially a minister who was staring straight ahead at the prairie, who spoke with little emotion, who couldn't possibly be feeling any of the things that she was feeling.

Her entire body was brimming with nervous energy. She'd been quiet too long. She'd sat in his lap too long. Their conversation was too staid. She had to lighten things up or she'd explode.

She took a deep breath and blurted out the first thing to come to her. "So, you're a cowboy, a minister, and now I find out that you're a healer of sore ankles, too. Is there anything you can't do?"

"Can't sing. Don't dance too well." He shrugged. "Other than that, I'm perfect."

Beneath his black stubble she could see a dimple at the left of his mouth, a dimple made even more pronounced by his off-kilter grin. His piercing green eyes twinkled. Mike was right—he was close to perfect except, of course, for his streak of bossiness.

"How much do you really know about fixing twisted ankles?"

"I've delivered foals and calves and patched up more wounded cows and horses than I care to count. One ankle shouldn't be much of a problem."

"I'm not a horse or a cow."

His grin widened as he aimed his eyes toward her. "I've noticed."

Mike's broad smile and his comment flickered quickly through her mind as the ranch house came into view. He dug his heels into Buck's flanks and the horse shot off as if he were more than anxious to find a pile of hay and to get rid of the burdens on his back.

Charity was just as anxious to get her bottom out from between Mike's legs. It was a feeling she wasn't the least bit accustomed to.

It was a feeling she liked too darn much.

The house was dark except for the light at the back porch. She wished Max or Jack or somebody were awake to help her up the stairs and into bed so she wouldn't have to put any pressure on her ankle, but it had to be well after midnight and she seriously doubted anyone would have climbed out of the warm beds they'd retired to a few hours ago.

Somehow she'd get to her bedroom on her own. Mike had done enough already, and considering the odd—lustful—feelings she was having about the man, she figured she'd be much better off going upstairs alone.

Apparently Mike had a differing opinion on how she should get to bed. No sooner had he brought Buck to a halt, but he swung down from the horse and pulled her into his arms.

"I can walk now," she protested, but he didn't loosen his hold.

"I'll carry you."

"It's really not necessary."

"I'll be the judge of that."

"Look, Mike," she said as he opened the squeaky screen door, "if you're doing this because you want to show me how heroic you are . . . well, I've already seen the moon glinting off your shining armor, and nothing could be brighter than that halo you wear."

"I'm not a hero, I don't have a halo, and the only reason I'm carrying you is so you don't fall down the stairs and break your neck, just to prove that you can walk all on your own."

"Are you always so stubborn?" she asked, giving in to his protests far too easily and wrapping her arms around his neck.

"Always."

He carried her into the mud room, forgetting to catch the screen door before it slammed with a repeated thump, thump, thump.

"Shhh." She put a finger to her lips, and then whispered, "There's no need to wake everyone up. Do you want the whole house—including the kids—to rush into the hallway and see you carrying me to my bedroom?"

He stopped halfway up the semidark stairwell. One black brow rose as he stared at her. "All I plan to do is look at your ankle. Did you have something else in mind, something you think we need to hide?"

"No, but people have a tendency to jump to conclusions."

"Let them."

He continued his climb and she would have struggled, but she didn't want to accidentally kick the wall or make any unnecessary noise. She'd been branded a tramp on more than one occasion. The accusations were false, completely and utterly untrue, but she didn't want her family and newfound friends thinking she was a harlot, to have them think she was leading their preacher down the road to heathenism.

"Where's your bedroom?" Mike asked when he reached the landing.

"Third one on the right."

Her heart beat far more rapidly than the light thud of his footsteps on the floor. There was nothing immoral about what they were doing, but it looked far from innocent. Deep inside she wondered if Mike had any lascivious thoughts on his mind. He might be a minister, but he was also a man, and she couldn't imagine any man carrying a woman to bed—and then leaving without trying . . . something.

Much to her dismay, he didn't leave her. He set

her down gently in the middle of the big soft mattress and fluffed some pillows behind her back. A fat dollop of nervousness settled in her throat as he dropped his hat, gloves, and coat on a chintz-upholstered wingback chair, sat on the edge of the bed, and drew her booted foot into his lap.

Okay, so maybe he *was* just going to look at her ankle, but his gentlemanly ways didn't ease her nerves.

He put one hand on the heel of her boot and the other just above her ankle. "This might hurt."

"I'm pretty tough."

His gaze settled on hers for just a moment, and he smiled softly. "I've noticed."

She noticed him, too, and she concentrated on him as he carefully worked at removing the boot without jarring her ankle. His hair was as black as a starless night, flattened at his temples from his hat, but she could easily see that it was thick and neatly trimmed around the ears and the nape of his neck. With her imagination running amuck, she envisioned a wavy lock falling over his forehead. Wasn't that a prerequisite for all gorgeous men?

And his body. She couldn't see his muscles, but she knew they were hard and well defined, after all, they'd been stuck in a saddle together, their bodies rubbing against each other for the longest time, and she'd been able to feel his power even through their heavy clothes. He stood a good six-foot-four if not more, so tall that even she would have to stand on tip toes to kiss him—if she wanted to kiss him, which she didn't, but the thought had surprisingly crossed her mind.

She'd noticed all those things and more about him when she'd seen him that first time at Lauren and Max's wedding, but she'd forgotten the breadth of his shoulders, the strength of his chest, and just how flat his stomach was. She remembered now, and she doubted she'd ever forget.

Was it a sin to admire a minister's body? she wondered.

A jolt of pain ripped through her ankle and up her leg when he slid the boot from her foot. Was that payback for thinking about Mike's physique?

His gaze shot toward her. "You all right?"

She nodded, then laughed inside at her ridiculous notions. The world would be in pretty miserable shape if everyone who'd ever took delight in gazing at a marvelous body was found guilty of committing a grievous sin.

She rested against the pillows Mike had stacked between her and the headboard and breathed slowly, easily, as she watched Mike pull off her heavy wool sock. He cupped one hand around her heel and with the other gently examined her ankle. "Does this hurt?" He moved her foot easily, checking to see if it was swollen, to see if he heard any cracks or pops, but she didn't feel anything more than the tenderness of his touch, the heat of his fingers.

"I've sprained it a few times. I know the difference between twisting it and doing real damage."

He didn't turn his head from what he was doing, but he looked up at her through thick black lashes. "And you still dance?"

"Would you give up being a minister if you had a sore throat?"

He shook his head slowly.

"Dancers don't give up because of sprained or tender ankles, either. Fortunately I'm between jobs right now, so this little mishap won't be much of a problem."

"I thought you were in some big stage show."

She wondered if he realized that he was rubbing the bottom of her foot, his callused thumb making small circles on her skin. Slow circles. Sensual circles.

Her heart fluttered. So did a million butterflies in her stomach. She took a calming breath, trying to think about his question, trying to structure an answer that didn't start with "Please don't stop what you're doing."

Finally she said, "I've been in three big shows this year."

"Dancers move from show to show that often?"

"Only when they're let go."

His fingers inched their way up under her pant leg and he made those same slow, deep, massaging circles on her calf. She wasn't about to tell him that it was her ankle that was hurt or that his hands were on the wrong part of her anatomy. He'd have to work his way much, much higher up her leg before she'd make him back off.

"Wanna tell me why you were let go?"

She decided not to wait for the pitter-patter of her heart to slow before she answered, since that could take forever.

"I got fired from the last show because the choreographer's wife shot him." Three weeks and too many days of unemployment later, she was still miffed. "I held Josh's bloody head till the paramedics came. I took flowers to the hospital and still he had the audacity to tell me I was trouble. The jerk didn't press charges against his wife. Oh, no, they reconciled. But he canned me."

Mike laughed at the ridiculous incident. She couldn't blame him, when it seemed too implausible for words.

"What about the other two shows?" Mike grinned. "Did you get fired from those as well?"

"I lost the job before that because I had a slight disagreement with the director over my costume," she admitted far too freely, baring her soul while Mike stroked the sensitive spot behind her knee.

His brow rose. "What, you didn't like the color? The style?"

"I changed my hair color to get that job and let me tell you"—she grabbed the end of her ponytail and stared at it—"going from nearly black to sun-kissed brown because the director said he already had too many raven-haired girls in the cast, was annoying as hell, but I'd do just about anything for a good part."

"All that and you still got fired?"

"All that. I made one concession after another. I didn't even mind when the director changed me from a watermelon to a strawberry—after all, the costume was more compact and easier to dance in. But when he decided to make me a half-peeled banana, well, that was just too much."

The good pastor's fingers stilled. His brows pulled together as his eyes darted to her breasts and lingered there for a second—a hot, hot, feverish hot second—then drifted back to her eyes. "Half peeled?"

"Topless," she confessed, even though she knew that Mike had understood completely. "He felt my skin tone was perfect, just the right creamy color for a peeled banana. I told him I hadn't seen any bananas with breasts and told him I'd prefer continuing on as a strawberry. He said that was fine with him, as long as I was a half-eaten strawberry because he firmly intended to have me go on stage with my breasts exposed."

Heat crept into her cheeks. Good heavens! What was she doing divulging all this information to a holy man?

"I'm sorry. I hope I didn't embarrass you. I mean, I'm sure the last thing ministers think about are naked women."

A grin touched his face. His dimple deepened. "I can't speak for all ministers, only me, but I've been known to think about naked women a time or two."

"Isn't that a sin?"

"Not in the Bible I'm familiar with."

Well, it was a sin in her father's Bible. Dear old dad thought a good time was Bible study on Friday nights, not high school dances. His idea of after-school activities was serving food to the homeless, not coed volleyball or basketball. Chaplain Mattingly equated the word naked with a woman wearing anything that exposed her knees and elbows and all points in between.

Maybe she'd been naïve in her thinking that all ministers were the same. That they had no vices. That their thoughts were 100 percent pure.

Mike Flynn thought about naked women. And he certainly knew how to stimulate a woman's libido with just a smile, with the simple touch of his hands on her flesh.

*Hmmm.* Maybe he wasn't a minister in the real sense of the word. Maybe he'd gotten a certificate through the mail that gave him the right to marry people, but nothing more. Suddenly she began to wonder if he ministered to some strange cult, where the female parishioners gave their hearts, their minds, and their bodies to a man—their pastor—who claimed he had special ways to save a woman's soul.

Heaven knows she'd run into numerous men like that in Vegas.

She really didn't think her soul needed saving, by any man, not at the moment anyway, so she pulled her leg loose from Mike's strong and callused hands, drew her knee close to her chest, and massaged the ankle herself.

As if it had just dawned on him that his hands had gotten a tad overfamiliar with her leg, as if his conscience was at war with his lustful nature, he plowed his fingers through his hair and rose from the bed.

Wouldn't you know it, that thick lock of hair she'd imagined falling over his brow tumbled forward, shiny, black, and . . . and . . . good heavens, Pastor Flynn was the sexiest man she'd ever set eyes on. She couldn't tear her gaze away from him while he shrugged into his heavy lambswool coat and pulled his hat low on his brow.

She didn't know what had come over her. As a rule, men didn't get her all hot and bothered. She didn't have room for a man in her life, because all her passion was concentrated on her work. But Mike bothered her.

And that annoyed her because he was all wrong for her. Not only was he a man of God who'd frown at her profession, but he lived far from Vegas, the place where her dreams resided. Pull in your feelings, she told herself. Get a hold on your emotions.

She took a deep breath. There. She was fully in control now.

"Thanks for coming to my rescue."

"Not a problem." He tugged on his gloves, and she refused to look at his long, strong, soothing fingers. "You ought to stay off your ankle for a couple of days."

"I've never been one for sitting still, and you

already know I don't follow orders, even when they're in my best interest."

He hit her with a crooked smile, then took a step toward her, his legs brushing the comforter on the bed as he reached out a gloved hand. For a moment she thought he was going to cup her cheek, that he was going to say something endearing that would make her rethink her plans to keep her emotions under lock and key. But he didn't caress her cheek. Instead, his hand dropped down to his side.

"It's late, and I've got a sermon to work on."

"Can't that wait till morning?"

"I've got two mares and a wild stallion to hunt in the morning."

"Won't you be too tired?"

"You don't sit still; I don't sleep."

Her father had always told her that sleepless nights were caused by worried minds. The good pastor looked like a man who shouldn't have a care in the world, but still she asked, "Something troubling you?"

"Wayward horses. Nothing more."

It wasn't the truth, but she had the feeling he didn't talk about his problems. He controlled them as much as he controlled the rest of his emotions and everything else around him.

"Do you have any idea where you might find Satan?" she asked.

"I can think of a few places, but Satan's got a bad habit of staying one step ahead of me."

"What will you do when you find him?"

"Drag him back to the ranch again and tame him."

She didn't like the sound of that. "You won't be able to."

"What makes you so sure?"

"He's wild and doesn't know anything but running free. He'll probably die if you try to break his spirit."

"There you go again, thinking you know all about horses."

"I don't know much at all about horses, but I do know what it's like to have someone force their will upon you, under the misguided belief that you'll be better off."

"I'm not thinking about what's good or bad for Satan, I'm thinking about this ranch. That's my job, Charity, and I do what has to be done, no matter the consequence."

With that he was gone, the door shutting quietly behind him. He might have thought that closed door put an end to their conversation, probably felt that she'd leave well enough alone. But she had every intention of proving to Pastor Flynn that he couldn't tame Satan any easier than he could tame her.

He shouldn't have gone to Charity's bedroom, Mike told himself as he trudged down the stairs and out of the house, hoping the icy air would knock some sense into him. But he was still hot. He was still bothered.

He shouldn't have taken off her boot or massaged the soft, warm skin on her foot. He never should have slid his hand under her pants and up her sleek, velvety-skinned leg. He should have let her ride off in the night with Satan and left it at that. He should have stuck with his earlier conviction that getting close to Charity Wilde could be fatal. But no, he'd had to prove to himself that he could hold a woman, touch a woman, inhale the lingering scent of a woman's wildly exotic perfume and not be affected.

The only thing he'd proved was that he was hornier than hell.

"What's going on?"

The last person Mike wanted to see right now was Jack Remington, but his boss and lifelong friend was perched on the top rail of the corral, feeding carrots to Buck.

"Not a thing." Mike swept Buck's reins up from the ground and swung onto the horse's back. He needed to get home and pray for his salvation; the last thing he wanted now was a long conversation with Jack. "Didn't mean to wake you."

"Sam's the one who heard you. She's got one ear tuned to the twins every second of the day, but you and Charity are the ones she heard."

"Wasn't much to hear."

Jack shrugged as he pulled a cigar from his pocket. "Your sex life isn't my business."

Mike chuckled cynically. "Fifteen, twenty years ago you would have asked to hear every sordid detail."

"I just wanted to make sure I was gettin' more than you."

"Yeah, well, you were getting more then and things haven't changed over the years."

Jack grinned. "Celibacy's gotta be hell."

It was, and ten times worse with Charity around, but Mike wasn't about to mention that to Jack. Besides, he figured his friend knew him well enough to guess the torment messing with his mind.

"I thought you'd given up smoking," Mike said as he watched Jack methodically cut the end off the cigar.

"I've made it as far as not lighting up." Jack rolled one of his favorite Montechristos between his thumb and first two fingers. "Now I'm working on keeping the damn things out of my mouth."

Mike watched Jack lift the cigar to his lips, stare at it for a few seconds, then toss it down to the ground. "Guess I'll let Sam throw the rest of the box in the fireplace on her birthday. Not the greatest present, but it doesn't appear I'll be giving her a pair of Tennessee Walkers."

"Not unless I can find them."

"Wanna tell me what happened?"

Mike had hoped this subject wouldn't come up tonight, but at least he could get one bit of trouble off his mind and only have his craving for Charity to deal with.

He folded his hands over the saddle horn and looked across the still and silent prairie. "Satan got them."

"I figured as much."

"I'm going after them first thing tomorrow"

"You gonna send Benny and Hank out, too?"

Mike shook his head. "This is one problem I'm going to deal with on my own."

Jack jumped off the rail, and crushed the discarded cigar beneath his boot. He'd never questioned Mike's decisions on how to run the ranch, and Mike figured he never would. But Mike could see that Jack had something else on his mind, something he wanted to ask, but didn't quite know how.

Jack shoved his hands in his coat pockets and stared off toward the Crazy Woman Mountains. "You ever think about getting married again?"

That was the last question Mike had expected. "No."

"Word about you being in Charity's bedroom could leak out and be all over the territory by noon tomorrow."

"I've got nothing to hide."

"I know, but sometimes I wish you did." Jack tilted his head, looking up at Mike with concern in his eyes. "It's been six years since Jessie died. Don't you think it's time you move on?"

Mike felt the anger welling up inside of him. "Ask me about the horses, the cows, the ranch, or the church and I'll give you an answer. But everything else is none of your business."

"It wasn't your business when you were worried about my relationship with Sam, but you butted in anyway."

"That was different—"

"Like hell."

"Stay out of it, Jack."

"You've spent the last ten years counseling others through divorce and death and God knows what else, so why the hell won't you talk to someone about what's making you so miserable?"

Because he couldn't tell anyone the truth, that he'd played God and because of his foolishness his wife had died. "Jessie's dead. I've talked to God every day for the last six years. Do you really think things will get better for me if I talk to you, or Sam, or Lauren, or anyone else, when talking to God hasn't done a damn bit of good?"

Jack didn't flinch. "You can wallow in self-pity all you want. But Jessie's not coming back."

Mike knew that all too well. The things he'd loved about Jessie, the good things they'd shared in their short time together, didn't even come to him in dreams anymore. He'd tucked her deep in his heart, the place she'd always stay, cherished and loved forever. It wasn't grief he was suffering from. It was guilt.

Guilt for taking his wife off of life support.

Guilt for being alive when Jessie was dead.

Guilt for wanting another woman, for wanting Charity Wilde, who wasn't anything like the wife he'd loved.

He took a long, deep breath, and looked down at his friend, the man who'd been at his side when he'd married Jessie and when he'd buried her, too.

He'd shared everything with Jack, but not this.

"Do me a favor, Jack."

"What's that?"

"Don't preach." He made a half-hearted attempt to smile. "Leave that to the experts."

*Chapter 4*

CHARITY CREPT, WITH A DECIDED LIMP, down the stairs at five A.M., careful not to make any noise that might wake her friends and family. One step. Two. Three. *Squeak!*

She froze when the screech of the wooden step reverberated up the stairwell. Jerking her head around, she quickly checked to see if any bedroom lights flicked on, but all was silent. One would think that with all his wealth Jack Remington could do something about squeaking stairs, but Sam had told her yesterday that Jack had liked the noise when his oldest son Beau was still living at home. It let him know what time the kid got home—or didn't come home, which had often been the case.

But she wasn't a teenager, merely a woman

who wanted to sneak out of the house to see Mike, and she didn't want anyone trying to finagle an answer out of her about what she was up to.

There wasn't anything scandalous in her plan, although there was no telling what people might think, especially if they knew the good pastor had been in her bedroom last night. No, Mike said he was going after Satan first thing this morning and Charity was dead set on stopping him.

He wasn't going to like her intrusion—again—but Satan's plight and Mike's resolve to capture the stallion had been on her mind all night. She couldn't let him imprison the magnificent beast and try to turn him into a fat, placid farm animal that did nothing but laze around a pasture munching on grass.

And if Mike *was* lucky enough to get a rope around Satan, Charity firmly intended to be on hand to help the mustang escape.

All hell would break loose afterward. Mike would be livid and she could easily imagine the intensity of his green eyes as they turned on her—hot, impassioned, murderous. Without a doubt, he'd never again give her a sensual, luxuriating, heart-palpitating foot rub. She'd survive, of course, and really, it was best if he never touched her again.

He was all wrong for her. They had nothing—and far too much—in common. He was a minister; she was a showgirl. He was stubborn and probably butted heads with everyone he met. So did she, and that spelled big-time trouble for both of them if they ever tangled.

Still, she couldn't get Mike out of her head. Not his radiant eyes, not his splendid physique, and definitely not the tender way his arms had held her safe against him as they'd ridden across the prairie.

But after she helped Satan break out of Mike's clutches she'd see the real Mike Flynn, the stern and unyielding control freak she was sure she'd caught a glimpse of last night. When he showed his true colors he'd be just like every other man she'd ever met, and she'd find it much easier not to think about him again.

Then she could enjoy the rest of her short vacation, go back to Vegas, get her life straightened out, and get back to the business of becoming a star.

Another board at the base of the stairs whined beneath her boot and when she stilled, she heard the laughter—Lauren's and Sam's—streaming from the kitchen. A strip of light shone under the door. Never in her wildest dreams had she expected anyone to be up and about so early.

It wouldn't be polite to not at least say good morning to the women who had become her dearest friends, in spite of all the miles that separated their homes and their lives. She really needed to get to Mike's, but she was hooked by the laughter, by the scents of cinnamon and sugar and good strong coffee wafting from the kitchen.

What could it hurt to take a few minutes for herself, a little time to enjoy the feeling of warm family ties, something that for many years had been as foreign to her as the wide-open plains.

Ignoring the dull throb in her ankle—so the ladies of the house wouldn't nag about her staying off her feet all day—Charity pushed through the swinging kitchen door. "Good morning."

Lauren flashed one of her bright and lovely smiles. "Oh, dear, I hope we didn't wake you."

"No, I couldn't sleep." Charity's comment elicited another smile from her sister-in-law, a sly grin this time that said, "I know what you were up to last night." Luckily Lauren didn't tease her about the incident.

"Pull up a chair," Sam said as she flitted about the kitchen. "The cinnamon rolls will be ready in a minute, but if you're starving, try one of the éclairs left over from yesterday."

Sam looked prettier than ever, Charity thought, as she sat at the round oak table across from Lauren. Not many women could appear stunningly beautiful in an over-sized chenille robe and floppy slippers, but Sam had an aura about her that made her stand out in a crowd. It was hard to believe she'd once lived in a Volkswagen or that she'd had a loan shark at her back.

It was even harder to believe that Sam, with Lauren's help, administered a charitable organization for the homeless, wanted to start a breeding facility for Tennessee Walkers, was the mother of twins, not to mention stepmother to a nineteen-year-old son, *and* ran her multimillionaire husband's household without a lick of help. In fact, Lauren had told Charity that Sam balked every time Jack mentioned getting a housekeeper or cook.

Sam Remington was totally amazing. Independent and in control of her own destiny—exactly what Charity wanted to be.

"The coffee's fresh," Sam said, cradling her daughter, whose tuft of shocking red hair peeked out from under a fluffy pink blanket. She shifted Hannah into the crook of her left arm and lifted a brimming glass coffeepot. "Would you like a cup?"

"I'd love some. But why don't you sit down and let me pour."

"Nonsense." Sam grabbed a mug from a cabinet and expertly maneuvered toward the table with a full load in her arms. "I'm pregnant," she added, setting the cup on the table and filling it with steaming coffee, "not disabled."

"Speak for yourself," Lauren said, feeding a bottle of formula to Tyler, Sam and Jack's other twin. The towhead was swathed in blue, and Lauren balanced him gingerly on what remained of her lap. At eight-months pregnant her stomach stretched halfway to her knees, but the lady was a picture of perfection in Pamela Dennis maternity wear, capped by a zillion-dollar haircut, with fat diamond studs in her ears. In spite of her obvious wealth, Lauren Wilde was a bundle of generosity and charm.

"Goodness," Lauren said, rubbing her belly, "Max Jr.'s been kicking all night long. I swear this little one's going to come out riding a Harley bigger than his dad's, and let me tell you, it can't happen soon enough. Of course"—she reached across the table with great effort and grabbed a chocolate éclair—"as soon as the doctor gives us the go-ahead, Max and I plan to put every effort into having our second."

"Did you plan Junior?" Sam asked, lowering her own pregnant body into one of the kitchen chairs.

"Of course we did." Lauren licked chocolate from her smiling lips. "We planned to have him two years from now."

Sam laughed as she rubbed her own swollen belly. "Jack and I planned to have this one, too— of course we were planning to wait until the twins were out of diapers. Eleven months apart was a little unexpected. I suppose we should have taken precautions, but where's the fun in that?"

Charity put an éclair on a napkin and licked the yummy chocolate from her fingers, absorbing every word of this bizarre conversation. In her day-to-day world, women talked about auditions, boyfriends, bounced checks, and love affairs gone sour. Babies were the last thing anyone wanted to talk or think about, and every step imaginable was taken to make sure an accident didn't happen. Accidents meant you were out of a job because no one wanted to see a long-legged, big breasted, heavily pregnant showgirl prancing across a stage in a sequined thong.

Charity had taken precautions, too. Foolproof

precautions—like absolutely no sex—and she didn't plan to change her routine any time soon.

Of course, watching the way Lauren and Sam smiled and cooed while keeping up a mile-a-minute conversation about Lauren's avant-garde wedding business, a continuation of yesterday's chatter about Max's biker buddies, the ranch, the horses Sam wanted to breed, and the outrageous lives of Lauren and Jack's mother and father, Charity thought she could get used to the coziness—for a while.

A steady diet of this would surely bore her and in no time at all she'd hightail it back to Vegas. Right now she imagined she could put up with another four or five days of prattle.

"I know this is none of my business," Sam said, drawing Charity back to the conversation, "but . . ." She took a sip of coffee and stared at Charity over the brim of her mug. "Well . . . I couldn't miss the voices coming from your room last night."

Had she and Mike really been that loud? Had everyone heard?

Instantly, as if she were a young girl living under her father's roof again, she felt the need to defend what had gone on. "Mike and I didn't do anything, if that's what you're worried about."

"Worried?" Lauren chimed in. "Goodness, no! We just wanted to make sure you'd brought a box or two of condoms with you. You can't always count on a man being prepared. And, well, Mike's not the type to walk around with one in his pocket. I imagine most ministers don't."

Charity was certain her mouth had dropped open. Were they really suggesting that she might want to have that kind of relationship with Mike?

"I don't keep any condoms around," Sam added, as if the conversation needed to go any further, "and I know Lauren doesn't, either, which is really quite obvious. It's a long trip to the store, but we'll head there this afternoon if . . . well . . ." She smiled coyly. "If it's necessary."

"Mike's a minister," Charity blurted out. "For heaven's sake! You don't think I'd sleep with him, do you?"

"Well," Sam said, drawing out the word, "maybe it would be a little unorthodox considering his vocation and the fact that the two of you aren't married, but he is a man, an awfully good-looking man even though he can be a bit high-handed at times. And you know perfectly well, Charity, that things sometimes happen when you least expect them to."

"Nothing's going to happen with Mike. Not now. Not ever."

Lauren's eyes narrowed. "Oh, dear, it hadn't even crossed my mind that you might not be interested in men."

"I've never met one I wanted to be interested in."

"But you've noticed how good-looking Mike is?"

"Of course I've noticed. What woman in her right mind—or out of her mind, for that matter—wouldn't notice a man who's drop-dead gorgeous? But he's a minister, and . . . and I'm not interested."

Sam stretched a hand across the table and squeezed Charity's fingers. "I think you protest too much, but maybe we're teasing too much, too."

"It's just that we'd like to get you out of Vegas," Lauren added, shifting Tyler to her shoulder and patting him gently on the back. "One of those bullets that hit your friend Josh could have hit you."

"But it didn't," Charity interrupted. "It was a fluke. A once in a lifetime thing. What all of you seem to forget is that I've worked long and hard to get where I am. I don't know anything else, so what would I do if I left Vegas? Sing and dance on a street corner somewhere and hold out a hat for tips? Go to New York and try to get a job on Broadway, which is nearly impossible, and while I'm fighting a million other singers and dancers for a slot in a chorus line, hold down a waitressing job?"

"Max has asked you a dozen times to come to Florida and work with us," Lauren said. "It would mean the world to him, and me, too."

"I know you mean well, but Max would hover over me far more than he already does. My dad hovered and I hated it. I don't want to go through that again."

"Then move here," Sam said. "No one would hover."

"What could I possibly do here?"

"I know I've told Jack over and over again that I don't want him hiring someone to help me, but when I really think about it, I know I won't be able to handle everything when the new baby comes."

"You need a nanny. A cook. A housekeeper. You don't need a showgirl."

"What I need is a friend," Sam said. "There aren't many women out here, and as much as I love Jack, there are times when I just want to chat with a girlfriend."

A pleasant feeling wrapped around Charity's heart and hugged it warmly. But as nice as Sam's offer sounded, she knew she'd need much more than friendship with this woman to make her give up the life she'd worked so hard for in Vegas.

"I'm just a phone call away," Charity said, but she knew that talking across the miles could never be as good as sitting across the table from each other. It was, however, the only thing that made sense. "Thanks for the offer, Sam, but I've got an audition coming up for the job of a lifetime. It's a singing role, as well as dancing. It's what I want more than anything else."

"Then go for it," Sam said, her smile infectious. "My mama always told me I should reach for the stars and far be it from me to tell you something different. But there are millions of stars out there. Don't be afraid to latch on to one that's shooting in a different direction. It might just take you where you really want to go."

* * *

The frigid air hit her like an impenetrable wall of ice, but Charity tucked her chin into her wool scarf and trudged toward the barn. There weren't any stars there, but that didn't matter. The only star she wanted to latch on to was in Vegas. That's where she'd set her sights, and the few setbacks she'd had of late weren't going to dissuade her.

She couldn't give up.

But Vegas and auditions were a long way off. Right now the only thing that concerned her was getting to Mike's before the streak of morning sunlight on the horizon widened.

She hadn't told Lauren and Sam where she was going. If she had, a whole new series of questions and speculations about her brief encounter with Mike would have popped up. Instead she'd told them she wanted to go for a ride. They'd both thought she was out of her mind to go out so early in the morning, but she wouldn't be swayed. In the end, Sam told her to take any one of the horses in the barn.

But the barn was empty.

And even if she did have a horse to ride, she didn't have the foggiest idea where Mike lived. Obviously the morning was not turning out as she'd planned.

"Well, I'll be damned. Sure didn't expect you up at the crack of dawn."

Charity spun around at the unexpected sound of a stranger's voice. The man was old and bent, but she saw a ton of charm hidden behind his scraggly whiskers.

"I'm Charity Wilde," she said, smiling. "You must be Crosby."

"Yeah, that's me all right. Just call me Cros. I'm not big on lots of syllables. And this here's Rufus," he said, patting the Border collie who'd dropped to his haunches at his master's side. "Used to be Jack's dog till all them kids took over the house and drove Rufus crazy. He hangs out with me now."

Crosby scratched his grizzled cheek. "We're out for our mornin' constitutional. What's your excuse for being out here?"

"I wanted to go for a ride."

"Jack turned the horses out before headin' to Sheridan. Must have left an hour or so ago to pick up Beau from the airport. Don't know why that kid had to go away to college. A man can learn a hell of a lot more stickin' around this place."

"I heard there weren't enough girls around and that's why he chose to go away."

"Yeah, I heard that, too." Crosby cocked his head and his bushy white brows knit together as he studied her. "You gonna stick around?"

"Just a few days."

"Too bad. I ain't never been big on crowds but wouldn't hurt to have another woman or two in this part of the country. Give us old farts somethin' better to look at than cows or each other."

Charity found herself smiling. "Gets lonely out here, huh?"

"I ain't got time to get lonely. Pastor Flynn

comes by every night to check on me and sticks around for hours. You'd swear the feller didn't have a home of his own." He scratched his whiskers again. "You run into the good pastor yet?"

"Last night. Actually I thought I'd pay him a visit this morning."

A wily grin touched his rheumy eyes. "Well, you ain't gonna find him out here. He hangs his hat a mile or so up the road. I'd give you a ride but I ain't allowed to drive no more. Can't get on the back of a gall-darn horse, either. Sure is a pain in the butt gettin' old."

Charity linked her arm through Crosby's. "What if I walk with you a ways and you point out the direction I should go to find Mike's place?"

"No need for you to waste your time with me." He pulled away from her arm and hobbled slowly toward the tack room. "Grab one of them saddles and bridles in there, we'll round you up a horse, and I'll head you toward Mike's." His eyes narrowed. "You a good rider or a so-so one?"

"I always thought I was pretty good. Of course, I let some stallion named Satan get the better of me last night."

"You mean to tell me you got on that mustang's back?"

"Rode him a good ten or fifteen minutes before he dumped me."

"Well, I'll be damned. Does Mike know?"

"He saw it all."

Crosby chuckled and stepped aside while she went into the tack room to pick out a saddle. "Mike tried to sit Satan once, but that fool horse wasn't havin' none of it. Damn near kicked Mike's teeth out, and they've been doin' battle ever since."

"He's going after Satan this morning. I plan on going, too."

"Well I sure as hell hope you're goin' after the man and not after that horse."

"I hate to disappoint you, but I'm going for the horse."

"Too bad. A woman couldn't hitch up with a better man than Mike."

"I'm not interested in getting hitched."

He hit her with a smirk. "So you say."

Crosby headed for the far barn door and she followed, lugging the heavy saddle, blanket, and bridle with her, wondering why people didn't see what she did—that she and Mike were all wrong for each other. Maybe they simply had their hearts set on finding a woman for Mike, and she was the first single one to cross his path. That was highly possible here in Nowhere, where cows outnumbered people a hundred to one, where kids like Beau left the ranch and headed for the big city after graduating from high school and rarely came back.

If you wanted to get married out here, you usually went elsewhere to find the woman or man of your dreams. Or you imported them. Well, she might be imported, but she wasn't on the market.

Her destiny was the stage and the closest she ever wanted to get to a bridal gown was wearing a skimpy one made of sequins and feathers in a Vegas extravaganza.

Crosby let out a whistle, which startled her back to the here and now. "I'll have a horse here for you in a second," Crosby said, letting out another piercing whistle.

The pasture beyond the barn was dotted with horses—appaloosas, bays, and chestnuts—but it was a striking brown-and-white paint that galloped toward them.

"This here's Jezebel." The horse nuzzled Crosby's hand, then his pocket, looking for something to eat.

"Hold your horses, gall darnit!" Crosby pushed Jezebel's muzzle aside and pulled an apple from his pocket, balanced it on his palm, and in a flash Jezebel snatched it away.

"We used to ride this place together," Crosby said, running gnarled fingers over the horse's mane. "She don't get much of a workout no more, but she's got speed and ain't too particular about who rides her."

Charity scratched behind Jezebel's ears and the horse nuzzled her coat pocket in return. "Sorry, girl. There's nothing there."

"She don't mind. Just whisper sweet nothin's to her on occasion and she'll be happy."

Leave it to a man to think that sweet nothin's was all a woman needed, Charity grumbled to herself as she raked her gloved fingers through

Jezebel's mane. Personally she didn't need or want sweet nothin's, or a man for that matter— not a drop-dead gorgeous one, not a sweet one, not a controller. All she wanted was the spotlight.

And right now a change of subject.

She hefted the saddle over Jezebel. "I hear you've been on the ranch a long time."

"Been here since the thirties and haven't left since, except for Lauren's weddings. She had too dang many of those things if you ask me. Don't think I'll be goin' to any more, thank goodness, now that she settled down with that brother of yours. Course, Reece, that's Jack's dad, keeps badgerin' me about goin' to Santa Fe and livin' with him and Mike's folks. Can't think of any reason why a man would want to do a damn fool thing like that."

"It's warmer there in the winter."

"Don't like the heat. Don't like New Mexico," Crosby grumbled, as he slipped the bit into Jezebel's mouth and adjusted the bridle. "Lived in that part of the country once and ain't about to go back. Lived in that Vegas place, too. Course, it wasn't no highfalutin city back then."

Finally a subject that had nothing to do with babies, marriage, men, condoms, or wild horses—things she knew nothing about. "Did you like Vegas?" Charity asked as she tightened the cinch.

"Like I said, there weren't much there back then. Moved to Boulder City when me and my pa got work on the dam. Hoover, Boulder, don't rightly know what they call the thing these days. Didn't care what they called it then, either. It was the only place you could make money durin' the Depression, and that's why we went."

"If the money was so good, why'd you leave?"

He shrugged. "I killed somebody in a barroom brawl."

Charity's fingers stilled on the saddle. Had she heard him correctly? She stole a glance at the old codger, who'd just admitted to being a murderer, and caught sight of his grin.

"I take it you haven't heard that rumor yet?"

"No," Charity said, wishing the lump would leave her throat. "It's not true, is it?"

"Could have been true if I'd hung around much longer. Boulder City was too laid back for me, so I hung out in Vegas. Did too much gamblin', too much drinkin'. Spent too many nights with ladies who weren't exactly ladies. Thought I could make it rich there, but I lost as much money as I made. Then I found myself gettin' caught up in one fight after another and ended up witnessin' someone get killed. Finally got smart and moved up here and ain't regretted it a bit."

He gave Jezebel a couple of sugar cubes that had half crumbled in his pocket. "What about you? Has that hell hole worn on you yet?"

"Not in the least." Charity saw no reason to tell Crosby about the love-hate relationship she had with Vegas and focused instead on the good side. "There's always something to do. Always something new to try. It's exciting, fun, and I can do the kind of work I love to do. I really can't think of any place else I'd rather be."

"Yeah, well, I said the same thing once." Crosby led Jezebel out of the barn. "Hope it works out better for you than it did for me. But if it don't, you come back here. Like I said, we could use a pretty face around the ranch."

Charity swung into the saddle, the chill of the creaking leather seeping through her jeans and even her long johns. She wondered how Crosby's frail body could handle the bone-numbing weather, wondered if it was good for him to be out here alone, especially when it was still half dark. "Can I walk you back to your place?"

"Hell, no. Rufus and I still got another half mile or so to go on our constitutional. Doctor's orders, you know. Gotta keep the blood circulatin'. Besides, you gotta get to Mike's place."

He pointed toward a distant hill. "He lives just over that rise. No need worryin' about knockin' on the wrong door. Ain't no other cabins for miles. Ain't a more needy man for miles, either."

"I'm not in the market for a needy man," Charity said, wishing the conversation hadn't turned from Vegas to matrimony. "I'm not in the market for *any* man."

"Yeah, so you said before, but I ain't never known a woman to get up at the crack of dawn just to go chasin' a horse."

Crosby slapped Jezebel's rump and the mare

took off on a run, headed toward the rising sun. Headed toward Mike.

And Charity wondered if Crosby—not to mention Lauren and Sam—knew her better than she knew herself.

## Chapter 5

MIKE SLUMPED OVER THE KITCHEN TABLE, staring at the scribbles on a lined yellow tablet, at a sermon that was going nowhere and had to be ready to deliver tomorrow morning.

He hadn't slept in twenty-four hours. He hadn't showered, changed clothes, or even taken a razor to his face. All he'd done after chasing Charity and Satan across the prairie was drink a pot-and-a-half of coffee and try to get something inspirational down on paper.

But words didn't come as easily as they had when Jessie was alive. Then, his messages had flowed easily from his fingers to the paper. Now he had to dig deep within his heart for every phrase, had to search his Bible for just the right passage. It took a solid week to write a half-hour sermon. Then on Sunday he'd ask himself what right he had to deliver God's message when he'd committed one of the most grievous sins of all.

He'd thought about giving up his ministry, but he couldn't. It was as much a part of him as the Wyoming prairie. He'd left this land, his friends, and his family a few times—for college, where he'd met Jessie; divinity school; for a honeymoon—but he always came back, because he found it hard to breathe anywhere else.

Breathing would be just as difficult without his faith. A time or two he'd ridden across the plains, where no one could hear him but God, and he'd beg for forgiveness, he'd shout at the Lord and ask Him to take his troubles away. But the guilt stayed with him. At times he feared that God had abandoned him, then he'd return to a belief he'd always held, that the Man upstairs was looking for the right time to relieve him of his burden.

All in good time, he kept telling himself. All in good time.

He downed the dregs of cold coffee in his mug and scribbled a few more sentences, drawing his thoughts and words from old familiar hymns, and threw in a few references to candy hearts, chocolates and flowers, all the trappings of Valentine's Day, which they'd be celebrating this Sunday, along with a handful of birthdays. He tossed in long-remembered biblical passages from the Song of Solomon and 1 Corinthians, and would have added his own personal reflections on love, but those weighed too heavily on his heart.

Absently grabbing the coffeepot off the warmer in the center of the kitchen table, he started to fill his cup, but he'd already drunk the last of it. He set it back down and rubbed his eyes. He was exhausted, but he needed to get a few more lines on paper.

He opened his Bible for more inspiration and the volume parted easily at the worn pages in the book of John, the place where he kept the picture he'd taken of Jessie the night before he'd rushed her to the hospital.

He lifted the yellowing Polaroid and drew his finger over his wife's smiling face, her delicate features. Somehow over the years he'd forgotten the sound of her voice, forgotten the feel of her body snuggled against him during the long cold nights of winter. The love he'd felt for her was still there, he'd just tucked it deep in his heart. But the longing for her had stopped years ago.

What he missed was having a wife, a woman to kiss, to make love to till the wee hours of morning.

If he had a wife . . .

What was he thinking? He couldn't sleep through the night. Instead he'd toss and turn and wake up in a cold sweat from nightmares. He couldn't subject a woman to that.

Of course, if he had a wife, he wouldn't be sitting here now with only an empty coffeepot and a half-finished sermon for company.

Charity Wilde was responsible for these feelings. Until yesterday he'd resigned himself to being alone; now he didn't know what he wanted.

Leaning back in his chair, he closed his eyes,

thinking he might try to catch fifteen or twenty minutes of sleep before heading out after Satan.

Before long he felt himself drifting in and out of dreams. Suddenly he was on the prairie with a wild stallion, a brazen, carefree creature leading him on a fast and furious chase. And when he got close enough to toss his rope, the beast whirled about in a tornado of wind and snow, transforming right before his eyes into Charity Wilde.

Her long, lean body was all creamy white and completely, beautifully naked, her waist-length hair blew about her in the breeze, reaching out for him, the silky brown tendrils wrapping about his chest, pulling him willingly into her embrace. Tighter, tighter, her exotic, intoxicating perfume wafting through his senses until he saw nothing and felt nothing but the mesmerizing showgirl.

The knocking at the door ripped him from his dream and the chair skittered out from under him when he jumped to his feet.

*Blast!* He wasn't ready to let the image of Charity go. It was foolish to want her, but what man in his right mind wouldn't?

He stormed across the living room, prepared to give the ranch hand who'd interrupted his daydream a piece of his mind, but when he threw open the door it wasn't Benny or Hank or even Woody or Bill who stood on the porch.

It was Charity Wilde, her skin an even creamier white than what he'd seen in his daydream, her once black hair a brilliant brown, her cheeks and the tip of her nose chilled a pretty pink. She was fully clothed, but that didn't mean he couldn't imagine the charms hidden beneath the heavy layers.

He wasn't a man of many words, but right now he was speechless.

Charity was stunned when the door jerked open. Since when did a minister walk around in an unbuttoned blue chambray shirt hanging loose from his jeans, with his chest so explicitly visible? And Mike's chest wasn't just any chest. It was rippled with muscle—hard, hard muscle—and his skin, what she could see beneath the mat of black curly hair, was a glorious slightly faded-by-winter bronze, the kind many of the male dancers she knew obtained from a bottle. His feet were bare, and she found herself wanting to touch them the same way he'd touched hers last night, massaging them slowly, methodically, sensually.

A wanton, lust-filled lump stuck in her throat as she focused on his face. She stood on the porch in the cold and looked at the heavy black stubble on his chiseled jaw, the stunning emerald green eyes that now had deep shadows beneath them, and hair as dark as a starry night, blue-black and shiny. Not surprisingly, a heavy lock fell over his brow. He raked his fingers through it, but it fell right back, disorderly, unruly, and absolutely beautiful.

No man should be so gorgeous, especially to a woman who didn't want to mess up her life by getting involved with a guy.

It had been a big mistake to come here.

She drew in a deep breath and exhaled, a puff of fog forming between them, which thankfully clouded his good looks.

"Mornin'," he said, in his deep, velvety voice. The mist cleared, and she couldn't miss his gaze as it meandered down her body to her heavy battered-leather boots, then wandered back to her face, all in half an instant. "How's the ankle?"

She'd forgotten there'd been any pain in her ankle. Nearly forgotten her name. "Better," she choked out. "Thank you."

He looked past her to the snow-dusted yard, probably trying to figure out how she got to his place. His eyes settled on Jezebel, then riveted on Charity again. "Crosby doesn't let just anyone ride his horse. What did you do, put some kind of magic spell on him?"

"I smiled." She tucked her gloved but freezing hands under her arms for a little more warmth. "If I smiled at you, would you let me in?"

A slow grin touched his face, and he stepped aside, holding the door wide. "Sorry. I'm not used to company this early. You took me by surprise."

She was glad she had. If he'd known she was coming, he might have dressed for the occasion, and she really did like looking at his body.

He closed the door behind them. "Would you like some coffee?"

"No thanks."

They stood stock-still, awkwardly watching each other like young kids at their first dance, neither knowing what to say or do.

"Tea?" He sounded like a flight attendant.

He looked like a god.

"No thanks."

He leaned against the door and his shirt parted

a wee bit more. *Good heavens!* She had to turn away to stay sane, but even with her back to him, she couldn't forget the image of his body or his heated eyes, which she knew were watching her move about the living room, studying her just as she studied his not-so-humble abode.

"Did you come here to see what I look like first thing in the morning?"

She turned at his question. "No. I'd expected you to be dressed, ready to go after Satan." She perched on the carved log arm of a rustic western sofa and crossed her legs, taking some weight off her ankle. Again she leisurely gazed at his toes, the long, lean length of his legs, his hard, flat belly, and his breathtaking chest. She smiled in spite of herself. "Is this your normal attire for chasing wild stallions?"

His hands didn't move toward the buttons. She'd thought for sure that he'd pull his shirt together, or make some excuse for his appearance, but he did neither.

"This is what I wear when I've spent half the night chasing wayward women and the other half writing a sermon."

"Tough night, huh?"

"I've had worse."

He pushed away from the door and went to the hearth to toss another log on the already blazing fire. Apparently he was in no rush to go after Satan.

Against her better judgment, she was in no hurry to leave, either.

Her gloved fingers moved toward her scarf,

unwrapping it slowly. She dropped the wool muffler over the sofa back, feeling all at once like a stripper from the wrong side of Vegas, especially when Mike's green eyes fastened on each and every one of her moves.

Nervously she fumbled with the buttons on her coat and he moved toward her slowly, intently, like a tiger stalking prey. Her heart went on overdrive and her fingers trembled. He nudged her hands aside with his strong, nimble fingers, then took his merry sweet time unbuttoning her jacket, watching her eyes, and her lips as he methodically worked his way to the bottom.

With that done, with her heart racing, he tugged off one of her leather gloves, followed by the wool one she wore under it for extra warmth. His body loomed gloriously, breathtakingly before her and she ached to touch him. All of him. One would think she'd never been near a man before the way her pulse quickened and her body throbbed! Usually she was indifferent. More often than not she looked at dancers, choreographers, and directors as androgynous human beings.

But right now, her mouth, her nose, and her eyes were only inches from Mike's stomach, from the column of short black hair that raced from his navel to some hidden, forbidden place beneath the waistband of his jeans, and she saw a sexy creature, not a sexless one.

She looked up shyly, hoping he couldn't feel the thoughts ripping through her. Sex. Minister. Sex. Minister. Sex. Those two things didn't go together at all!

Nor did the slow, sensual way he took off her second glove and smiled. "Your fingers are freezing."

And she was probably going to burn in hell.

The good pastor captured her hands in the heat of his palms, rubbing them gently to bring back the circulation. "So," he said, drawing her fingers close to his mouth, blowing his warm, moist breath on them. "What brings you here so early?"

Suddenly all she could think of was the sensuousness of his actions. The way he'd comforted her and held her close last night, even though he was angry at her for helping Satan escape. His mesmerizing touch on the bottom of her foot. Tender fingers smoothing over her ankle and higher still, inching up under her jeans when all he would have had to do was take her boot off and hightail it out of her bedroom.

And now—*pant, pant*—the way he was standing so close to her that she could feel the heat of his body as he held her fingers precariously close to his lips.

These were the actions of a man on the make, a man who'd go to any lengths to get what he wanted from a woman. She'd been around a lot of sleazy men in Vegas, men who thought she was easy, that all they had to do was whisper sweet nothings in her ear and she'd fall into their arms and then their beds or even the back seat of their cars.

She'd never succumbed before because those men had left her cold. But Mike made her feel awfully weak in the knees. He came darn close to hypnotizing her, made her think that he could persuade her to do just about anything.

Of all the men she'd ever met, he should know better.

She took another deep breath, tried to remember what he'd asked her, and finally answered his question. "I came here to help you look for Satan." Her eyes trailed to his lips, to her fingers, which were just a fraction of an inch from his mouth. "I hope you don't think I'm here for . . . any other reason."

His brow rose in question. "Such as?"

"I don't know. Sex, maybe?"

He frowned. "What makes you think that?"

"The way you're about to kiss my fingers. The way you unbuttoned my coat and took off my gloves. Then there's the way you've been all nice and sweet to me, as if you want something in return."

He dropped her hands all too suddenly and plowed his fingers through his hair. "Have you been in Vegas so long that you've forgotten what polite, well-bred men do? Have you forgotten what lending a helping hand is all about? Does everything in your life revolve around sex?"

That did it. She popped up from the arm of the sofa and faced him almost eye to eye. "Is that what you think of me? Do you think the words sex and showgirl are synonymous?"

"I never gave it any thought until you got all hot and bothered about me rubbing your fingers to get some warmth back into them. Should I let you get frostbite? Was I supposed to let you lie on the ground last night and freeze, or let you walk back to the ranch on a bum ankle?"

"You might have been better off if you had."

"Yeah, and you would have been dead. Coyotes get hungry this time of year, and they're always on the lookout for a wounded animal. Mountain lions look, too; and I've seen their tracks lately. You couldn't have outrun either of them."

"I could outrun you," she said, realizing the stupidity of her statement, how childish their bickering had become.

"Maybe so," Mike said, "but I'm not on the chase."

His eyes were hot. The heat from his body was hotter. He glared down at her and she glared right back. It was an absolutely ridiculous standoff, and she'd been completely responsible for all of it.

She blew out a deep breath, skirted around him, and went to the fireplace, sticking her hands close to the fire in the immense rock hearth. She heard him walk across the room, saw through the corner of her eye that he'd leaned a shoulder against the wall and watched her just as curiously as she'd watched him.

She tilted her head away from the fire and smiled at him. A slight smile, but it was all she had left in her at the moment. The rest of her was consumed by the embarrassment she felt for having thought that he might be on the make. "Thanks for letting me get that off my chest."

"Anything else you want to unload? I've been trained to listen."

"You weren't listening a minute ago. You were arguing."

"I'm human."

She'd noticed. All too human.

She shrugged out of her coat and tossed it onto the couch, getting ready to explain why she'd come unglued. "Most of the men I meet think sex and showgirl are synonymous. They think I'm an easy lay." She looked at his face for some sign of shock, for disgust, but saw only more questions. "I'm not," she tossed out, "just in case you're curious."

"I never thought you were."

He shoved away from the wall, moving close again. Real close. "You sure you want to go out with me to find Satan?"

"I'd rather help you find the mares. As for Satan, you should leave him alone."

He grinned. "The horse expert returns?"

"I don't claim to be a horse expert, but I do know wild animals shouldn't be kept in captivity."

He shook his head. "I don't plan to lock him in a cage and put him on display. I plan to breed him."

"And what are you going to do with him when he's not providing stud service? Hide him away in some dingy little stall somewhere?"

"It all depends on Satan. If he wants to be difficult, he gets a corral with walls so high he can't jump over them. If he cooperates, he gets a big pasture to run in."

"But he wants to run free."

"We don't all get what we want."

Oooh, she wanted to stomp her foot at his

pig-headedness. His true colors were shining brightly, flashing control, control, control!

"So—" He boxed her jaw lightly, and the dimple deepened in his whisker-coated cheek. "Maybe you oughta head back home and help bake Valentine's cookies."

She knew he was teasing. Still, she felt her fingers digging into her palms as her fists clenched. "I'd rather keep you company, thank you very much."

"The temperature's dropped since last night, and I'm going to be riding long and hard."

"I'm tough."

His gaze trailed slowly, dangerously, up and down her body. "Your butt's gonna get sore, your thighs are gonna ache, and you'll probably eat a lot of dust."

"And you're gonna have a thorn in your side, cause I'm going with you come hell or high water."

"No."

"Yes."

He shook his head, then headed for the stairs, ignoring her as if she'd disappeared.

"Excuse me."

Mike turned around halfway to the second floor. "Yeah?"

"We were having a discussion."

"I thought it was settled. You're going whether I want you to or not."

*Hmm, that was an easy win.* "I'll try not to make your life too miserable."

"Easier said than done." He took another step up the stairs but didn't stop looking at her. "I've got to clean up before we go. Make yourself at home, raid the fridge, whatever. You could pack some sandwiches if you want. There aren't any restaurants where we're going."

With that said he disappeared and the room seemed empty with him gone. But at least she could breathe again, and at last the heavy thump of her heart ceased its rapid beat.

When she got keyed up at home she ran five miles, maybe ten. She couldn't run right now, so she strolled, studying her surroundings, the furniture made of rough-hewn woods and bold western fabrics, furniture that was so like its owner.

She'd expected to see antlers and the heads of wild animals mounted on the mile-high log walls, just as they were at Jack's and Sam's. She halfway expected to see a cross somewhere, a few pictures depicting Jesus healing the sick, or at least a copy of DaVinci's *Last Supper*—the kind of home decor she'd grown up with.

But there were no crosses in sight, no outward signs of religion at all. Mike's walls were littered with paintings of the prairies and snowcapped mountains, cowboys and mountain men, and over the fireplace, mounted right above an antique rifle, was a magnificent painting of a dappled gray stallion, its wild black mane whipping in the wind.

Moving toward it, she studied the brush strokes, the thick layers of oil paint making the mane look as if it were flying out of the picture. It was Satan, no doubt about it, right down to the cuts and scrapes on his body and his brave, overly daring eyes.

Her own eyes trailed to the lower right corner of the painting and saw the artist's name: Jessie Flynn. Mike's sister? Charity wondered. His mother? Or maybe a male member of his family. Charity didn't have an artistic background, but she could tell that Jessie Flynn had talent.

She made her way to the kitchen, a cozy place with honey-gold knotty-pine cabinets and hardwood floors strewn with Indian rugs. She couldn't remember a time when she'd been in a home that felt so comfortable and warm, in spite of being so massive and . . . masculine.

Riding to Mike's place she'd tried conjuring an image of his house. She'd assumed it would be small. An aged cabin with one main floor where the kitchen blended into the living area, and a loft with an unmade double bed. What she'd seen had taken her breath away.

The cabin rambled along a meandering creek, its edges icy with only a trickle of water rolling over the gravel and rocks. A wide deck spread around three sides of the house and a few carved wooden chairs sat beneath the eaves. Two thick-trunked and leafless aspens poked up through one corner of the deck, and it wasn't hard to imagine a hammock spread between them on a warm summer's day.

It was all too beautiful.

Like the man himself.

Above her she could hear Mike moving around, heard water running, and suddenly she envisioned him standing naked, the pulsing, steaming water pouring over his black hair, broad shoulders, and rippling bronze muscles. She tried to rid herself of the image, but like the best of dreams, the fantasy took on a life of its own. The shower curtain swept aside and a woman stepped into the tub, her slender fingers sliding over Mike's back and weaving together behind his neck.

His powerful hands smoothed over the edge of her breasts, along her curvy sides, and cupped her bottom, tugging her hips against his. They danced in the steam, in the hot water, slowly, sensually.

The water in the upstairs bathroom shut off with a loud thunk that echoed through the walls, ripping her from her daydream.

*For heaven's sake!* She had to find something to occupy her mind before Mike came down the stairs and was burned by the flames leaping from her body.

Opening the refrigerator, she grabbed meat, lettuce, mustard and mayo, slapped it between slices of bread, and wrapped half a dozen sandwiches. Next she found herself washing coffee mugs and the pot, picking up wadded pieces of lined yellow paper and tossing them into the trash, then straightening the table—things she rarely did at home.

When she touched Mike's Bible, she remembered how much she'd enjoyed Bible study classes she'd attended with a few of her high school friends. Her father encouraged it. Actually, he'd insisted she organize a study group. At first she'd balked at the notion, but she'd actually had a good time talking about different chapters and verses when no one was around to preach about the wages of sin or having a good time.

Her spin on the scriptures was a whole lot different from her dad's. She wondered if it was different from Mike's.

She couldn't help but touch the worn pages of his Bible, the one that said it was okay for ministers to think about naked women. Hopefully his Bible also said it was okay for showgirls to lust over naked ministers. She drew her fingers along the curled edges and flipped through the pages, staring at the yellow highlighting on passage after passage.

And then she saw the picture. It was as worn and faded as the Bible, but there was no mistaking the beauty of the woman in the photo. There were no markings on it, no dates, no name. She wondered who she could be and even though she wanted to believe the pretty blonde was a sister or cousin, she had the feeling she was someone much closer. An old girlfriend. A lost love.

She felt a sudden, unexpected pang of jealousy and closed the book, putting the woman from her mind. It was crazy to be jealous of a man she had no intention of getting hooked on. After all, she was leaving in a few days, going back to Las Vegas, to the life she loved.

How silly she was being.

Pulling out a chair, she sat down to read the

words Mike had scribbled on his pad. It was a
sermon—a Valentine's Day message—and it surprised her to see his references to hearts and flowers. She put her elbows on the table and rested
her chin on her knuckles, smiling as she read
Mike's words, all so different from her father's.

"Interesting reading?"

Her gaze shot toward Mike, his cheeks smooth
now, his hair damp and combed too neatly in
place. She liked it mussed, the wayward locks
hanging over his brow and a strange longing
came over her to reach up and curl her finger under a thousand strands and coerce them into tumbling across his forehead. He was dressed in jeans
that stacked over scuffed black boots, and his glorious chest was hidden beneath a gray flannel
shirt.

He looked wonderful leaning against the doorjamb, his heated gaze bearing down on her as it
always seemed to do when he was near.

"I like your sermon," she said, flipping
through the pages of his notepad.

"I didn't think you were into religion and
church."

"It's preaching I don't like. You know, the constraints, the demands."

He whipped a chair out from the table and
straddled it, folding his arms on top the back. "I
see. Ministers are synonymous with tyrant, dictator, and . . . control freak?"

She shrugged. "Deny it if you want."

"Would denying it do any good? You seem to
have your mind made up already."

Her stare drifted from the yellow writing pad to the veins on the back of his hands, to the jagged scar across the knuckles of his right, to the blunt cut of his fingernails. Slowly she looked straight at him. "My dad's a minister. He thrived on control and hell-fire-and-brimstone is his middle name."

"I'm not your dad."

That was obvious. He wasn't like any man she knew.

"Aren't you going to ask if my dad and I get along? Don't you want to know what it was like growing up in his household or how a minister's kid could become a showgirl?"

"If you feel the need to tell me, go right ahead."

Jeez, the man was stubborn!

"Let's just say things weren't easy, but I survived."

"And you became a showgirl to rebel against him?"

"I became a showgirl because I like to sing and dance. In spite of what you might think, I'm not rebellious."

He hit her with a maddening grin. "So why'd you take off on Satan last night?"

"To prove to you . . ." That was the wrong thing to say, and the grin on his face was proof that he was getting great pleasure out of her sudden discomfort.

"To prove what to me?"

"You were positive Satan would hurt me, and I wanted to show you that he wouldn't."

"But you're not rebellious?"

"No."

"Then I'm not a control freak."

"So you say."

"Maybe you'll see me in a different light after we spend a long, hard day together." He shoved out of the chair and headed to the laundry room. "Come here."

"Dishing out orders already?"

He peered through the door and grinned. "You don't give an inch, do you?"

"Not if I can help it."

He chuckled, shaking his head as he tossed a heavy sweater at her. "If you don't want to freeze, you might consider putting that on."

Okay, so he was being nice, but only after she'd expressed her displeasure at his command. She might be exasperated with the frustrating yet sexy man, but she wasn't crazy enough to ride out in the just-above-zero temperature without bundling up.

Picking the forest green sweater up from the tabletop where it had landed, she slipped the bulky knit over her head and inhaled the faint scents of musky aftershave and . . . Mike, a combination of leather and soap. Irish Spring, maybe. She remembered the scent from their ride last night, from their closeness in her bedroom, and the slight aroma that lingered in the wool came darn close to making her toes tingle.

Silly. Plain silly, she told herself, and went back to the business of getting ready for her trek out on the prairie.

Standing, she adjusted the enormous sweater over her hips and shoved the cuffs from her fingertips to her wrists. "It's a bit big," she said, pulling her ponytail from under the neckband.

"It'll keep you warm, that's all that matters."

Obviously he wasn't into fashion, because he dug through a laundry basket on top of the washing machine, pulled out what looked like a ragged ball of yarn, and thrust a red-and-orange knit stocking cap with a fat tassel at the end into her hands.

"You might want to try that on for size, too."

She stared at the ridiculous garment. "This isn't yours, is it?"

"One of my parishioners gave it to me for Christmas."

"And you wear it?"

One side of his mouth tipped upward. "What do you think?"

"That you accepted it graciously and hid it away because no sensible—or fashionable—person would be caught dead in it."

He shrugged. "Possibly."

"So why should I wear it?"

"Because frostbitten ears are uglier than that cap. Even worse is a pretty woman who's had her ears amputated."

He had a point, she thought, as she pulled the cap over her head. But she didn't see the point of the gooey white paste he was squeezing onto his fingertip.

"What are you going to do with that?"

"I'll show you." He curled his hand around the back of her head and held it steady while he applied the zinc oxide to the bridge of her nose and her cheekbones. She could feel the warmth of his breath against her face as he worked, could almost feel the softness of his freshly shaved cheeks. Why, oh why, did her knees have to feel like jelly?

"That oughta keep your skin from burning."

"It should scare away coyotes and mountain lions, too."

His fingers slid from the back of her head and brushed over her jaw. His thumb whispered across her lips. "I can't imagine you scaring anything or anyone away. Not mountain lions, not coyotes, not—" he dropped his hand as if her lips had suddenly ignited—"not anything."

He tossed the tube of zinc oxide on the table and grabbed his coat from a rack by the door. "Why don't you get your jacket and gloves and we'll get going."

"What about *your* knit cap and zinc oxide? Are you immune to the sun and frostbite?"

"I'm pretty much immune to everything."

Everything but her, she imagined. But she was trouble, she was a showgirl, and he kept backing away.

And she tried convincing herself it was all for the best.

She grabbed her coat and gloves from the living room while Mike shoved the sandwiches and thermos of coffee into a saddlebag.

"So, Pastor Mike," she said as he pulled on his jacket, "is this trip going to be as long and hard as you told me, or were you just trying to scare me off?"

He frowned at her from beneath the black Stetson he'd tilted low on his brow. "Something tells me this is going to be the longest and hardest journey I've ever taken."

## Chapter 6

MIKE AND BUCK AMBLED ALONGSIDE Charity and Jezebel as the morning sun crested the eastern bluffs and shone down on the prairie. He tried to concentrate on their surroundings, knowing he should keep his eyes peeled for the black-and-white spotted mares, for Satan's harem, and mainly for the dappled gray rene- gade, but his focus was centered on Charity.

She'd called him pastor, a term reserved for his parishioners, for minor acquaintances. Charity wasn't either. She was something more, although he hadn't quite pegged what.

Whatever she was, he didn't want her calling him pastor. He didn't want to be her minister, didn't want to hear her confessions, or counsel her. What he wanted to do was kiss the slender curve of her neck, her temples, her brow. And, oh yeah, he wanted to kiss her lips. Wanted to kiss them till they were hot and swollen and she begged him for more.

He'd come close to kissing her when he'd put the zinc oxide on her nose and cheeks. His mouth had been only a fraction of an inch from her lips, so close that he could feel the heat of her body, could almost hear her heartbeat, so close that her exotic perfume intoxicated him and sent his mind wandering to places it shouldn't go.

What a fool he was. A mixed up fool who didn't know whether he should push her away or clasp her against his chest.

The only things he did seem to know was that she made him forget his troubles and made him hungry. He wanted her, which was pure hell for a man who couldn't have every ounce of Charity Wilde unless he married her. Sheer agony for a man afraid of getting married again, because he knew in his heart that if he did, the guilt he couldn't get rid of would someday rear its ugly head and rip his marriage apart.

*Keep your hands off of her. Look all you want. Just don't touch.*

Easier said than done.

Somehow he kept his distance, but he couldn't stop looking. He studied the soft lines of Charity's profile; the way short tendrils of her golden brown hair had sprung out from under the ridiculous stocking cap he'd insisted she wear; the way her lips tilted into a smile when a jackrabbit skittered across the dirt and snow, and the way she frowned when an osprey swooped from the sky, caught the rabbit in its claws and carried it away.

He nudged Buck close to Charity and Jezebel and pointed out the track of a mountain lion, the bleached skeleton of an antelope, and the hazy shape of Devil's Tower a good fifty miles away.

"Lauren told me Jack's ranch was huge, but I had no idea it would be this big."

"We left Jack's place about a mile back. This is mine." He stilled his mount and Charity did the same. He rested his gloved hands atop the saddle horn and stared at the vast stretch of land. "There aren't any fences and you'd have to look awfully hard to find the property stakes, but a few thousand acres out here belong to me."

Her hazel eyes widened as they followed his gaze. "A few thousand?"

"That's not all that big, not by Wyoming standards, but it's enough. Someday, when Jack's son Beau takes over my job as manager, I'll run my own cattle and horses out here. I won't get rich, but money's never been my priority."

Out of the corner of his eye he could see her frown. She found his statement hard to believe, but he could understand that, considering that she lived in Vegas, where money was everyone's chief concern.

"Haven't you ever wanted to live somewhere else, do some other kind of work?" she asked.

"All I've ever wanted is right here. Good

friends. Two careers I love. A house I spent a few years building, and this land." He breathed in the familiar scents of sage and icy snow, and caught a drift of Charity's perfume again. She added something special to the prairie, something exotic, a unique brand of wildness. In spite of her stubbornness, he could get used to her hanging around.

"What about you?" he asked. "Have you ever wanted anything besides a life in Vegas?"

She shook her head. "What I didn't want was the life I had."

"Hell-fire-and-brimstone, right?"

"Sunday through Saturday, come rain or shine." She laughed lightly. "There were good times, too, but my dad was determined to make me forget the life I'd led before he and my mom adopted me."

"How old were you?"

"Five. I don't remember much of anything before my folks took me in, but I never forgot the time I spent in Vegas with my real mom."

"A good time?"

"My mom didn't have any money, only an old truck, a bunch of glittery costumes she'd picked up at some thrift store, and me—her four-year-old ticket to riches and fame." Charity tilted her head toward him and smiled. "I suppose it wasn't the best of times for her, but I had fun."

"Doing what?"

"Playing dress-up, wearing tons of sequins and jewels and makeup. My mom was sure I could be the next Shirley Temple if we could just get to Hollywood, but she needed money to get there, so she put me on a street corner, told me to sing and dance, and held out a hat for tips."

"You didn't mind?"

"I was a ham. I liked the bright lights and the showgirls I'd catch a glimpse of every now and then. I loved the applause and the way people tossed dollar bills into the hat and smiled when they watched me. We made pretty good money until the cops ran us off."

"What did you do then?"

"Went to Hollywood for a while. My mom was certain I could be a star if the casting directors would give me a chance. What she refused to realize was that I could sing and dance, but I couldn't act to save my life."

"So you didn't become a star?"

"I'm still working at it. I got waylaid for a few years when my mom decided she had better things to do than support a daughter. She'd already ditched my brothers, and getting rid of me was pretty easy."

"You don't sound bitter."

"It was a long time ago and, well, let's just say I didn't miss her when she walked out of my life. After that I spent thirteen demure and sedate years as a preacher's kid and the last seven once again trying to make a go of it in Vegas."

"I take it it's not all that easy?"

She laughed. "I live in a run-down apartment. I'm currently unemployed. No, it's not easy."

"What are you going to do when you get back home?" Mike asked, sidling Buck against Jezebel, allowing his leg to brush against Charity's. "Any job prospects?"

"A few, of course some aren't as good as others. If I don't get into a big stage show right away, I'm sure I can find a bar or club looking for someone to sit on their piano and sing."

He could easily picture her sitting on a piano, belting out tunes in her seductive voice, with her stunning legs crossed at the knee, her feet in a pair of sky-high heels, her body in a barely-there dress that was almost hidden by her cloak of long silky hair. If he thought she'd stay out here in the middle of nowhere, he'd hire her in a minute. Wouldn't his parishioners love to see her sitting on top the piano on Sunday mornings, belting out a chorus of "Jesus Loves Me"!

"I've got an audition in a month," she continued. "It's the part of a lifetime—for me, at least." He saw the sparkle in her eyes and knew in that instant that she'd never be happy staying in a place like this, where glamour only came in magazines delivered through the mail.

"I take it the job of a lifetime means you won't be playing a peeled banana."

She smiled, shaking her head. "I don't know anything about the costume—or the show. Everything's under wraps right now, but it's touted as being the most elaborate production in Vegas history—in the biggest hotel in the world. Everything's scheduled to open by summer and this time—for the first time—I'm trying out for the lead, at least I was when I left home."

"You mean they could have picked someone already—without auditions?"

"That's always possible. But . . . well . . ." She frowned and turned her gaze back to the prairie in front of them. "I might not get to audition."

"Why not?"

"It's a long story, all of it leading up to the fact that the choreographer hates my guts."

"Did you fix him up with a blind date, too?"

Her eyes fumed, but he couldn't miss the touch of mirth mixed with her agitation. "I didn't like him well enough to fix him up with a date. In fact, one time he made me so mad I punched his lights out. Unfortunately, he's put together the dance routines for the show I'm going to try out for. He could cross my name off the audition list or he could make my audition absolute hell."

"If he's such an important guy, why'd you hit him?"

"You're sure you want to know?"

He nodded, wanting to know everything about her.

"He had a problem with the way I danced." The words nearly ground through her clenched teeth. "I did everything under the sun to please Duane-the-lech, but nothing seemed to be good enough. Rehearsals were long and exhausting, and if the least little thing went wrong during the show I'd hear about it for hours on end."

"What went wrong?"

"Anything and everything."

She pulled her boot out of a stirrup and wrapped her leg around the saddle horn. As far as Mike could tell, the woman couldn't do anything wrong—with her body, at least.

"For starters," she said, "one time I danced right off the stage. It wasn't my fault that someone swiped my mask and they gave me a substitute at the last second. It was too big and slipped over my eyes, and I could see Duane standing in the wings getting more and more irritated by the minute because my hands were on the mask instead of where they should have been. So I just got brave and figured I'd done the routine so many times I could do it in my sleep. But I was wrong. I toppled off the stage and landed in the lap of a man who'd had far too much to drink. He didn't mind nearly as much as Duane."

"Is that it?" Mike asked, desperately trying to keep a straight face.

She shook her head. "That was the *first* time Duane got mad. A few weeks later I passed out on the stage."

Suddenly he was worried. "Why? Not enough sleep? Not enough to eat?"

She laughed, and the sparkle in her eyes brightened a day that was turning cloudy. "No, it was a costume problem again. I was a Mayan princess, and I had to wear this gigantic headpiece made of peacock feathers and rhinestones that must have weighed a good twenty pounds. The weight wasn't the real problem, of course.

The blasted thing was engineered all wrong—
heavier in the front than in the back. I complained
up one end and down the other, but no one
would listen to me. So there I was, out on the
stage, all the lights shining down on me, and
when I bowed to the sun god I lost my balance
and my forehead smacked into the floor. I was out
like a light for at least thirty seconds, but the
show went on, right around me. Duane gave me
the what-for when the curtain went down and
made darn sure I was back in the show when the
curtain came up."

"You should have hit him twice."

She frowned. "This from a minister?"

"From a man who doesn't like bullies. You
could have had a concussion. You could have
been seriously hurt."

"You think I hit him because he made me go
back on stage? You can't stop a show just because
someone gets hurt or faints. You go on if you've
got the flu or a sore ankle."

"Okay, I get the picture here. You're a glutton
for punishment. You'd do anything and everything because the show must go on."

"Almost anything and everything. I do draw
the line occasionally."

"So why'd you knock him out?"

"Like I said before, he had a problem with the
way I danced. He didn't think my bumps and
grinds had enough realism to them and wanted
to give me private lessons, but I declined. A few
days later I got this note to come to his office on
my day off, and when I got there he was stark

naked. I started to leave but he grabbed my hand, pulled me up close and far too personal, and insisted on showing me how bumps and grinds were really done. *That's* when I decked him."

"He fired you when you could have turned him into the police for attempted rape?"

"Oh, yeah. And you should have heard him cussing even though I helped him get dressed, even though I hauled him to the hospital because I broke his nose, even though I told him I wouldn't report him to the cops."

Her smile, the way she told the tale, made him want to laugh, but the reality of what had happened sobered him.

"You really want to go back to Vegas, to a life like that?"

"Incidents like that are the exception, not the rule."

"But you'd be working with that man again if you got the job."

"It's my life, Mike. You take the good with the bad." She looked around them, at the snow-dusted prairie, at the storm clouds building in the north. "Do you throw up your hands when a blizzard comes in and wipes out a big part of your herd? Do you give up when the price of beef drops?"

He shook his head.

"The career I want in Vegas isn't much different than you chasing after Satan. He doesn't want to be caught, but he gets really close to you, teasing you, and you're determined to chase him no matter what obstacles get in your way. Well, stardom's this close to me," she said, holding up her gloved hand so her thumb and index finger were just an inch apart. "I get frustrated sometimes. I want to throw my hands up and quit at least once a week, but I can't."

She stared at the prairie for a moment, then faced him again. "Don't you get frustrated with your work on occasion?"

"Yes," Mike admitted. "When the winters are too long and the summers are too short, which is most of the time."

"But you stay here anyway."

"I grew up here. My dad worked for Jack's dad, and I'd watch him come in from the range every night feeling satisfied with what he'd done during the day, whether it was riding herd, branding calves, or stringing fence. I never wanted anything else."

"So how come you became a minister?"

He chuckled, hating to admit the truth, but she'd asked and she was going to hear all the sordid details. "For the worst of reasons."

She dropped her foot back into the stirrup and half turned in her saddle. "You mean you didn't stumble across a burning bush in the desert, that a voice didn't cry out to you saying, 'You shall minister to my people'?"

"Not exactly. I spent eighteen years trapped in a car every Sunday because the closest church was two hours away and my folks wouldn't miss a service for love or money. I always hated Christmas morning, getting dragged away from my presents because we had to go to church. 'You can open them later,' my dad used to say." He laughed at the memories. "We wouldn't get home till late in the afternoon and Jack—who didn't have to go to church—was always on the lookout for us to return so he could brag about his new toys, show them off, and I hadn't opened even one."

Charity laughed lightly, the sound ringing across the plains.

"Laugh all you want," Mike said, keeping his grin at bay, "but Jack got a BB gun one year and had all day to practice before I got mine. He was shooting cans before I got my Red Ryder out of the box, and he gloated about being the best when I was still figuring out how to aim the thing."

"So what does that have to do with you becoming a minister?"

"I told you. I didn't like the long drive into Sheridan."

"Why didn't someone build a church out here?"

"It's easy enough to build a church. It's a whole lot harder to find someone who wants to live in the middle of nowhere, or come out here just on Sundays to preach. I figured I'd have to keep on commuting if something wasn't done about the problem, so I decided I'd take the job."

"That's it?" she asked, her eyes narrowing. "That was your *calling*? Jealousy and a sore butt?"

"That's it."

"No college? No seminary school? Someone just waved a wand over your head and *zap* you're a preacher?"

He shook his head. "A lot of years in college with a degree in psychology and a masters in theology. Then"—he smiled—"someone zapped me and made me a preacher. Jack's dad gave me a piece of land to call my own, and he and the Atkinsons, who own the neighboring ranch, built the church."

"Have you ever regretted it?"

"No." He meant that with every fiber of his being, even though his faith had taken a bad stumble when Jessie had died. Even now, there were times he got burning mad about the way things happened in the world. Sure he had doubts sometimes, wondered whether he was fit to spread God's word. But he'd never turn his back on the calling he believed in or the people he ministered, too.

"I've always loved being a rancher and riding the range," he said. "And every time I come out here, I realize I'd have none of this if it wasn't for God." He gazed out across the stark but beautiful prairie. "Counseling someone in trouble; marrying a young couple anxious to start a life together; preaching on Sunday morning; I do it to thank God for blessing me with all that I have. I also do it because my life felt fuller—richer, I guess—once I became a minister."

Charity maneuvered Jezebel in front of him, and not for the first time he noticed that her smile was far more beautiful than the land he loved. "I had the feeling there was a little more to it than convenience," she said.

He laughed. "Yeah, well, don't make a saint out of me. My congregation's small and for the most part, I'm only needed on Sunday. That gives me time to manage Jack's ranch and take care of my own place. In between I'm on call if someone needs me."

"I never would have pegged you as being modest."

"Just honest." He grinned. "Okay, I'll admit, sometimes it gets overwhelming, but I don't plan on giving anything up."

"Do you make time for a personal life?"

He shrugged, letting her see a slight smile on his face rather than a frown. He didn't see any need in making her think something was missing in his life—or that he cared. "My work *is* my personal life."

"So is mine." He couldn't miss her frown and wondered if she was lonely, too.

Again he faced the far-off cliffs. The sun was rising high in the sky, peering out from behind a thickening barrier of dark clouds and beating down on the rugged red rocks.

Something moved high on the promontory. Something black and gray, a wild stallion whose mane whipped about in the breeze.

"We're being watched."

Charity turned her horse toward the bluff and followed his line of vision. "Is it Satan?"

"Yeah. There's no telling how long he's been watching us."

"What do we do now?"

"We go after him."

A sudden gleam radiated in her eyes, a sparkle that didn't come from makeup and stage lights but from deep inside her. "You can go after him, but I'm going to chase him away." She laughed, dug her boots into Jezebel's flanks, and tore off across the prairie.

*Blasted woman!* Stubborn. Headstrong. Trouble.

Why he wanted her baffled him. But he wanted her like he'd never wanted anything in his life.

He nudged Buck's flanks, and in less than a heartbeat they were charging after the mare and her rider.

The wind beat against Mike, chilling him to the bone, but nothing could slow him down as he and Buck sped toward Charity. They dodged the slush and mud that Jezebel kicked up until finally the two horses raced neck and neck.

He could hear Charity's laughter over the thundering of hooves. Saw the smile on her face, in her wild, excited eyes. The stocking cap had blown from her head and tendrils of hair that had escaped from her braid whipped about her. She'd long ago rubbed the zinc oxide from her face and her cheeks had turned from pink to flaming red. He tried to push the thought away, but he couldn't help but wonder if she looked that flushed and beautiful and wild in the midst of making love.

It was a tormenting thought, especially for a man who'd been celibate for six long years. Maybe it was time to stop being tormented.

Charity made him forget his worries. Made him forget his guilt—at least she'd helped him push it to the back of his mind. Maybe he could move on, think about having a woman in his life again.

Rash decision or not, Charity was the woman he wanted.

Catching a quick glimpse of the wild horse which had been his original prey, he tore off toward a winding, icy ravine, letting the stallion lead the chase. They ran full out, through the gravel of a long-empty streambed and between the boulders that lined its side. His heart beat hard and heavy. The thrill of the chase was the next best thing to making love. If he couldn't have one—for now, at least—he'd give the other all he had.

Satan darted up the side of the ravine, his powerful legs and hooves sending sagebrush, rocks, and dirt cascading down the side. Following the beast would be foolhardy—but Mike was willing to take his chances.

He whipped around in the saddle and saw Charity coming up behind him, excitement still in her eyes. If he went up the face of the canyon, she'd want to go too.

He looked back at the rocky cliff, at the narrow elk path knifing almost straight up the side. He could make it but he wouldn't put Charity's life at risk. He'd tell her to stay put, but . . . He shook his head at the thought. Charity would follow. She'd look at the path and say, "If you can do it, so can I, and nothing you say or do will make me change my mind." He wasn't going to give her the opportunity to be daring and foolhardy—to end up injured or dead.

He pulled Buck to a halt and rested his hands on the saddle horn. He inhaled deeply and let the air out slowly. His heartbeat took a little longer to calm.

"What are you stopping for?" Charity asked, brushing her hair from her face with gloved hands when she and Jezebel stopped beside him.

"Decided I'm hungry."

She glanced down the winding ravine, then turned her gaze toward the steep incline. Her eyes narrowed into a frown. "What, you decided Jezebel and I would never make it up that cliff?"

"Jez might make it," he said flatly. "There's a good chance you wouldn't."

"What makes you so sure?"

"I'm not sure of anything, but I'm not willing to find out what the real outcome would be."

"Shouldn't it be my choice?"

"Next time." He grinned. "I'm feeling autocratic at the moment."

Again she stared at the steep climb of the ravine. "You're just going to let Satan go?"

"For now."

A sly smile touched her lips. "You would have

gone up the cliff if I hadn't been with you, wouldn't you?"

"More than likely."

"You're probably thinking I'm nothing but trouble."

"I've thought that a time or two. But right now I'm thinking that it's cold out, that I'm hungry, and that I'd rather be sitting next to a fire . . . with you."

He couldn't miss the doubt in her eyes. "Why?"

Because she was trouble. Because getting close to her was as desirable as taking a bite of forbidden fruit. Because he no longer had the willpower to fight the attraction he felt for her.

Nudging Buck gently, he circled his horse until he and Charity were face to face. He knew his gloves were cold and rough, but he cupped them tenderly over her inflamed cheeks. He could almost feel her warmth seeping into his body.

And then he leaned forward, slowly, methodically, and kissed her.

His lips lingered longer than he'd planned, not nearly as long as he wanted. If kissing her was a mistake, it was the most rewarding mistake he'd made in his entire life.

"There's a line shack not far from here," he whispered against her mouth. "It's not the most comfortable place, not much in it but an old pot-bellied stove and a bed, but I can—"

Charity jerked away. "A *bed*? Good heavens, Mike! You're a minister."

Suddenly she whipped Jezebel around and beat a mean streak up the ravine.

*Blasted woman!* All he wanted to do was build a fire in the stove and sit on the bed while they ate the sandwiches she'd made.

Sex hadn't even crossed his mind.

At least that's what he told himself as he and Buck once more went on the chase.

## Chapter 7

*SEX!*

That's all he wanted, Charity fumed. A roll in the hay in some out-of-the-way line shack where no one would see or hear. How on earth could she possibly have thought Mike Flynn was different from other men?

Because of Mike, she and Jezebel were dashing along the precarious rim of a rocky ravine, which was sheer madness and screamed trouble with a capital *T.*

*Damn! Double damn!* Why couldn't Mike have been happy with just a kiss? Why did he have to bring a bed into the mix? Why did he have to be like all the other men she'd come in contact with? Why couldn't he get to know her, spend time with her, maybe even fall in love with her before wanting to rip off her clothes?

Because he was a man, the kind of man she needed to stay away from because . . . because . . . oh, because she liked him too darn much!

But that didn't give him any special privileges. She hadn't given in to millionaires willing to pay for a sample, to lithe dancers whose bodies could move in all sorts of extraordinarily sexual ways and would probably do a wonderful job initiating a woman in the ways of making love. She hadn't put out for bouncers, high-rollers, casino bosses, Marines, or high school jocks.

She certainly wasn't going to give in to a man of the cloth, a man whose principles should be loftier and more exalted than a mere mortal's.

"Slow down Charity!"

She heard him hollering from somewhere behind her but she wasn't about to comply. Instead she leaned over and whispered a few sweet nothin's into Jezebel's ear, and the horse leaped forward at a blinding pace.

She had no desire to talk to Mike right now, not while she was angry. He'd just feed her another line, maybe try to kiss her again so her legs would turn to jelly, then sweep her up on his steed and carry her off to his secret hideaway on the plains.

No, she wouldn't stop, she wouldn't slow down, and she wouldn't give him another chance to mesmerize her, to make her fall into his arms and then, when he had her completely under his spell, control her every action and try to control her every thought—like her father had done for too many years. If she had to stay an unmarried, frustrated, lonely virgin the rest of her life, so be it!

Of course, Mike was making the prospect of staying a virgin seem like an eternal hell.

She heard Buck's thundering hooves coming up along side her, saw the fog of the horse's breath out of the corner of her eye. She tried to go faster, but Jezebel had only so much steam. The mare was slowing and there was no way Charity could rein her to the right or left because the cliffs jutted straight up on either side of them.

"Damn it, Charity!" Mike yelled. "You're gonna get us both killed if you don't stop right this second."

He reached across the distance between them and grabbed Jezebel's harness. In another second he'd either be sharing Jezebel's saddle or on the ground, getting dragged under the horse's hooves. As infuriated as Charity was, she didn't want Mike hurt.

Drawing on the reins, she managed to slow Jezebel and finally brought her to a halt.

Taking a deep breath, she tried to calm down before she looked at Mike. When she faced him, she could feel the burning fury radiating from his eyes. His chest rose high and fell hard and she could see the muscles of his jaw visibly tense.

To say he was mad would have been an under-statement.

"Mind telling me what the hell got into you?" he asked through nearly clenched teeth. "You could have broken your damn fool neck and mine as well, not to mention the fact that you could have caused the death of a couple of horses."

"Nobody died," she threw back. "Nobody got

hurt. But the next time you come on to me, the next time you try to get in my pants, I swear I'll . . . I'll—"

"*What* on earth are you talking about?"

"Don't try to sound all innocent with me. I've been around enough men to know you all want the same thing. Well, I'm not cheap and I'm not easy, and there's no way I'm going to run off to some bed in some line shack, just so you can have your way with me."

"I kissed you! That's it."

"But you wanted more."

"Yeah, I wanted more. But that doesn't mean I'd rip your clothes off of you, throw you down on the floor, and have my way with you."

"Am I supposed to read your mind?"

"You're supposed to trust me."

"I don't trust any man."

"I'm not just any man."

"And I'm not just any woman."

His eyes blazed and his gloved hands tightened into fists, sure signs that he was getting angrier by the second. "You've got that right, lady. You're maddening, frustrating, and pigheaded."

"*Me?* What about you? You're stubborn, exasperating, and . . . and . . . you're a minister. For God's sake, Mike, you even swear up a blue streak!"

"I think the Man upstairs would forgive me, considering what I've been forced to deal with."

"And what, pray tell, have you been forced to deal with?"

"You! Until you came into my life, I could count

the number of times I said hell or damn on one or two hands, and suddenly they're punctuating everything I say. Ever since you barged into my life, everything I've tried to protect, like my sanity and my privacy, has been shot to hell."

"You're the one who insisted on going to my bedroom last night."

"Yeah, to look at your ankle."

"But you took extra liberties and ran your hand halfway up my—"

"Did you try to stop me?"

"No."

"Why?"

"Because it felt good."

He glared at her a moment. Slowly the dimple deepened in his cheek and he chuckled. "Yeah, it did feel good. But that doesn't mean I'd try to take more."

"How could I possibly know that?"

"Because you can trust me. Because you should forget what you've experienced with every other man and just look at me for what I am."

"A minister?"

"No, as a man who wouldn't take advantage of you, no matter how much he wanted you."

Her eyes narrowed. "Do you want me?"

He laughed, letting out an ounce of pent-up frustration. "Against my better judgment, yes."

"But I'm trouble."

"And your life is in Vegas and my life is here. The way I see it you and I should stay far apart until you leave. I didn't want you coming with me today. I didn't want you getting between me and Satan, and I didn't want you getting under my skin, but you've done all those things."

"I'm not a tease and I didn't set out to get under your skin. All I planned to do was keep you away from Satan." She couldn't miss the questioning rise of his brow. "Okay, so I like you, but I didn't set out to like you. I sure as heck didn't come out here to the middle of nowhere expecting to fall under your spell, and I wouldn't have if you hadn't run your fingers up my leg last night."

"And I might not have done that if you hadn't wiggled your fanny up against my—"

"I was uncomfortable. Saddles aren't built for two people."

"The problem is, you and I aren't going to fit together no matter where we are."

His words shouldn't have hurt her, but they did. She didn't want to get involved with Mike because he'd never understand what she did for a living. He'd try to change her. Try to make her the good little woman—and that's not what she wanted to be. But . . . but she hated to hear him say there could never be anything between them, especially when there was so much about him that was good and strong and moral, things she would have wanted in a man—*if* she'd ever wanted one.

"Did you ever meet a woman who was a good fit?" she asked, figuring she might as well torture herself by learning more intimate details about Mike's life—a life she'd never fit into.

"Yes. My wife."

Charity's throat tightened. "I didn't know you'd been married."

"Once, but never again."

She grabbed hold of her braid and twisted it nervously in her hands as she studied Mike's strong, somber profile. He was scanning their surroundings again, a fixed stare on his face.

Jezebel yanked at the reins Charity had been holding far too tight and grazed on the few blades of prairie grass scattered about. The mare stepped close to Buck and Charity's leg nudged Mike's, but he didn't look toward her. He'd grown quiet and far too pensive.

"Are you divorced?" Charity asked.

Mike shook his head. "She died six years ago."

"I'm sorry."

A hint of sadness drifted across his face before it faded, leaving in his eyes a tender remembrance as he looked toward the cloudy sky, at the red and gold buttes and the stands of pine and aspen. "Jessie—my wife—used to come out here and paint. Not in the winter, because she never could get used to the cold, but in the spring and summer when the sky was blue and the thaw made the streams run full."

It seemed obvious now. Jessie Flynn—the painter—had been Mike's wife. That's why his house was littered with her watercolors and oils, reminders of the woman he'd loved. Too many reminders.

Suddenly she remembered the photograph he kept in his Bible, the one of the pretty, petite blonde. Was that another reminder?

"I saw a picture in your Bible. Was that Jessie?"

He nodded, silent again, but she sensed there was a whole lot more he wanted to say.

"I looked at her paintings while you were getting cleaned up this morning. She was really good."

"Yeah, she was."

"I liked the one she did of Satan. It's almost like he stood still for her while she painted every strand of hair, every scar."

"She never missed a detail." He laughed as he took off his hat and combed his fingers through his hair. "There were times when I wished she'd just let her hair down and not worry about everything being perfect, but that wasn't her style."

He shoved the black Stetson back on his head and adjusted it so the sun missed his eyes. "She was painting ivy vines on the top of the kitchen walls when I snapped that picture. Each leaf had to look real, right down to the veins. She was meticulous with everything. The house was always spotless, she made gourmet meals when meat and potatoes would have been just fine."

He took a deep breath. "That night she was exhausted. She'd been tired all week. I should have known something was wrong when she let me help her fix dinner. She'd always insisted on doing it herself, but that night was different. I should have . . ." He shook his head, grief furrowing his brow. "I should have stayed home with her the next day."

"What happened?" Charity asked softly.

"Her heart gave out. Who would have thought

a twenty-eight-year-old woman could be happy and healthy one day and the next be lying in a coma, hooked up to machines that kept her alive."

Charity curled her gloved hand over Mike's. She was afraid he might pull away, but he didn't. Instead he tilted his head toward her and smiled. "I didn't mean to dump all of that on you."

"I don't mind listening."

"Then listen to me now. Don't run off. Don't jump to any conclusions. Just listen." He shifted in his saddle and in a move Charity took to mean he wasn't going to let her run off even if she wanted to, he slipped his fingers around Jezebel's bridle and pulled her and the horse closer to him.

"There hasn't been anyone else since Jessie. I haven't wanted anyone else. I haven't thought about anyone else . . . until you." His clarification left her nearly speechless. "As for the line shack, I'd planned to build a fire so we could warm up. And the bed . . . well"—he grinned—"there's no table, no chairs. I figured sitting on the bed would be better than sitting on the cold floor while we ate."

Red-hot embarrassment crept up her neck and cheeks. "I should have known you didn't have sex on your mind."

He chuckled, and she could see his fingers tighten around Jezebel's bridle. "I'm a man, Charity. Sex was very much on my mind. But trust me," he added quickly, apparently thinking she might run off after that comment, "I practice what

I preach. How can I counsel kids to wait for marriage if I don't do the same thing?"

"I thought you weren't interested in getting married."

He was quiet a moment, staring again at the length of the ravine. "Some days I'm not sure what I want."

The next words slipped from her mouth without thinking. "Did you know what you wanted when you kissed me?"

He let go of Jezebel's bridle and threaded his gloved fingers through the hair that had fallen from her braid. His green eyes were warm. Intense. "I knew that you were the last woman on earth I should be interested in. I knew you and I would fight over anything and everything. I knew I shouldn't kiss you, but I couldn't help myself."

They weren't endearing words of love and she should have gotten into a huff because he was so blunt, but she knew he was right. They were all wrong for each other—that, however, didn't mean she couldn't enjoy just one more kiss before they called a halt to this meaningless, senseless, totally unsuitable tryst.

Mike took off his hat and with his fingers still threaded through her hair, drew her face close to his. "You're not going to run if I kiss you again, are you?"

"No."

"You understand this is just a kiss, nothing more?"

She nodded, but her heart went into overdrive.

Slowly, his eyes wide open as he watched her, his mouth closed over her lower lip. He sucked on it, his tongue making small circles over her sensitive flesh. Charity wove her hands about his neck and whispered, "More. Please."

His mouth swept over hers. Heat radiated from her heart, to her stomach, then shot blazing flames through her arms and legs to the tips of her fingers and toes. His kiss was so powerful, so moving it caused the ground to shake beneath her.

A half day's growth of beard had shadowed Mike's face, and she loved the roughness against her cheeks and chin. His lips were slightly cracked and chafed from the bitter weather, but she relished the rough feel of them, the salty taste of them. But what she really enjoyed was the way his tongue reached out for hers. Warm, so warm, and they did what she loved doing the most— they danced, a sensual mixture of the waltz and tango. Slow. Easy. Their lips, their tongues perfectly in sync.

And then the earth shook again.

Somewhere in the back of her mind she thought she heard the deafening whinny of a horse and the powerful crash of hooves against stone. But at the surface of her consciousness, all she heard was a giddy song playing in her heart.

Until Jezebel jerked the reins from her hands in an attempt to catch her attention. Somehow she managed to drag herself away from the intoxicating scent of Mike's aftershave, from the heat emanating from his body, and tilted her head to see Satan standing not fifty feet away.

*Blasted horse!* How dare he interrupt the most pleasant moment of her whole entire life.

The stallion didn't move, except for the wind whipping through his mane. He merely stood there and stared at them with defiant brown eyes, daring them to go on another chase.

Mike's right hand twisted around the rope hanging from his saddle and Charity reached across him, clutching his fingers, hoping to stop any attempt he made to lasso the stallion.

"Couldn't we ignore him this time?" she asked, drawing in a deep breath and leaning toward him, wanting their mouths to dance again.

"It's hard to ignore him when he's standing there watching us."

"Close your eyes and kiss me again. Maybe I can make you forget he's there."

"You make me forget a whole lot of things," Mike said, sweeping his hand over the back of her head and tugging her mouth hard against his. He kissed her so thoroughly in just those few swift seconds that she almost tumbled off of Jezebel's back. "Sometimes," he whispered against her lips, "I'm afraid you could make me forget I'm a minister."

And then he was gone—the salty taste of his lips, the warmth of his breath, his hard, strong body. All she could see was his back as Buck sprinted across the prairie.

Her body trembled. She wanted more, so much more, but she had to turn her back, just as Mike had done, before he made her forget that she had a life in Vegas, a life she wanted far more than she wanted his kisses.

If it wasn't for Satan, she'd ride off in the other direction. She'd get as far away from Mike as she could. But right now she had a stallion to save.

She'd worry about saving her sanity later.

## Chapter 8

SATAN LED THEM ON A WILD CHASE, over flat land and rugged, up a rise to the top of a narrow and treacherous plateau. Mike thought for sure a hard and fast ride would cool the fire burning inside him, but all it did was add to his anxiety and toss fuel on the flames.

Charity was hot. Too hot for any man. Wild and untamable. Seductive yet innocent. Vulnerable but guarded. A complicated woman—and he was a fool for touching her.

The woman drove him mad.

A barrage of gravel hit his coat and grazed his face, yanking him back to reality. It hurt like hell, the place he'd be going if he didn't get hold of himself and remember that he was a man who'd vowed that he wouldn't have sex without marriage.

For the first time in a long time he could understand what the teenagers in his church were going through, how overactive hormones could lead them astray. Right now he wanted to stray— but he wouldn't. Couldn't.

He wiped mud from his face with the back of his glove and turned around to see Charity right on his heels. Her hair had pulled completely free of its braid and whipped out behind her in the breeze. Don't look, he told himself. Don't even think about all that silky brown hair cascading over naked shoulders, and firm breasts, and slender hips. Don't think about your hands smoothing over those velvety places and seeking out warm, hidden places as well.

Think about Satan.

He rode harder, trying to put Charity out of his mind. Later, after he caught that damnable horse, he'd figure out how to deal with the lustful cravings of his body and soul. Of course, a man of the cloth didn't have all that many options to consider. If truth be told, there were only two: abstinence, which was proving to be a pain; and marriage.

Oh, yeah, wouldn't a marriage between the two of them be something, when both of them had different goals in life. One night of marital bliss and she'd hightail it to Vegas and he'd be stuck in nowhere, hornier than ever, thinking about his wife dancing half naked, doing bumps and grinds on stage for hundreds of thousands of men when he'd prefer that she dance naked for him alone.

*Forget her!* Just forget her. You're not in love

with her. You don't want to marry her. And she thinks you're a control freak with an uncontrollable libido.

*Think about Satan!*

It wasn't long before Charity caught up with him, and they rode together in pursuit of Satan, both of them looking straight ahead, neither one of them daring to look at the other.

It was better that way.

The stallion had had endless chances to disappear, to charge down a steep embankment or through a narrow draw, but he never left their sight. If this was some new kind of game the mustang was playing, Mike didn't mind playing along, but he planned to come out the victor.

Not far ahead, the plateau came to a sudden halt. Mike and Charity slowed their mounts and stopped a few hundred feet from the edge of the rocky precipice, but Satan kept running until his escape route came to an abrupt and perilous end.

Satan stood on the overhang, his movements skittish as he jerked his head around to stare at the sudden drop-off and the deep, rocky ravine below. Charity looked just as jumpy as the horse, her nervous eyes flickering from the mustang to the rope Mike held.

Her gloved hand stretched over his thigh, her fingers mere inches from the rope. "Please let him go."

Mike shook his head. Whether Satan wanted it or not, he was going back to the ranch, he was going to be tamed, and Mike wasn't going to let Charity interfere.

Her leg brushed against his, but Mike kept his concentration centered on Satan, nudging Buck a few feet away in case Charity got it in her mind to do something foolish—like try to stop him again.

Circling the rope over his head, he built a loop as he and Buck ambled toward the stallion. Satan's nostrils flared and his eyes widened in a mixture of anger and fright. He skittered about, his powerful hooves sending rocks and dirt cascading over the cliff.

"Don't move, Satan," Mike coaxed. "Just hold still, and we'll get this over with."

Out of the corner of his eye Mike caught a glimpse of Charity coming up along side him, saw her pleading eyes, but he wouldn't be stopped. Satan was destined for his ranch, to sire the best saddle horses in the west. The stallion would not get away again.

The loop he'd built was perfect. His distance from the stallion was exactly right, and he let the rope slide through his gloved fingers and fly toward the mustang. In a heartbeat, Satan would be his.

But in less than a heartbeat Charity hit him broadside and he sailed out of Buck's saddle and through the air. His butt hit the ground first. His back and head followed right behind, bouncing a time or two against the dirt and mud, before Charity landed smack on top of him.

Murderous thoughts ricocheted through his mind as he tried to catch his breath. He had a rope in his hands—a rope that hadn't found its mark. Since the rope wasn't around Satan, maybe he'd just wrap it around Charity's slender neck, after all, it was fully exposed and just inches from his hands.

The rest of her body was a whole lot closer. Too close. Her warm breath and her cascading hair teased his cheeks, his ears, his nose. Soft breasts smashed against his chest. Her hipbone jabbed his groin and half a dozen rocks stabbed his backside.

Murdering Charity would be easy and what the heck, he'd already racked up a whole host of sins he had to atone for.

He brushed a hunk of Charity's hair from his face and her defiant hazel eyes glared down at him. Her jaws ground together as if he'd jumped her instead of the other way around.

"I hate to ask this," he said, "since you seem to be so comfortable, but could you move?"

"No. If I do, you'll go after Satan and I told you I wouldn't let you catch him."

If she wouldn't budge, he would, but the first shift of his body did nothing more than make their hips rub together. And then the unexpected happened. His blasted body reacted—fast, hard, completely out of control.

Charity's eyes widened. She wiggled in an attempt to get away, but instead her pelvis ground right into him.

"Quit moving or you're gonna have real trouble on your hands," he said through nearly clenched teeth.

She froze. "I didn't mean to make you . . . angry."

He sucked in a deep breath. "No?"

A slight smile touched her lips. "Feel like murdering me?"

"It crossed my mind."

"But you're a man of God and you wouldn't do something like that. Would you?"

"Every man has his limits."

A touch of merriment twinkled in her eyes as she pulled a lock of his hair over his brow, slid an inch or two up his body, rubbing him the wrong way once again, and planted a soft, teasing kiss on his lips. "Have you reached yours?"

"Just about."

"Does that mean you'd like me to get up now?"

An hour ago he might have told her to stay where she was. He might not have cared about the rocks stabbing him in the back. But things had a way of changing in an hour.

He looked past her toward the wild stallion. The horse stood stock still on the edge of the cliff, glaring at him as if he dared Mike to try again.

Why was he surrounded by stubborn, obstinate creatures that needed taming?

"Whether you like it or not, Charity, I've got a horse to catch. So, yeah, I'd like you to get up now."

"All right, I'll move, but I'm not going to let you get Satan."

Headstrong. Willful. Sexy. And he had to get her off of him—fast.

Her first real move spelled near disaster, when her knee slid between his legs. He steeled his nerves, anticipating the next undulation of her teasing body, and sucked in a deep breath through clenched teeth when her hips slid and swirled in all the wrong but right ways. She was soft and feminine, and he was anything but soft.

"Sorry."

The woman didn't look the least contrite. In fact, she looked as if she enjoyed every speck of torture she inflicted upon him. Inside and out, he was dying a million deaths while she wiggled her erotic body all over him in what appeared to be a half-hearted attempt to stand.

The last squirm, the last little bump and grind pushed him over the edge. He wrapped his arms around her, rolled over as if they were in a king-sized bed, and stared down at her.

"Looks like the tide has turned and I'm in control now."

Her lips pursed as he moved in close, his mouth only a fraction of an inch from hers. Her breathing grew heavy. He could feel the beat of her heart quicken.

"What are you going to do now?" she asked.

"What do you think?"

She swallowed hard. "Kiss me?"

That had been his first thought, but his emotions weren't that far out of whack. "Not on your life." He chuckled as he pushed up from the ground.

Ignoring the mud, dirt, and snow that clung to a good deal of his body, he swept up his hat, pulled it hard on his head, and went for his rope.

But Charity had beaten him to it. "You looking for this?" She stood between him and Satan, the lariat clenched in her fist.

He stuck his hand out, palm up, as if he thought she'd give the rope up without a fight.

"I'm not going to let you get him. He's wild and free, and he'll die if you try to fence him in."

"Give me the rope."

Charity shook her head as she backed toward the stallion. "How would you like it if someone roped you? If someone shoved you behind a ten-foot fence?"

"Five foot," he corrected.

"A fence is a fence, it doesn't matter how high or how low it is."

He took a cautious step toward her, keeping a wary eye on the stallion and the edge of the cliff. "I won't hurt him, Charity. How many times do I have to tell you that? All I want to do is tame him, then breed him."

Satan reared, his powerful front hooves batting the air before they came down hard just feet from Charity.

"Don't get any closer to him, Charity. Please."

She ignored him, moving back an inch at a time, even though Mike had stopped his advance.

"The ledge isn't going to hold the two of you." Mike's heart hammered in his chest as rocks crumbled away at the edge of the ravine, as Satan spun around and leaped over the side, down the steeply-angled cliff, sending snow and dirt into the air behind him. It rained down on Charity, and Mike lunged forward to grab hold of her, but all he caught was the flash of fear in her eyes as the ground gave way beneath her feet, and she disappeared along with a rush of earth.

Chapter 9

MIKE DROPPED DOWN ON THE UNSTABLE precipice, braced his hands on a thin layer of shale, and peered over the edge to see Charity's twisted body lying at the bottom of the rocky ravine. A raging bull could have kicked him in the gut and he wouldn't have felt a tenth of the pain that ripped through him now.

There was no time to think about the foolishness of plowing over the cliff, no time to think about Charity's frightened eyes or the fact that even though he hadn't touched her, it was his actions that had pushed her over the side. He had to get to her quickly.

He rose to his knees, looking for a way down that wouldn't kill him, when the shale shifted and fell away beneath him, sending him boots first into the ravine.

He grabbed for sagebrush to slow his descent, but the branches slipped right through his gloved fists. Dirt and dust pelted his face and body before he came to a jarring halt, smacking into a pile of boulders. Pain shot through his shoulder but he ignored it, scrambled to his feet and raced toward Charity.

She was still. Too still. His heart thudded in his chest as he knelt next to her and caressed strands of hair from her face. Her eyes were closed, and he couldn't see any movement at all beneath her almost translucent lids.

"God, Charity," he whispered against her lips, "please don't be dead." It was a prayer mixed with a plea. The woman maddened him, excited him, and right now her stillness was scaring him half to death. He could push her away. He could watch her go back to Vegas and never see her again. But he couldn't lose her this way.

Slowly her eyes opened and he offered a silent, thankful prayer.

Her shaky hand slid beneath her head. She winced, and her eyes slammed shut. Mike ripped off his glove and slipped his fingers through her hair to find a knot the size of a walnut behind her right ear. A knot twice as big had formed in his throat, but relief washed through him when she pushed herself to a sitting position and leaned her head against his chest.

He held her to him, cradling her body as her breathing steadied. Thank God she was all right.

She gripped his coat, as if she were afraid he might leave her, took one long, deep breath, then tilted her head up and hit him with a halfhearted grin. "Was your trip over the edge as exciting as mine?"

Mike gritted his teeth. She'd just careened down a cliff and he'd done the same thing, which could have killed them both. He'd lost Satan— again. And she was grinning!

He had half a mind to walk away from her, to hike out of the ravine and leave her to the coyotes and mountain lions. He tried to hold on to those thoughts when she peeled her glove off and her chilled fingers smoothed over his brow. "You're bleeding."

"Doesn't surprise me."

She knelt in front of him, her dirty face looming just inches from his as she inspected a wound he couldn't even feel. He wanted to kiss her. He also wanted to push her away, and that emotion was winning the conflict warring inside him.

"It's only a scratch." She kissed his forehead lightly, and he steeled himself from feeling anything. "This is just a scratch, too," she said, drawing her fingers over a stinging cut on his cheek. There was a touch of remorse in her eyes. "Does it hurt?"

"No."

He pulled his gloves back on and stood, giving Charity's body a quick, impersonal once over. "How about you? Anything hurt?"

"I've taken worse falls on stage," she said, "and, as you might have guessed, I'm wearing a lot less padding when I'm doing a show."

"I figured as much."

He held out a hand and helped her up. Even though he loosened his grip when she was steady on her feet, she held on tight. She moved toward him, the buttons on her coat rubbing against the buttons on his, as she picked specks of sagebrush from his hair. "One would think you were upset with me."

"Upset?" He laughed cynically. "Upset isn't a strong enough word. Furious doesn't quite work."

"Murderous?"

"That's a more appropriate adjective considering that you continually ruin my chances at catching the horse I've been after for a whole lot of years. But acting on that emotion would be going against everything I believe in."

"And you'd never do that, would you?"

"Push me a little further and there's no telling what I'll do."

Once again he shoved away from her and went in search of his hat. The sooner he found it and got out of this place, the better off they'd be.

"Are you looking for this?"

He turned to see Charity fingering his dirty black hat. "Yeah. Thanks."

He knocked scraps of brush from the Stetson, slapped it against his leg to get rid of some of the dirt and dust, then worked a dent out of the brim and pulled it low on his brow.

A soft hand touched his arm. "I am sorry, Mike."

"About what? Helping Satan escape?"

She shook her head, a gesture he should have expected. "About your cuts. About the bruises you're going to have tomorrow. For being a pain in the neck."

Her sincerity made him chuckle. "I've got the feeling being a pain in the neck comes naturally to you."

"It's a problem I've suffered from all my life. My father worked awfully hard to change me, but he couldn't. I've tried to change me, too, but that just seems to lead to more trouble."

If consolation for a troubled life was something she needed, she'd have to find it elsewhere. He could counsel friends, family, his parishioners, but he didn't want to have a heart-to-heart discussion with Charity. Their discussions had a tendency to lead in other directions. And if they continued along the path they'd been following, they were destined to bump into bigtime trouble—for both of them.

Right now, the best thing to do was to get back to the ranch, then stay as far away from her as possible.

He skirted around Charity and looked toward the top of the bluff where he saw Buck grazing on a clump of grass. He whistled and the gelding stared down at him, shook his head as if he hated to be bothered, then backtracked along the cliff with Jezebel following behind, looking for a safe path into the ravine.

"Maybe it would be better for Buck and Jezebel if we went up to them instead of them coming down here," Charity said glumly.

"They'll be fine," he said. "They might be horses, but they're not foolish enough to get close to the edge unless they're sure it's safe, and they won't come down the side until they find the easiest way."

"Unlike me?"

He expected to see defiance in her eyes when he looked at her, but all he saw was utter defeat. His heart twisted, but he didn't answer her question. Instead, he turned his back and watched the horses working their way down the steep incline.

If he kept this up maybe she'd hate him before the end of the long ride home. It wasn't the way he wanted things to end between them, but it was probably the best way.

Behind him he heard Charity's sigh, then all was silent between them as they waited for the horses to make it to the canyon floor.

A ground squirrel scurried across the rocks and disappeared into a hole. A raven swooped down from some unseen perch and positioned itself on a boulder, waiting for his prey to reappear. The sun moved behind a cloud then came out again, and all the while Mike kept his eyes from focusing on Charity.

A normal man would have spirited her off to the line shack. A normal man would have spent the morning with the long-legged beauty in his arms. A normal man would have known much more than the taste of her lips, he would have already savored the texture of her nipples against his tongue, smoothed his palm over the naked curve of her hips, and buried himself inside her and known her heat, her scent.

But he wasn't a normal man. He was a minister

who could lust in his heart but do nothing to satisfy his cravings. A man filled with guilt who refused to marry again. A man who wanted Charity Wilde, in spite of the fact that she was impulsive, reckless, a tease, and nothing but trouble.

For all those reasons, he stayed away from her.

The whinny of a horse broke through the quiet and his thoughts. Mike's gaze jerked toward Buck, afraid his mount had lost his footing. But the gelding stood motionless, three-quarters of the way down the slope, and stared right past Mike and Charity, looking at something in the distance.

Another whinny echoed in the ravine, followed by the hollow, echoing sound of rocks tumbling against each other in the riverbed.

"Mike."

He turned at Charity's voice and followed her stare to a place where the craggy cliff angled sharply to the east. Satan stood tall and proud, his mottled gray fur blending into the rocks as his brown eyes fixed on them. Why the stallion had hung around was anyone's guess. Teasing was one thing for Satan. Foolishness was another. He didn't take chances like this.

The stallion pawed at the ground. He snorted, his hot breath turning the frigid air into a fog around him as he jerked his head wildly.

"Something's wrong." Charity's eyes were wide with worry when she twisted around to look at Mike.

"He's badgering us. He's rested now and ready for another chase."

"No." Charity shook her head. "There's something else. I know it."

She stumbled over rocks and driftwood as she made her way toward the horse. He'd never known a woman with so much determination, and his heart and resolve softened a touch. As much as he wanted to give up and call it quits for the day, he trailed after Charity, giving in to her instinct.

All of a sudden Charity stopped. He watched her shoulders rise then slump as she took a deep breath. Her jaw was tight when she turned toward him. "Maybe you should go first. I have a tendency to get us in trouble when I take the lead."

They were undoubtedly the most insincere words she'd ever uttered. He could laugh. He could kiss her and tell her his anger had subsided a notch. But he did neither. This time, he refused to give in to temptation.

He trudged by her, not smiling, not saying a word, concentrating all his efforts on getting to Satan without frightening the beast, moving cautiously over boulders, gravel, and downed tree branches.

The stallion's only movement was the nervous flicker of his eyes from Mike to Charity then back to Mike again. Charity was right. Something was wrong. But what?

Mike was less than ten feet from Satan when the stallion reared up in a show of power. A moment of fear pierced through Mike when he thought Satan's hooves were going to crash down on his skull, but they pounded against the ground instead. A second later the mustang beat a hasty retreat, running fiercely down the canyon's center, his mane and tail flying about him in the breeze.

Mike took a deep breath as he watched Satan streak out of sight. He thought about turning around, about heading for Buck, who'd nearly caught up to them, and getting out of this place, but there was something about Satan's actions that drove him further down the ravine.

Five yards. Ten. Mike maneuvered over rocks, through territory rarely traveled by man, and then he heard a horse's snort not far from where he was walking. The ravine twisted to the right, but off to the left was a deeply shadowed cave in the cliff wall, its opening nearly obscured by sagebrush and juniper.

Moving slowly, cautiously, Mike stared inside the cavern and froze when he saw the black and white Tennessee Walkers, one standing, one lying on the ground breathing heavily, a deep, vicious and bloody slash in her side. Against the far wall, almost hidden in the dark, was the trampled and broken body of a mountain lion.

"What is it?" Charity asked, placing her hand on his arm.

"The mares."

He moved toward the injured animal, kneeling at her side to inspect the torn flesh on her back and the deep gashes where claws had ripped across her side. She wasn't going to last long, not out here.

"What can I do?" Charity dropped down on her knees beside him, not the least worried or squeamish about the blood as she caressed the mare's neck in a futile effort to comfort her.

"I've got a cell phone in my saddlebag," Mike told her. "I need you to get it for me." He started to tell her about the bandages and first-aid kit, but she was already gone and he turned his full attention back to the mare.

Satan had led them here on purpose. He'd wanted Mike and Charity to find the injured mare, wanted them to help her, but he couldn't have done that if Charity hadn't thwarted Mike's attempts to capture the stallion.

The woman was going to take particular delight in telling him that was one more reason why Satan should stay wild and free.

Gravel crunched at the entrance to the cave, and from the corner of his eye he watched Charity come inside and crouch beside him.

"I brought the bandages and first-aid kit, too," she said, handing him the cell phone. "What should I do now?"

"Take off your gloves."

She didn't question, she just ripped the gloves off and looked at Mike for his next direction. She was calm, composed, and right now he was glad she was with him.

Without asking permission, Mike pressed her bare hand against the animal's exposed flesh to try and staunch the flow of blood. "Keep pressure on that spot while I call the ranch."

She wasn't squeamish. She didn't pull away,

and as he called one of his ranch hands, he couldn't help but admire her guts, a spunk he'd never seen in Jessie. He'd loved his wife with all his heart, but he knew full well that Jessie wouldn't have been beside him now, wouldn't have put her hands in blood, or put her mouth close to an injured horse's ear and whispered "You'll be all right, girl. Hang in there."

Charity was born to do exactly what she was doing right now. Suddenly it dawned on him that she was the trainer he'd been looking for, the one with an innate horse sense, the one who could gentle the wild horses he wanted in his herd.

But could he convince her that wild horses didn't need to be wild? And more importantly, could he convince her to stay?

He finished his call and shoved the phone into his pocket. "Shouldn't take much more than half an hour for Hank and Woody to get here with a trailer."

"Then what?"

"Get the mare back to my place. See if I can get the vet to come out."

"Is she going to be okay?"

"I don't know."

Mike dug through the bag for antiseptic, cotton, and bandages then went to work on the horse's wounds, doing the best he could to staunch the flow of blood.

Charity's hands were beside his, instinctively holding torn flesh together while he bandaged, dabbing at blood with her own wool scarf so he could get a clearer look at the horse's injuries.

"We wouldn't have found her if I'd caught Satan earlier today," he said, doing his best to give Charity credit for the miracle that had taken place, but he couldn't look at her face because he didn't want to see her I-told-you-so smirk.

"She wouldn't have been attacked if Satan hadn't brought her here," Charity said. She didn't accuse, didn't smirk, she'd merely repeated thoughts he'd had earlier. "Of course," she added without hesitation, "that doesn't change how I feel about him being caught."

Mike angled his head toward her and smiled. "We're never going to agree on that issue, are we?"

She shook her head. "I think we're destined to disagree about all sorts of things."

"Maybe we could reach some sort of compromise?"

"You're stubborn. I'm stubborn. Coming up with a compromise that works for both of us could take a long time, and I'm leaving in a few days."

"Then don't go back."

Her eyes widened in surprise, then slowly narrowed as if she were contemplating his rash statement.

She tilted her head and watched his hands while he worked on the horse's wounds. "I've got a big audition coming up. I have to go back."

Without thinking, he dug himself into an even deeper hole. "Then stay here until the audition."

"Why?"

"Because . . ."

The familiar screech of the brakes on Woody's

truck sounded outside, giving him time to wonder about the real reason he wanted her to stay.

Charity touched his arm, holding him back when he made a move to leave. "Why should I stay?"

He looked at her questioning eyes, at the injured horse, then said only a portion of what he felt. "You're good with horses. I could use someone like you on the ranch."

"I'm a good dancer and Vegas needs me, too." Charity smiled, but he didn't see a twinkle in her eyes. He'd disappointed her. Maybe she'd expected him to say, "Stay, because I need you." Of course, there was always the possibility that she had no interest in staying, that what he felt for her was completely one-sided.

She scrambled up from the ground and wiped her blood-stained hands on the thighs of her jeans.

"Are you going back in the truck?" she asked, looking at the silhouetted ranch hands walking toward the cave.

"Yeah. I need to stay with the mare. I'll have Woody or Hank get the other horses back." He smoothed a strand of hair from across her mouth, needing to touch her, probably for the very last time. "You goin' with me?"

She shook her head. "I'll ride Jezebel back to the ranch." She grinned. "And I'll try to stay out of trouble."

"You think that's possible?"

"No. That's part of the reason I like Las Vegas so much. Everyone gets in trouble once in a while, so it's not quite so obvious when it happens to me."

"A lot different from out here."

"A whole lot different."

Stepping toward him, she kissed his cheek lightly, then beat a hasty retreat out of the cavern.

Temptation had disappeared from his sight, but he doubted she'd ever be out of his mind—or his heart.

## Chapter 10

TRAIN WILD HORSES? SHE WAS A DANCER, not a cowgirl, but . . . Mike's offer had preyed on Charity's mind for hours. Even now, late in the afternoon, with the family gathered in the kitchen drinking coffee, decorating cookies for church the next day, and chatting non-stop about Beau's adventures at college, Charity's escapades on the great Wyoming plains, and Mike's trip to the vet with a zillion-dollar horse, she thought about Mike's words—the ones he'd uttered and the ones he'd left unsaid. Did he want her to stay for the horses—or for him?

She tried pushing the thoughts from her mind by laughing and gabbing with everyone else. She thought she was putting up a good front, but Jack Remington continually eyed her from the corner of the room, listening intently to what she had to say, especially when Mike's name came up. She'd seen that look before. He was analyzing her, studying her, trying to figure out what she was up to—which was absolutely nothing.

At last she escaped and found herself moving quickly, almost stealthily toward Jack's office on the far side of the house. This was where she'd wanted to come ever since she'd gotten back to the ranch. She'd thought about it while she'd showered and applied salve to her aching muscles. She'd thought about it while she'd been trapped in the kitchen.

She wanted to look at Jack's books.

Scanning the titles, she drew out a light volume with the innocuous title *Wild Horses and Burros of the Great Plains* and stood in the sunlight beaming in through the window to look at its contents. Her interest, of course, had absolutely nothing to do with the job Mike had off-handedly offered her, but strange as it seemed, she found herself a wee bit curious about what such a profession entailed.

Unfortunately, she didn't like what she read. The horses in the photos looked content enough, but she was less than thrilled by the headings that touted gentling methods like "bamboo pole" and "sliding neck loop." These time-tested practices left her feeling skittish, and she imagined the mustangs must experience a far more overwhelming panic when they saw a stick or rope heading their direction.

Her own methods would be far different. Patience. Persistence. If you wanted gentle, you had to be gentle. That was her philosophy.

Of course, she had no intention of ever giving her methods a try. Two run-ins in two days with a wild horse who didn't want to be gentled and with a man who thought everything should be tamed had left her with bruises to her body, her ego, and her emotions.

She was confused, too. For the first time in twenty-plus years, something other than dancing and singing had captured her interest, had taken over her thoughts, and for some odd reason she felt guilty, as if she'd betrayed a lifelong trust.

"Looking for something in particular?"

Charity spun around at the sound of Jack Remington's voice, her heart beating rapidly as she clasped the open book to her chest, hiding it just as she'd hidden copies of *Teen Beat* and *True Confessions*—magazines that her dad insisted would corrupt her mortal soul.

She flashed a guilty smile at Jack who flashed a what-the-hell-are-you-doing-in-my-office smile right back at her. She hadn't secretly pocketed a candy bar in the grocery store, she was merely digging for information, an action that could be totally misconstrued by everyone at the Remington ranch. She knew how the people around here stretched things out of proportion, taking one small notion and making it one big deal. This little notion, no doubt, would be taken as evidence that she wanted to stick around "Nowhere"— which she didn't.

The next notion might be that she'd fallen in love with their pastor, that she was looking for some way to wiggle into his heart and make him see her as a woman with more to offer than a well-toned body and a penchant for getting in trouble. That, of course, was the furthest thing from her mind. She was going home soon, and that was that.

"I was just looking for something to read," she said, answering Jack's question as she casually leaned a shoulder against the bookcase, attempting to look perfectly at ease with him staring at her. "Hope you don't mind me coming into your office."

"Not a problem."

It might not be a problem, but Jack's suspicious stare was maddening. He looked like a man with something he wanted to get off his chest, and for some reason, she knew that something had to do with Mike. Jack's silence was just as maddening as his glare. She'd make a beeline for the door and get completely away from him but his tall, broad body was blocking the way.

Perhaps she should strike up a conversation. "You've got a lot of books on . . . cows." She groaned inwardly at the sheer ridiculousness of her comment.

"I've got a lot of books on *horses,* too." Jack strolled across his office, picked a ledger up from his desk, then stared at the dust jacket of the book she clutched against her breasts. "That one you've been scanning's about operant conditioning, among other things."

She didn't want him guessing at her reasons for looking at the horse training book, so she played innocent, tilting the book to scan the cover. "Hmmm, operant conditioning. I never would have guessed that from the title."

"You interested in horse training?"

She shrugged. "Is that what operant conditioning is?"

Jack rested a hip on the edge of his desk and folded his mighty arms over his even mightier chest. "It's better known as clicker training— gentling a wild horse in a controlled environment, shaping his behavior by giving him rewards, like carrots and apples."

"In other words, bribing him so he'll do something totally against his nature."

Jack chuckled. "Mike told me you weren't all that crazy about him penning up and gentling wild horses. Satan in particular."

"I don't think Mike had gentling on his mind. Breaking Satan's spirit is more like it, and I'm dead set against anyone or anything having their spirit broken."

"Then why didn't you take the job Mike offered you? You could have done anything you wanted with Satan."

"It was an off-handed job offer, and I don't remember anything being said about me having full reign. Besides, I don't know the first thing about horses."

Jack's gaze again darted to the book in her hands. "You trying to learn something about them now? Maybe you're thinking about taking the job?"

See! One small action, like reading, blown totally out of proportion.

"I prefer wearing sequins to rawhide."

"Yeah, that's what I thought."

"You don't have to say that like it's a sin."

"Sin has nothing to do with it, as far as I can tell. I merely think you might not be cut out for this country—or Mike."

Her jaw tightened. "You're entitled to your opinion, I suppose. But let me tell you, if I had the desire to stick around here and train horses, domestic or wild, I'd be the best horse trainer in the state, maybe even this side of the Mississippi. And if I wanted Mike—"

"Do you?"

*Yes. No. Maybe.* "I have a life in Vegas, so this entire discussion is pointless."

"He's falling in love with you."

*Impossible.* "Did he tell you that?"

"He didn't have to. I can read his mind almost as well as my own, and I know what he's feeling."

"You're wrong."

Jack shook his head. "You think you'd make a good minister's wife?"

Charity laughed. She hadn't given marriage any thought at all. "I wasn't good at being a minister's daughter. I've got no intention of being a minister's wife."

"Then do me a favor?"

She felt her eyes narrowing at the tone of their conversation. "What?"

The phone on Jack's desk rang and she was glad for the distraction, but the steadfast and annoying owner of the Remington ranch ignored it. "Stay away from Mike the next couple of days. If you don't, he won't be asking you to stick around and train horses, he'll be asking you to marry him."

"And you think marrying me would be the worst thing in the world for Mike, right?"

Jack shook his head. "I've got nothing against you."

"You could have fooled me."

"If you want the truth, I think you're the best thing that's ever happened to Mike. Unfortunately, I don't think *you* know what's best for you. You think it's Vegas, when it's really Wyoming. You think it's dancing, when it's really horses. And you think it's some unreachable star, when it's really the love of a good man."

"What makes you think you know what I want or don't want?"

"Because I spent a hell of a lot of years chasing after the wrong thing, too. It wasn't until I met Sam that everything I'd ever wanted came into full view."

"I've only wanted one thing in my life, and what I want is in Vegas."

"Then don't hurt Mike by letting him think there's even a remote chance you might be happy here."

"I'd never hurt him."

"Not on purpose, but—"

A soft rap on the open door brought a halt to their disquieting discussion. "Am I interrupting something?" Sam asked, walking into the room and smacking her husband with an I-heard-everything-you-said frown.

"Not at all." Charity wished Sam had come in

five minutes sooner, that she'd drag her busy-body husband out of the office now and give her a chance to breathe again.

But Sam merely slipped her arm through Jack's and smiled at Charity. "Jack can be terribly opinionated at times. I take most everything he says with a grain of salt." Her smile widened. "You should, too."

Jack's eyes narrowed as he tugged his wife against his side. "I'm just looking out for Mike."

"He's a big boy. He can take care of himself, and so can Charity."

Right now, however, Charity wished she could sink into a hole someplace.

"For what it's worth, Charity," Sam added with concern, "I think Mike's just as capable of hurting you as you are of hurting him. Be careful."

"Now look who's butting in," Jack teased, as Sam pulled him toward the door.

"Yes, darling, but I do it with much more finesse." Sam and Jack were nearly out of the office when Sam looked back at Charity. "I almost forgot. You've got a call. Someone named Duane."

*Duane the lech?* Duane of the nasty bumps and grinds and bloody broken nose? The choreographer who hated her guts? That was all she needed after suffering an inquisition from Jack.

The office door closed and she was left alone with a case of nerves and trembling fingers that fumbled with the receiver. What could Duane possibly have to say to her that he hadn't said in the emergency room when the doctor was patch-ing up his broken nose? And how on earth had he tracked her down?

"Hello," she said politely, when she really wanted to ask "What the hell do you want?"

"I'm moving up the audition." Duane was cold and curt, just as she'd expected, but—*Hmmm.* Why was he calling her with this information instead of his assistant? She hated to get her hopes up, but Duane's voice on the other end of the line was a very good sign that she stood a chance of getting a starring role in his new production.

"When?" Charity asked, immediately thinking about enrolling in an extra ballet class, taking a few private lessons from a former showgirl who could show her some tricks that would blow Duane out of the water. She'd have to get moving if she wanted to be a star.

"The sixteenth."

She'd almost missed Duane's statement while thoughts of stardom raced through her head. "The sixteenth? Okay. That is the sixteenth of *March*, right?"

"February."

"But that's just a couple of days away."

"You either make it or you don't. If you still want a shot at the lead, you'll be there."

That was it. Duane hung up hard, and the dial tone rang heavily against Charity's ear.

February 16th. Tuesday, and if she remembered correctly, today was Saturday. She hadn't danced in weeks. She'd nearly sprained her ankle last night. Her body was bruised and sore from the tumble she'd taken today. She was in no shape to audition, but ... but she wouldn't miss this chance for anything in the world.

She had to change her flight. She had to practice.

Jack said she didn't know what she wanted, but he was wrong. She wanted to go home. She wanted to dance. She wanted to forget that for a few moments today, she'd almost let someone and something else come between her and her dream.

Chapter 11

MIKE PACED THE LENGTH OF DOC TEN Hope's kitchen, the spiral phone cord trailing his steps as he waited for someone, anyone, at the Remington ranch house to answer. At last the ringing ceased and a breathy, sexy female voice answered.

"Hello."

"Charity?"

There was a long, hesitant pause at the other end. "Mike?"

"Yeah." He didn't need to hear Charity's voice, not now when he'd done everything in his power to push her out of his mind. She was history. A flame that had flickered brightly, singed him, then disappeared, the way most flames did. He shouldn't have expected anything more.

"Is everything okay?" Her voice was soft, whispery, concerned.

"I've got a lot on my mind." And he didn't want to spend a long time talking to her so she'd be on his mind again as well. "Is Jack there?"

"I'm here by myself. Everyone else went to the Atkinsons's for dinner."

Mike collapsed in a kitchen chair, forced to talk to Charity because no one else was around. He cupped his hand around a steaming mug of coffee and knew he should just ask for her help and get the conversation over with, but temptation got the better of him. He liked her voice. He liked her more than he should. "Why didn't you go?"

"I couldn't bear the thought of eating more birthday cake."

He laughed for the first time since Charity had left him in the canyon. "Sam likes to celebrate. Birthdays. Christmas. Thanksgiving. It's never just one day. Always a week. You live out here and you'll get caught up in it, too."

There, he'd opened up that discussion again. She'd seemed adamant about leaving, but maybe she'd had a change of heart.

Once again there was a long silence at the other end of the phone, and he found himself hoping against hope that Charity would tell him she'd like to take part in more celebrations, that she wanted to work with horses, that she'd stay.

If she stayed, maybe he could figure out what he wanted from her next.

"How's the mare?" she asked, words he should have expected.

He swept a hand over his whiskers and tired eyes. So much for Charity Wilde sticking around.

"She's torn up inside as well as out, but Doc ten Hope's the best around. If anyone can save her, he can."

"How about you?"

"What about me?"

"How are you feeling?"

"Tired." *Lonely.* He took a sip of coffee and the hot liquid burned its way inch-by-inch down his throat. As exhausted as he was, as adamant as she seemed, he decided he couldn't give up. "Don't go back to Vegas, Charity. Stay here."

"I can't."

"A few more weeks, that's all. Stay here and work with the horses until your audition. See if you like it."

He heard her sigh. "I can't, Mike. My audition's been moved up and . . . I'm flying home tomorrow."

He'd just been gut-kicked by half a dozen Satans. He could hide behind the notion that he wanted her to stay for the horses, but he wanted her to stay for himself.

"I need to see you before you leave."

"I'm not going to change my mind about staying, Mike. I'm a dancer, not a horse trainer."

"I didn't say anything about horse training, Charity. I said *I* need to see you before you go."

"I'll be busy till then. I've spent the last few

hours stretching, exercising, trying to work some of the kinks out of my muscles and get somewhat in shape before Tuesday. I need to spend more time with Max and Lauren and the kids—"

"You afraid of seeing me? Afraid I could talk you into leaving Vegas?"

"Of course not." She didn't have to sound so sure of her feelings. "That audition means everything to me."

*And I mean nothing?* He wanted to shout the question at her, but he knew what her answer would be. They'd had two days together. Two days! It was fun. A good time. But it meant nothing else—to her. She was used to flitting from one good time to another, and flitting from him to someone or something else was nothing new.

"Then I'll wish you good luck." He forced himself to smile, even though no one could see him.

"Thanks."

"Look, I called for a reason." An important reason, something he'd almost forgotten. "I left my place in a hurry and I can't remember if I bolted the barn door. I won't be home till one, maybe two, and I've got the feeling Satan might come back tonight and try to take the Tennessee Walker again."

"I could call the Atkinsons's and see if Jack could stop by your place on the way home."

"It's out of the way, and Fay usually serves dinner late. Do you think—"

"I'll go. Consider it my way of making up for all the trouble I've caused you."

"Trust me, Charity. If I wanted you to make up

for all the trouble you'd caused, I'd ask a lot more of you. A whole lot more."

Charity trudged toward Mike's place, every muscle in her body screaming at her to slow down, to take it easy as she trekked over hill and dale. Fortunately the hills were low, the dales weren't steep, and the massive log cabin was just over a mile away, because her stiff, achy body was having a fit over the latest workout she was forcing on it.

Ballet lessons were strenuous, so was running five to ten miles a few times a week, but getting thrown from a horse, taking a flying leap out of a saddle and knocking a full-grown and decidedly handsome man to the ground, not to mention tumbling down the side of a rocky ridge and landing with a thump at the bottom of a ravine, were beyond her body's limits.

Minuscule snowflakes plopped on her nose and cheekbones. One landed on her upper lip and she licked it away. The snow was lovely, falling lightly as dusk turned rapidly to night. With a wide-beamed flashlight aimed in front of her, she drew in a deep breath and felt the tingle of frigid air slip into her mouth and down her throat.

Must hurry, she told herself, feeling like Little Red Riding Hood as she swung the basket of goodies she'd packed as a goodwill/forgiveness gesture, a little something extra to make up for being such a pain. She knew full well Mike wanted more—but this was all he was going to get.

Again she reminded herself that she had to hurry. She wasn't about to dawdle and accidentally run into Mike if he got back early from the vet. Her game plan was faultless. Get to Mike's place, drop the basket on the kitchen table, check on the Tennessee Walker and the other horses in the barn, bolt the barn door, check for any signs that Satan was on the prowl, then hightail it back to the Remington ranch house.

Simple. Expedient. Smart.

Bumping into Mike would certainly cause her great amounts of confusion. The good pastor, for all his preaching, was pure temptation. Avoiding him was her only recourse, because whenever he was near, even when it was only his voice coming through the phone, she wanted him.

Lust. That's all it was. What woman wouldn't lust over the man?

Don't think about him. Put him completely out of your mind because thinking about him leads to bewilderment.

Turning on the speed, Charity ran the rest of the way to the cabin, doing long jumps over puddles and ditches, kicking high, stretching out her toes as she made each ballerina-like leap, no easy feat in heavy boots, thick socks, long johns, and blue jeans. But Tuesday morning when she faced Duane-the-lech, she fully intended to wow him with her agility.

By the time she reached the front door, flecks of snow had grown to white thumbprint-size and covered the porch, the railings, her hair and clothes.

*Hurry. Hurry.*

Charity pushed through the unlocked door, flipped on the light switch, and suddenly the massive room was illuminated with the glow of track lighting beaming down from the high-timbered ceiling. This living room had seemed every inch a man's place when she'd been in here with Mike this morning. Now all she saw was the petite blonde from the picture in Mike's Bible.

Jessie's paintings, caught in the luminous, spotlighted glow, stared at her. They were everywhere, big, small, in-between, thick frames and thin, gilt and oak, as if Mike had amassed every painting Jessie had ever rendered into this room and turned it into a shrine to remember his wife.

Jessie Flynn. She'd scripted her name in the lower right-hand corner of every painting, the *J* flaring bigger and bolder than the rest of the letters, like something out of the movie *Rebecca*.

Suddenly Charity could picture Mike's wife sitting at an easel meticulously applying paint to a canvas, making sure the blues, whites, and grays of the sky, the greens and browns of the sagebrush and juniper, and the wildness of each creature was a faithful depiction of the real thing. Even more clearly she saw Jessie in this room, standing on a stool while she adjusted the track lights for the best effect or dusted the frames, looking at Mike over her shoulder, asking his opinion, smiling about some intimate secret they shared.

He'd loved his wife dearly. He still loved her. Charity had seen the tenderness in Mike's eyes when he spoke her name, when he stared off across the prairie and wished his wife were with him again.

Just once in her life, she wished she could be loved and adored in a way that was deep and lasting, instead of being the object of a man's affections from the moment he asked her to sneak into a back room until she dished out a blatant *No!*

She'd never been loved, not really. Her real mother had used her to make money. Her adopted father had taken her in and wanted to turn her into a clone of himself, and his wife, although caring, followed in her husband's footsteps, always obedient, never a person of her own.

Charity didn't want to be what someone else wanted her to be. She just wanted to be herself, trouble and all.

Coming here was a mistake. It made her think about the loneliness of her life, a loneliness she'd never admitted to a soul, and rarely admitted to herself.

Slamming her eyes shut, she forced herself to think about Duane's phone call, about the audition on Tuesday, about some future opening night when the spotlight would shine down on her and the audience would stand up and cheer.

And then she wouldn't be lonely any longer.

She escaped to the kitchen, needing to get away from Jessie and thoughts of Mike's love for her. She flipped on the lights, and set her basket of goodies on the table, taking out a wrapped plate filled with Max's sweet-and-sour barbecued ribs and Sam's potato salad, which she put in the refrigerator. She left a plate of pastel-iced sugar cookie hearts on the table as well as a piece of yellow birthday cake with dark chocolate frosting. She thought about leaving him a note, but what could she say that hadn't already been said?

Mike wanted her to be something she wasn't, just like everyone else, and she'd never give in to that.

Their brief time together had been fun, but it was over.

Somewhere, a clock struck nine.

Grabbing her basket, she headed out the kitchen door and was greeted by blowing snow that clung to her eyelids, her cheeks and lips.

She heard the whinny of a horse and knew immediately it wasn't one of the domestic animals. She'd know that sound anywhere, the power, the arrogance, the I'm-back-so-watch-out attitude that belonged to Satan.

The stallion stood not far from the barn, his black tail and mane crusted with heavy, wet snow. His brown eyes blazed through the storm, watching Charity's steps as she walked toward the barn, watching the big red door *thud, thud, thud* in the whipping wind.

It was dangerous for Satan to be here. Was he too pigheaded to understand?

Charity raced toward the mustang, flapping her arms. "Get out of here!" She did everything in her power to keep the beast out of harm's way, out of Mike's clutches, out of the barn and away from the mares.

But he was rebellious, pawing at the thickening snow and the frozen earth, flipping his head wildly, refusing to run away. Instead he galloped toward the gaping barn door, giving no heed whatsoever to Charity's attempts to make him leave.

She rushed toward the barn and was halfway between it and Satan when a fierce gust of wind blew her off her feet. She landed with a whoosh in a puddle of slush and mud. The flashlight slipped from her fingers and the wicker basket sailed out of her hands, flipping through the air and snow until it hit the ground and rolled out of sight.

Scrambling to her feet, she slammed her muddy behind against the door and tried to keep it closed even though the wind had something else in mind.

Satan glared at her through the now pelting storm, his near-black eyes looking angry and determined to get what he'd come for. He reared on his hind legs and crashed down hard, his front hoof smashing the flashlight, bringing an abrupt end to the beam of light pouring through the lens.

This was not going well, Charity decided. After tonight, there would be no doubt in her mind or anyone else's that she wasn't cut out for training horses—wild *or* domestic. She'd made the right decision in turning Mike down, and tomorrow wouldn't be soon enough to get away from this frigid, unwelcoming land.

But right now, she stood guard over the barn. Satan was not getting inside!

Of course, Satan had other ideas. He moved toward her, and even though she attempted to shoo him away, he nuzzled her side and pushed her out from in front of the door.

Satan was making a big mistake. If he thought he could force her to do something she didn't want, he had another think coming.

Charity slammed herself back in front of the door and stomped her foot on the ground. Unfortunately, it wasn't frozen solid. A thin layer of ice covered the mud puddle and her boot smashed right through, sending splatters of gooey wet dirt flying everywhere.

Satan stilled. His eyes narrowed as he contemplated her rash action.

"You think you can get the upper hand? You think you can push me away because you want something that I don't want you to have? Well, you're wrong, buster. I'm in charge here, not you."

Satan snorted.

"I'm not into ropes, I'm not into fences or corrals, but so help me, you push me out of the way and take that pretty mare inside, and I'm going to hunt you down and make your life an absolute hell."

Obviously Satan didn't care because he didn't budge. Instead, he snorted in defiance once more and nudged her side again.

Charity hauled off and smacked him just as she would any other male who touched her where she didn't want to be touched.

Satan's head jerked up, his eyes widened, and he glared at her for the longest time. Then he whipped around and ran off, disappearing into the storm.

*That'll teach you to be a brute!*

Putting her hands on her knees, Charity took a few deep breaths and finally found the strength to peek inside the barn. Buck was in the closest stall, one without a gate, and he raised his head just long enough to shake it in his normal disgust—with her, no doubt—then went back to chewing on fresh hay.

The last remaining and high-priced spotted mare appeared to be dozing contentedly. So did half a dozen other horses, and Charity quietly closed the door and slid the bolt, latching it so neither the wind nor a wayward stallion could get inside.

She swept her broken and bent flashlight up from the ground, then tossed the useless thing in a rusted metal trash barrel at the edge of the barn. The thought of walking back to the ranch in the dark was unsettling, but the only other option she had was staying in Mike's home until he returned. That prospect was even more unnerving.

Striking out across the yard, the snow and sleet slashed across her face and the wind pushed against her, making each step increasingly difficult. Finally she left the reach of the barn's floodlight and was met with a pitch-black night.

She shivered, not just from the cold but from the fear that raced through her. She was in total darkness, not knowing which way was north, or south, or east, or west. Getting lost would be easy, and if she did get lost, she'd be a six-foot Popsicle when she was found.

Turning a one-eighty, she took a few tentative

steps and again saw the light from the barn through the blustering snow. She followed the glow, and trudged through the thick, cold powder, slipping on the layer of ice beneath the snow as she made her way toward the house.

Chilled to the bone and soaked because the snow had slithered under her coat and attacked her sweater and undies, she grabbed the phone just as the clock struck ten, and hoped someone would be back at the ranch.

"I can't get back," she told Jack through chattering teeth, after she'd quickly explained that she'd gone to Mike's place merely to check the barn door, not to seduce the good pastor, to get under his skin, or to hurt him. Jack might have stuck his nose where it didn't belong, but she had to admire a man who went to bat for a friend.

"I thought I'd get here and get back within an hour," she babbled on, "but I had a run-in with Satan, he crushed my flashlight, and I never expected a blizzard—"

"It's a small snowstorm," Jack said. *Leave it to someone from Wyoming to think that.* "Won't last all that long."

"Does that mean you can come get me?"

Jack chuckled. "It means you'd better make yourself comfortable till morning. Mike won't risk driving home in the storm, so you'll have the place to yourself. Start a fire and stay warm."

Jack sounded positive about Mike being gone all night, yet Charity anticipated something ominous happening at the stroke of midnight. "Would you call Mike and tell him I bolted the barn door and the horses are safe. And then would you tell him I'm here—and make sure he doesn't mind?"

"All right, I'll call him. But do what I say. Stay warm."

The snow dripping off her clothes and shoes had formed an amoeba-shaped puddle at her feet. She grabbed a handful of paper towels to mop up the water, then cleaned up the mud she'd tracked across the gleaming hardwood floor.

Less than five minutes had gone by when the cell phone sitting on the kitchen counter rang and she answered it out of instinct. "Hello."

"Charity?" It was Jack's voice coming through the receiver.

"Did you reach Mike already?"

"Not exactly. I reached his cell phone."

Charity's eyes narrowed as she stared at the small gray instrument in her hand. "You mean I'm talking on *Mike's* cell phone?"

"It appears that way."

She gulped. "Maybe he has a second one?"

"Don't think so. Look, Charity, he's already left the vet's and more than likely he's holed up in a motel or with a friend. Just kick back and relax. I'll come get you in the morning, provided the snow lets up."

Easier said than done. Kick back wasn't in her vocabulary, and even if it was, how could she possibly kick back in someone else's home, especially when that someone had no clue she was there?

She paced the kitchen, her sodden jeans and

coat weighing her down right along with her thoughts. What if the storm didn't let up? Would she miss her flight? Her audition?

She was going to murder Logan Wolfe when she got back to Vegas. He'd told her she needed a change of pace. He'd told her she needed to relax, to get away from all her troubles. And look at the mess she was in now.

A chill rushed through her. It started in her toes and fingers then spread up her limbs and settled in her clattering teeth. She had to warm up before she shivered to death.

Scooting quickly to the laundry room, she shrugged out of her coat and draped it over a hanger that shuddered under the weight. She tugged off her boots and drippy socks, then struggled to work the damp and clinging jeans and long johns over her icy-skinned hips and down her legs. Her bra and thong didn't give her half as much trouble.

Except for her coat and shoes, she tossed every stitch of her clothing into the dryer. Suddenly she found herself standing in Mike's laundry room stark naked, her body a mass of goosebumps and quivering nerves. Why oh why had she played the good Samaritan?

She grabbed some of Mike's clothes from the laundry basket, then promptly dropped them. Dirt. Straw. The scent of horses and cows. Why couldn't she have found a clean white shirt, something he preached in?

A heavy *knock, knock, knock* sounded at the kitchen door. She threw her hands and arms over

her privates and peered from the laundry room
into the kitchen.

*KNOCK. KNOCK. KNOCK.*

Her anxiety-ridden heart thudded. She edged
her way along the kitchen wall, hoping no one
could see her through the window over the sink,
and cracked open the blinds just enough to see
outside.

There was nothing there but snow and wind,
gusting wind that wanted desperately to come inside. Thank heavens it wasn't an intruder—or
Mike.

Of course, Mike would not be home tonight,
she reminded herself. *Quit being so nervous. Just
put some clothes on!*

She cranked up the thermostat at the base of
the stairwell in the living room, then ran upstairs
to Mike's bedroom.

The big four-poster with the vividly colored
handmade quilt and plump pillows covered in
navy blue cotton looked inviting, but she would
*not* crawl under Mike's covers and go to sleep.
She had to stay awake and alert and listen for
anything that might sound like Mike returning
early.

Pulling open one drawer after another in the
highboy, she guiltily shuffled through Mike's private things and grabbed a pair of plaid boxers.
She wiggled into them, trying to keep the stretchy
band at her waist but it slipped again and again
to her hips. She gave up at last and hustled to the
closet and slipped into a heavy charcoal flannel
shirt that nearly swallowed her in its breadth. A

bit warmer now, she headed back downstairs to wait for her own things to dry.

She ignored Jessie's paintings, but still they glared at her as if she were an intruder. She stared at the cold, empty hearth, thinking how warm and wonderful she'd feel if fire leaped from a stack of blazing logs. She could bring in firewood and kindling from outside and light it, but the way her luck had been running she was bound to turn Mike's house into a raging inferno.

Instead she curled up on the couch and pulled an afghan over her. Her fingers tingled with the chill. So did her toes. She tried to close her eyes, but with rest came awareness of her body and the fact that every joint ached. She'd never make it through the audition on Tuesday if her muscles were stiff and sore.

The clock struck eleven.

What she needed was a good, long soak in hot water. It would warm her insides and help her relax. Mike wouldn't come home, Jack had told her so; and even if he did come home, Mike had said it would be at least one or two in the morning before he could get back.

She thought about the big and inviting claw-foot tub she'd seen in Mike's bathroom. She could soak for nearly an hour and no one would ever be the wiser. She could fill it with bubbles—

What was she thinking? Mike wouldn't have anything resembling bubble bath! She'd merely have to soak her weary bones in pure, unscented, unbubbly water.

Outside the storm raged. Trees bent nearly to

the ground as the wind blasted across the earth, carrying with it a heavy, wet snow. It beat against the house, rattling the windows and doors. Mike's truck wouldn't be any match for the raging blizzard. Surely he'd spend the night in a motel or with friends, tucked in a nice, warm bed. Even if he did drive home . . .

*No, he wouldn't. Not in this ghastly weather. Oh, just go take the blasted bath!*

He's not going to come home, she told herself, and raced up the stairs, into Mike's bathroom. She plugged the tub and turned on the hot water, sticking her hand beneath the antique brass spigot until the water was too hot to touch, then added a little cold and started to strip down to nothing while the tub filled.

The mirror above the sink had fogged over and there was a hint of condensation on the brass hook behind the door, where she hung the clothes she'd been wearing. It was far from a sauna, but the damp heat radiated through her skin just enough to partially soothe her muscles.

Wrapping her hair in a knot on top her head, she eased her bruised and aching body into the depths. She rested her neck against the back of the tub and let her hands and feet float to the top of the water.

Closing her eyes, she hummed a little ditty from the show she'd last been fired from and thought about dancing in the spotlight, singing to a packed house.

Her eyes popped open when the pleasant silence was broken by an eerie *clang, clang, clang* reverberating slowly through the room. She froze. She didn't even bother to breathe as she listened for other noises, for steps on the stairs. And then she recognized the clanging sound—the grandfather clock was striking midnight.

The witching hour. Time for some wretched disaster to occur.

But that was only in storybooks.

She took a deep breath and forced herself to relax. She soaped her body with Mike's big green bar of Irish Spring—the manly soap. His bathroom was rather masculine and spare compared to the rest of the house. One navy blue towel hung on a rack at the far side of the room. A razor, a can of shaving cream, a toothbrush, and a comb sat on the back of the free-standing sink. The toilet was one of those old-fashioned kinds, with an oak tank suspended high on the wall.

The navy shower curtain hung above her on a circular chrome bar, and the shower head extended from tall brass pipes that rose from the floor at the head of the tub. She liked this place. It was quaint. A man's home for sure, but a place a woman could fit into quite comfortably.

She slid a little deeper into the water and laughed at her thoughts. She was headed back to Vegas tomorrow and Mike wasn't interested in her beyond a purely physical lust—in spite of what Jack mistakenly thought. *Marriage. Hah!*

Some other woman might be able to fit into his life and home quite comfortably . . . but not her. She had plans. Dreams.

She reached for a bottle of shampoo, twisted

the lid and sniffed. She used a luxurious, far-too-expensive shampoo that was an intoxicating combination of coconut, ginger, and papaya. This smelled like . . . well, like something a cowboy would use, but at least the concoction was a mix of shampoo and conditioner.

She loosened the knot she'd made in her waist-length hair and let it tumble into the water. Her instincts told her she was stretching relaxation to the max, but she threw caution to the wind, put a few dollops of Mike's shampoo in her hands and massaged it through her hair and scalp, getting rid of the specks of mud that had splattered her earlier.

Again she closed her eyes and pretended that Mike was sitting on the edge of the tub, that his big, strong, callused hands were in her hair, that he spread the creamy shampoo along the curve of her neck, over her shoulders and chest. That his warm, slick palms cupped her breasts, kneading them gently, toying with her tender beaded nipples, driving her wild.

Slowly, ever so slowly, his hands slid down her body and parted her legs. Heat stabbed at her when she felt his imaginary fingers slip inside her, teasing, circling, moving in and out. Pleasing her in a way no man ever had.

Suddenly every muscle in her body tensed, quivered. Gigantic waves of sheer, unimaginable pleasure ricocheted through her. Her eyes flew open and she was certain Mike had walked in unbeknownst to her, that he'd been stroking her, fondling her, doing unimaginably delightful things to her.

But she was alone. Her own hands were still in her hair. Her legs had parted slightly but the only thing between them was warm, soapy water.

The orgasm had been thrillingly real, brought on by an erotic joyride of her imagination. Enjoy it, she told herself, it might be the closest you ever get to the real thing.

But, unfortunately, playtime had come to an end. She pulled the plug on the tub and turned the warm water on once again to rinse the shampoo from her hair.

Leaning forward, her head under the spigot, she combed her fingers through the long strands, watching the soap bubbles, water, and her hair whirl down the drain. When the last of the shampoo was rinsed out she turned off the faucet and, with her hair still slung forward over her head, started to wring out the water, beginning at the scalp and working her way to the ends of the strands.

But she never got to the end. A long, thick lock of hair had slid down the drain and . . . stuck. More and more hair was getting sucked into the pipe as the last bits of water swirled from the tub, and she couldn't pull back to extricate herself.

She stuck her finger into the drain, hoping she could figure out what was causing the problem, and prayed Mike wouldn't walk in right now and see her naked behind waving about like a pink helium-filled balloon as she struggled to free herself from the tub.

The wind outside whipped hard against the side of the house and shook the bathroom window.

The lights flickered.

She managed to maneuver around in the tub and tried to grab for the one lone towel on the far side of the sink. *Damn!* Her arms weren't long enough. She couldn't even reach his razor.

Twisting her body around, doing contortions she'd never even tried before, she stuck her leg out of the tub and attempted to wrap her toes around the razor. Instead, she gave it a hefty flick and sent it skittering across the room.

The clock struck one.

The power went out, and the room was blanketed in black.

## Chapter 12

MIKE GRIPPED THE STEERING WHEEL, fighting the storm battling the truck and trailer. Driving home in a blizzard wasn't the most foolish thing he'd ever done, but it ranked fairly high on the list. Once too often the truck and empty trailer had hit black ice and he'd nearly lost control. If that wasn't bad enough, three hours driving through blinding snow had mesmerized him and a few times had nearly put him to sleep.

But he'd made it. Hungry, dirty, and exhausted, he fully intended to forget about writing his sermon and wing it tomorrow morning. Right now he wanted to do nothing more than climb into bed and try to sleep. It usually eluded him, his mind haunted with guilt or spinning over too many things to do. Tonight, with any luck, would be different.

Near the barn he unhitched the trailer, glad he'd left the horse with the vet so he didn't have to deal with an invalid mare. Then he pulled the truck into the garage. It wasn't until he plugged in the engine to keep it from freezing that he realized the power had gone out. What more could plague his night?

He went around to the back of the garage and started the generator. In no time at all, lights popped on in the house. Odd. He was pretty sure he'd forgotten to lock the barn door, but he rarely forgot to turn out the lights. The energy bill he got each month was enough to make him remember to flip off switches.

Pulling his hat low on his brow and tucking his chin into the warmth of his coat, he made his way to the barn, thankful to see that the bolt was latched, quickly checked the horses inside, then sprinted through the pounding snow to the back porch.

It was halfway warm inside. Had he been so preoccupied that he'd left the heater running as well as the lights? Deal with it tomorrow, he told himself. Right now he just wanted to sleep.

He stripped out of his coat, hanging it over the back of a chair, and dropped his hat on the table next to a plate heaped with cookies and cake. Rubbing his hand over his whiskers, he stared at the sweets, thinking about Charity, as he'd done far too often on the drive home. As hard as he tried, he couldn't get her out of his mind.

The cookies and cake were her obvious handiwork. She must have dropped the plate off when she'd checked the barn. The burning lights and running furnace were probably Charity's handiwork, too, although the reason why she'd wander from room to room turning on lights escaped him.

Then, again, Charity never did what was expected.

In spite of his fatigue, he smiled. She was a thorn in his side and she claimed she didn't want to see him again. But the craving that had gnawed inside him all day told him things weren't over between them.

Trudging up the stairs, he stripped out of his clothes and tossed everything into the hamper in the closet. He was too tired to shower, but he couldn't sleep smelling like an overused and undercleaned corral on a hot summer's day. Besides, the hot pulsing water would feel good on his bruised and aching muscles.

Striding across the bedroom, he pushed open the bathroom door and . . .

A hellish fear shot through him. Charity was curled up in the fetal position in his hundred-year-old claw-foot. She was naked. Her skin was blue. He touched her shoulder lightly. She was icy-cold and she shivered beneath his fingers. "Charity?" He whispered her name, barely able to get the word out because of the lump of dread in his throat. She didn't respond to his voice but she stirred slightly.

Her right cheek rested against the drain and when he scooped his hand under her head, her eyes fluttered open. "Don't," she muttered through chattering teeth. "My hair's stuck." She half laughed, half cried, as her gaze flickered over his body. "And you're naked."

He plowed his fingers through his hair, grabbed the towel that was next to the sink, and thought about covering himself, but laid it over Charity instead. "I'll be right back."

He slipped quickly into a clean pair of jeans, pulled a quilt from the chest at the end of his bed, and raced back into the bathroom.

"You gonna be okay?" he asked, tucking the hand-stitched blanket around the woman in his tub.

"Now that you're here."

He slid a hand beneath her head again and helped her hold it up so he could see the damage.

"I tried to rip my hair loose from the drain, but that didn't work. Then I tried pulling a strand or two out of my scalp at a time, but that hurt like hell. So I just curled up and . . . and, okay, I started praying that you'd be foolish and drive home in the storm."

She was accident prone, she was trouble, but he wanted her in his life. Somehow, he'd find a way to make her stay.

Tears had dried on her cheeks. Her hair was a mass of tangles. But he'd never seen a more beautiful woman. "I'm gonna have to cut some of your hair."

"Cut it all. I don't care. I just want out of this tub. It's hard and uncomfortable and"—her lips quivered—"cold."

He opened the medicine cabinet, pulled out a small pair of scissors, and leaned over her.

"I've changed my mind!" she cried out. "Cut as little as you possibly can. I've got an audition in a couple of days and I've got to look my best."

A bull rammed his chest. How could he have forgotten that Charity wanted to leave? That Las Vegas was her life?

That was another bit of trouble he could deal with tomorrow. Right now he had to think about the present, and Charity's latest dilemma.

Tugging the quilt close to her breasts, Charity shivered as she watched Mike cautiously poke the scissors down the drain. She'd never felt so foolish, so exposed.

She shouldn't have climbed into Mike's tub. Shouldn't have shampooed her hair. Shouldn't have risked being found. She knew that trouble followed her around, so why didn't she know something like this would happen?

In spite of her embarrassment, she was thankful Mike had come to her rescue—again.

"Can you hold your head up on your own?" Mike asked. "Before I cut, I want to see if I can work any of it loose."

She rolled over in the tub. Maneuvering was difficult, but she managed to crouch down on her knees, gather her unstuck hair in her hands, and hold it away from the drain.

The quilt gaped open, and she wasn't oblivious to the very real fact that Mike's eyes drifted from his work to her chest, to her breasts. His Adam's

apple bobbed when their eyes met. She could almost hear him gulp, and then, being the good,
strong, moral man he was, he concentrated again
on the drain.

Heat pulsed through her. Mike's slow, hungry
perusal of her body had warmed her like a hot
buttered rum, potent, intoxicating, meandering
slowly through every vein, artery, and capillary.

She watched Mike's strong, rugged hands as
he dug his finger into the drain, trying diligently
to pull her hair loose. She thought about the
jagged scar that slashed across his knuckles, wondering if he'd cut himself on barbed wire as he
stretched it across the land, fencing in animals
that wanted to stray.

Finally he looked at her and shook his head.
"You need a warm bed and something hot to
drink. You need it now, not an hour or so from
now."

"In other words?"

"I'm going to have to cut the rest of it."

There was only one small hunk of hair left and
she'd long ago tired of being imprisoned in the
tub. "All right." She swallowed hard. "Cut away."

He shoved the scissors deep into the drain and
in just an instant, she was free, jerking her head
up and massaging her neck.

A second after that, Mike swept her into his
arms. As much as she wanted to protest, his embrace was irresistible and she relaxed against the
warmth of his skin.

He carried her to the four-poster, threw back

the covers, then laid her down, still wrapped in the quilt. The last thing she'd expected when she'd come here tonight was to end up in bed—Mike's bed. It was big and soft and she had an incredible urge to ask him to climb under the covers with her—just for a little extra warmth.

Instead, she forced her eyes from his faded-bronze skin, from the mat of hair on his chest, from his flat abs, and a belly button she uncharacteristically wanted to . . . lick.

Oh, she was warming up fast!

She tore her mind from sex and concentrated on the intricate quilt pattern. "This is beautiful."

"My mom made it." He crossed the room in two long strides and . . . okay, she quit staring at the quilt and studied the Herculean muscles in his back and shoulders as he opened one of his dresser drawers. "I get a new one every year for Christmas." He looked at her over his shoulder and her eyes flickered from his firm, fine butt to his bright green eyes. "Still cold?"

"A little." But that was a whopper of a lie.

"I've got some thermal underwear you can put on."

"I've already got a pair of your boxers and a shirt hanging in the bathroom."

One corner of his mouth rose, making his dimple deepen. "Should I ask what happened to your clothes?"

"I had a run-in with Satan, a few mud puddles, and a blizzard. I was sure you wouldn't mind me borrowing a thing or two of yours, considering that it was all your fault I had those little mishaps."

He studied her naked shoulder, where the quilt had slipped away, and followed her blanket-hidden shape all the way down to where she rubbed her feet together beneath the cover. Again he found her eyes and a slow, soft smile touched his mouth. "I'm sure you look better in my clothes than I do."

*Oh, I highly doubt that.*

Mike retrieved the boxers and heavy flannel shirt and dropped them beside her. "So, Satan came back?"

"He was after the Tennessee Walker again, at least that's what it looked like, considering how determined he was to get into the barn."

"And you managed to get rid of him?"

"I waved my hands, I stomped in the mud, and I screamed at him." She grinned lightly, then pulled the blanket closer to her neck as she again began to shiver. "I think he got the hint that I didn't want him around."

Mike sank down on the edge of the bed. "Not exactly what a horse trainer would do," he said, "but not bad for a novice. Of course, it would have been better if you'd directed him into the corral and closed the gate."

"That's not my style."

He chuckled. "So you've said."

He drew one of her feet from under the covers and blew warm, moist breath on her icy toes. With her cheeks feeling flushed and her heart going pitty-pat, she immediately began to wonder about the wisdom of a minister sitting on her bed, of a minister rubbing her bare toes, a minister slowly, deeply massaging the arch of her foot.

A shiver rippled through her body, not from the cold but from his gentle yet erotic touch. Here she was lying under the covers and imagining this man doing the same thing every night of the week.

*No, no, no, no, no!*

She had to keep her wits about her. If anything more happened between them, it would be a disaster.

She drew her foot out of his hands and rubbed the cool pink flesh herself. "Did you say you were going to make me something warm to drink?"

"Hot chocolate okay?" he asked, tucking the blanket around her hips and legs.

She nodded and he rose slowly from the bed. "Think you can stay out of trouble while I'm gone?"

"What trouble could I possibly get into here— in your bed?"

The suggestive innuendo didn't hit her until the words had slipped over her tongue, but it had obviously smacked Mike right in the face. His intense green-eyed gaze skirted the curves her body formed under the blanket and a frustrated frown wrinkled his brow. "Not to worry, Charity. You won't get into any trouble there."

He turned his back on her and walked out of

the room but his words hung back. He seemed as confused as she was by their continuing infatuation with each other, wanting each other but wanting something else far more: he wanted Jessie; she wanted what awaited her in Vegas.

Throwing off the quilt, she made a mad dash for the bathroom again, relieved herself, which she'd been dying to do for hours, washed her hands, took a quick look in the mirror at her frightful hair and decided it was beyond help, then ran back to the bedroom, threw on Mike's boxers and flannel shirt, and climbed under the covers.

Tucking her hands under the fluffy down pillow, she buried her nose into its warmth, inhaling the musky scent of Mike's aftershave on the pillowcase, a fragrance almost as intoxicating as his presence.

First thing in the morning she was going to say goodbye to him. So long. Farewell. This strange, bewildering fascination between us has been nice, she'd tell him, but it's better to end it now, before either one of us ends up with a broken heart.

Right now her heart didn't seem at risk, and she wanted to keep it that way. But when Mike walked into the room with two cups of steaming cocoa and she caught sight once again of his bare chest, his muscular arms, the jeans that sat low on his hips and the band of black hair that raced across the belly button she wanted to lick to that hidden place beneath his zipper, well—she took a deep breath—she wished he wasn't a minister with good principles and that she wasn't a show-girl determined to remain a virgin.

He set the mugs on the nightstand beside her, his belly button within easy touching distance.

"That's hot," he said. "Don't take a big gulp."

Hot was an understatement. Fire rushed through every point in her body, settling—*throbbing*—between her legs. She'd bought a vibrator once at one of those crazy, naughty lady parties, but she'd thrown it away after using it only a couple of times. It felt too good and she didn't want to get addicted. Just looking at Mike's body thrilled her far more than the vibrator, and she had the feeling he could be much more addictive.

The safest thing for both of them would be for her to get up, say goodbye, and go home right now. But his bed was comfortable. And, okay, she admitted it, she was a glutton for punishment.

She picked up the mug and held it in front of her face, hopefully hiding her sinful thoughts.

"I'm going to take a quick shower. Can I do anything else for you first?"

*Do a slow striptease on your way? Come back to bed and . . . kiss me?*

"No, thanks," she said, in spite of her wanton thoughts. "The hot chocolate's fine for now."

All too soon Mike was behind closed doors and she was alone in bed. She could hear the shower running and just like the morning before, she imagined him stepping inside. Only this time her imagination didn't have to work too hard to cook up a picture of his body. She'd seen him naked. Every glorious inch of him.

Wrong. Wrong. *So wrong!*

They were obviously being tested by some greater power. They were being tempted but she couldn't, wouldn't lower her principles. She'd fought off some rather gorgeous men in her life, men with money, power, and even fame, and she'd felt good afterward.

Surely she could fight her attraction to Mike.

She heard the thump of the water pipes, and knew the shower had stopped. She heard the jangling of the shower curtain as it was moved, could almost hear Mike's bare feet stepping out of the tub onto the tiled floor.

She imagined water coursing through the short black hair on his legs, making a puddle beneath him. She pictured him towel-drying his hair, his arms raised above his head, making his biceps flex and his chest widen, like Atlas holding up the world. She thought of the little dab of water that would remain in his belly button, forgotten when the towel whisked over his body.

She thought . . . She thought she should get out of bed and run!

But where would she go? Out into the cold? No, that would be crazy, especially when she was so warm and cozy in Mike's bed. And well, there was the fact that he was and always would be a minister, so his thoughts were pure—except that he did think about naked women. But surely, surely he wouldn't try anything funny, because her defenses had never been weaker.

She dragged air into her lungs when he opened the door, and even though she wanted to see him naked again, she hoped he'd be dressed. Her resolve to be good could withstand a lot, but Mike's body was one very good reason to forget her resolve and be bad.

Very, very bad.

He was in his jeans—that was good. His chest was bare—that was nice. His feet were long and narrow and a sparse sprinkling of short black hair dotted his toes and the top of his arch. She was fascinated. Totally and completely smitten.

He walked toward the bed.

Danger! Warning sirens went off inside her head.

He kneeled on the left side of the bed and leaned over her to grab his mug of cocoa. A tsunami raged through her body, the violent wave rushing over her nerve endings as she took a quick peek at his belly button to see if he'd left any water behind, something for her to lick away.

A drip was there. One little drip. But she didn't dare. Instead she inhaled deeply, dragging in the scents of Irish Spring and Old Spice that made her hot. So very, very hot.

Maybe she could lower her principles just a bit. She'd hung on to her virginity because she knew in her heart it was the right thing to do, to save herself for the man she loved—after all, that's what her father had preached. Later she hung on to her virginity as a protest against her father's declaration that if she went to Vegas she'd end up unmarried, unwanted, and pregnant—or even worse, living in sin. Well, she'd proved him wrong so far.

Who would have thought a minister would be the one holding a tempting, sin-filled apple in front of her, making her want a bite?

But Mike had principles, too. He'd never dangle an apple in front of her knowingly. More than likely, he was going to grab a pillow and blanket and go downstairs to sleep.

"Still cold?" he asked, crawling onto the high four-poster, doubling an extra pillow up against the headboard and leaning against it. Surely he planned to stay only a moment.

"I'm getting warmer, thanks. Of course, I don't think falling asleep in a cold, hard bathtub has done much for my muscle tone."

His gaze slid over her quilt-covered body, and she knew instantly that her conversational skills needed bigtime help. Was she trying to sabotage her virginal ideals by focusing her words on body parts?

"What hurts?" he asked.

*Why lie now?* "Everything."

He plucked her mug from her hand and set both cups on the nightstand. "Roll over on your stomach."

*I should have lied!* "Why?"

"Because you're tense, because I've got a bad habit of not being able to sleep, and I figure I might as well do something constructive with my nervous energy."

"Like what?"

He chuckled. Obviously he wasn't as nervous as she was. "Like give you a massage."

"It's too cold to take off my clothes."

"This isn't about sex. It's about making you feel good."

"Is there a difference?"

He grinned. "Just roll over."

If any other man had told her to roll over, she would have scrambled from the room, but she took a deep breath and put her "principles" in Mike's extraordinary hands.

And those strong hands found their way to her shoulders, his thumbs gently kneading the muscles in her neck. She moaned softly, and let her body relax into the mattress and pillows.

"I could use a masseur like you in Vegas," she said, her words somewhat garbled against the pillow. "You wouldn't consider moving there, would you?"

"No."

"Could I bottle up what you're doing and take it with me?"

"Don't think so."

Charity felt his hands moving down her spine, felt him pulling back the quilt until the soft cotton tickled her skin as it slid over her legs. Down, down, down. She couldn't see him, but still she felt the heat of his eyes on her body and the cool night air on her derriere. Reaching behind her, she tugged at the hem of her boxers, stretching them over her thighs. No need to give Mike too good a view. Why it should bother her was anyone's guess. Her bottom was exposed every night when she danced on stage. But this was different. It was personal.

Even more personal was the way Mike straddled her hips. Maybe now was the time to leave, but . . . oh, she liked the weight of his body pressing into hers.

"Could we discuss Vegas again?" she asked.

"If you want."

He put the heels of his hands on either side of her spine. His fingers made circles, his thumbs swirled, and she nearly forgot what she wanted to say as she turned her body over to his magical hands.

"We could use someone like you in Vegas."

"I'm sure there are thousands of masseurs."

"Probably—professional ones and those who aren't exactly professional," she said. "There are a lot of sinners, too. A lot of people who need saving. I'm sure Vegas could use a good minister."

"I'm happy here."

He drew her arms down to her sides then slipped his hands under her shirt. His skin was warm against hers, the calluses on his palms rough but sensual as they soothed her muscles. Whether it was an accident or on purpose, his fingers skimmed the outer edges of her breasts, where they were pressing beneath her, against the mattress, and she jumped at the sensation.

His hands rested in place a moment, tentative, still. She heard Mike's intake of breath, and then his fingers disappeared from the heated skin of her back and sides, from under her shirt, and went back to work on the strained muscles of her neck. Slowly, methodically, he worked upward, splaying his fingers through her tangled hair and tenderly stroking her temples.

She was lost in the power of his caress, completely, breathtakingly mesmerized by the sensuousness of his kneading, probing fingers.

Slowly his weight shifted, his hips moving lower, settling over her thighs. She might have turned over to look at him, but she felt the length of his upper body stretch over her, felt the muscles of his chest against her back. His whiskered cheek brushed over her jaw, and then she felt the ultimate, body tingling sensation of his warm breath against her ear. "Have you ever thought of leaving Las Vegas?"

"Every time I get frustrated with my career."

"But you're not frustrated right now, are you?"

"No."

Soft, masterful lips touched her ear. "Don't go back," he whispered. Confusion hit her strongly, especially when his teeth tugged at her earlobe, when his tongue reached out and traced the edges of her ear. "Stay here, Charity."

"I've got an audition in a few days," she reminded him. "That's my life, Mike."

His mouth trailed to her throat, his gentle hands smoothing over the length of her arms until his fingers wove through hers. "How can I change your mind?"

She shifted beneath him, feeling the slight lift

of his weight while she rolled onto her back. His forearms rested on the pillow at each side of her head. He had her trapped and she knew, looking into his heated green eyes, that he had no intention of leaving—or letting her leave.

And then he kissed her. Soft. So soft, his hands cupping her cheeks. He tasted of hot cocoa and the sweet mini-marshmallows he'd tossed into the mugs. If any man could make her give up her dream, Mike was the one. But she couldn't give up, no matter how good he made her feel.

Again he whispered, this time against her lips, this time with his imploring eyes looking down into hers, "Stay, Charity."

If only she could. She cared for him, but it didn't seem enough to pull her away from her dream.

"My life's on the stage, Mike. I won't give it up."

He stilled, then sighed, and a moment later rolled onto his back and stared at the ceiling. The cold seeped into her, and as if he sensed her sudden discomfort, he gathered her into his arms again and tenderly drew her head against his chest.

His heart beat steadily, maybe a little bit fast, and she watched him close his eyes. His chest rose and fell with each soft breath he took. For a while she thought he was asleep, but his fingers never loosened on her arm. He held her tightly against him, as if he were afraid to let her go.

There was silence between them, too much silence. She knew she should slip out of bed, go downstairs and sleep, but she'd never known the comfort she felt now. She wanted even more, and stretched her hand from where it had been resting on her hip to his stomach, slowly trailing her fingers through the short curly hair, sliding them gently over his ribs, until they found his heart, and stayed.

His free hand settled on top of hers, and he squeezed it lightly. She thought he'd again ask her to stay, but he didn't say anything, he just looked up at the ceiling.

"Why do you have trouble sleeping?" she asked, after one minute on the clock had drifted into ten.

"Too many things always on my mind. Sermons to write, fences to mend."

"Do you think about Jessie?"

He was silent a moment, and then he sighed. "Too much, I suppose, considering that it's been six years. Sometimes, when I've been out on the range all day and I'm tired, I'll walk in the front door and imagine her lying on the floor, not breathing, her skin blue." His head rolled toward Charity and his tortured gaze settled on her eyes. "Your skin was blue like that when I saw you in the tub. It was something I never wanted to see again."

His tired eyes flickered closed. "I don't like to talk about her, Charity. It's too hard."

She didn't expect him to say anything more, not after that, but just as soon as she thought he might drift off to sleep, his eyes opened and focused on the ceiling again.

"Sometimes when I close my eyes I see Jessie

lying in the hospital with tubes running every-where. I see all the machines that kept her alive. I hear them hum and I blame myself for not being with her when she had the heart attack, for not being able to get her to the hospital on time, for . . ." He sighed and rubbed a hand over his eyes. He pulled her tighter and pressed a kiss to her forehead.

"Most of the time, staying awake is easier than trying to sleep."

This was the first time she could remember anyone sharing their deepest hurts with her, the first time anyone had ever reached out for her and needed her comfort.

Mike loved his wife and she couldn't change that. But maybe she could help him sleep.

She raised up on her elbow and kissed his eye-lids shut, a pang of delight squeezing her heart when his hand slipped into her tangled hair. She kissed his brow, then hooked her finger under a lock of his hair and dragged it down softly over his forehead.

"What do you see now?" she whispered against his mouth.

"A pretty woman sleeping in my bathtub." He tugged her mouth against his and kissed her lightly. "Great breasts. A curvy bottom. Long legs." He yawned and she felt his fingers move from her hair, to her neck, slowly traveling down the curve of her spine until they rested against her hip.

When she thought he'd pull her against him

again, his grip loosened, and only seconds later, his breathing deepened. At last, he slept.

Instinct told her to get up, to find a way to leave, but she said to hell with instinct, pulled the covers over both of them, and snuggled close to Mike to soak up his warmth.

Tomorrow was soon enough to bring all of this to an end.

## Chapter 13

CHARITY WOKE WITH HER DERRIÈRE spooned against Mike's jeans-clad hips. His arm had long ago slung over her side, and his fingers grasped her waist. Apparently he had no intention of letting her go, even while he slept.

*Not good. Not good at all.* It felt wonderful, but it definitely smacked of sin.

He was a minister, for crying out loud, and she was a showgirl. If one of his parishioners caught them in bed together, or even got a hint of what had gone on between them during the night, he might lose his job. His name would be mud. He'd be a broken man.

*Hmm, the perfect candidate for Las Vegas.*

No, no, no. That was a ridiculous thought. Mike belonged here with his horses and his good reputation. He had enough things burdening him, like the memory of his wife, without adding even more grief to his life.

Slowly, silently, Charity eased his hand from her stomach and the fingers of his other hand from her tangled hair. Apparently the storm had blown away, and she could see a touch of pinkish, early morning sky through the window. With any luck, she could slide out of bed, rush to the laundry room, get into her own clothes, and get home before anyone caught her in this compromising situation.

Sliding out of bed, however, wasn't as simple as she thought it would be because the tail of her shirt had wedged under Mike's hip. She tugged and his eyes opened sleepily.

"Good morning," he whispered drowsily, nuzzling her neck and making her toes tingle while he slipped his arm back around her waist and worked his fingers right up under her breasts. Then . . . he fell back to sleep.

Oh, she could get used to this but it was wrong, wrong, wrong.

When Mike's breathing deepened she went through the same escape routine. Move arm. Tug shirt from under hip. Slip away without waking him.

Success.

Her bare feet, all nice and warm from having rested against Mike's hot body for the past few hours, hit the hardwood floor and the chill ripped through her. *Jeez it's cold!*

She rushed to the Indian rug, which was a tad warmer than a block of ice, and pulled Mike's boxers up to her waist. Of course, they promptly slipped back to her hips, exposing belly button, belly, and almost everything else. She tugged Mike's flannel shirt over her bottom, stifling a gasp when she realized that only one button was buttoned—crookedly. No wonder Mike's palms and fingers had had free access to her skin. She might as well have been naked.

The bed creaked and she took one last peek at the slumbering man. His hair was mussed, his cheeks, chin, and jaw nearly black with a heavy coat of whiskers, and long black lashes rested against the dark circles beneath his eyes. He rolled his shoulders as if they were tired and tight, reached toward the empty side of the bed, fished around for something that wasn't there, then pulled the fluffy pillow up against him.

Time to go, before she got jealous and crawled back on the mattress and snuggled again.

Creeping out of the bedroom, Charity slipped down the cold wood stairs, ignored Jessie's pictures in the living room, and dashed into the kitchen—where she bumped breasts first into the face of a complete stranger. Actually, she didn't realize the woman was a complete stranger until they each stumbled back a foot or two and glared at each other.

Charity gulped, grabbed at the tails of her unbuttoned-except-for-one-button shirt and clasped it over her exposed belly. When she was somewhat composed, she said, "Hello."

The little woman with short, curly brown hair frowned as her judgmental eyes tried to make sense of the stranger in Mike's house. "I know you, don't I?"

"I don't believe so," Charity said, trying to keep her voice low so Mike wouldn't wake. "I'm Charity Wilde."

The lady frowned, staring at Charity's brown hair that had once been black—brown hair that was now a tangled mess, with a hunk cut out of it somewhere. "Yes, yes, that's right, the showgirl," the stranger acknowledged. "I saw you at Lauren's wedding and the family was talking about you last night at dinner."

Good things? Charity wondered. Bad? If they'd known about the events of the past few hours, the talk would have been scandalous.

The little lady shuffled across the kitchen, reached into a cabinet, and took out a canister of coffee, then proceeded to fill a filter with yummy smelling French roast.

"I'm Fay Atkinson. A friend of Pastor Mike's." Fay looked at Charity over her shoulder. "Is he here?"

"He's asleep, I'm afraid."

Fay's critical gaze studied Charity's attire—or lack thereof. "Rough night?"

"He took an injured horse to the vet and didn't get home till sometime past two."

"I see."

"Is there something I can help you with?" Charity asked, as if she had more right to be here than Fay.

"No, no, there were some things I wanted to discuss with *Pastor* Mike, but they can wait until church. *Pastor* Mike delivers the most amazing sermons. Never heard a one that didn't inspire me. Same can be said about everyone who comes to hear him." Again Fay hit Charity with that holier-than-thou look. "Will you be joining our congregation today so you can hear him preach?"

Charity shook her head. The last thing she wanted to hear Mike do was preach. "I'm heading back to Vegas this afternoon."

"That's too bad. As I recall, you have a delightful voice, which would have been a nice addition to our choir."

"Thank you," Charity said, even though she couldn't tell if Fay was being sarcastic or sincere.

"Do you think the *pastor* will be down soon?" Fay asked, frowning as she looked at her watch.

"I couldn't say. Would you like me to wake him for you?"

"Of course not." She reached into a cupboard and pulled out plates and mugs. "I've got five or ten minutes before I need to head to church and put out the flowers for this morning's service. Why don't the two of us have a bite to eat before I go."

"I really need to get going."

"Surely you can try one of my sticky buns first." Fay peeled the cellophane off a tray full of cinnamon rolls and set them on the table, taking away the cookies and birthday cake Charity had put there last night. "You won't find any others like them this far west. It's a special family recipe. They're a favorite of Pastor Mike's."

Was Fay a favorite of Mike's, too? Charity wondered as Fay dished an oozing, cinnamon-and-sugar roll onto each plate. Fay obviously spent a lot of time here, and even now she was playing hostess, expertly filling coffee cups and carrying them, a sugar bowl, and a small carton of cream to the table.

"So," Fay said, joining Charity at the table. "Are you and the pastor *good* friends?"

"Just friends."

Fay smiled. "I'm sure Roy Campbell—he's a member of our congregation—will be delighted to hear that. He's got a twenty-eight-year-old sister who's just gotten a divorce and is moving back to the area. I'm sure Roy's thinking of hooking her up—permanently—with Pastor Mike, although I think Dorothy's all wrong for him."

"I was under the impression that Pastor Mike wasn't interested in getting married again."

"So he says." Fay took a bite of cinnamon roll followed by a quick sip of coffee. "I remember when Jessie died. Never in my life have I seen a man so stricken. Poor boy's been grieving ever since. Far be it from me to pry, but I've told him again and again that he needs to settle down, find another girl like Jessie. Bless my heart, she was just the sweetest thing. Pretty, petite, and what a talent she had for painting." Fay cut a wedge of cinnamon roll with her fork and drew it toward her mouth. "Do you paint?"

"No."

"That's right. You sing and dance. Well"—Fay chewed the bite of roll—"be that as it may, Jessie was the best wife a minister could have, Mike even told me so once upon a time. Said if he ever married again, he'd want someone just like Jessie."

And Charity knew she herself was the exact opposite.

Fay leaned close to Charity. "You haven't overheard Mike talking about my niece Raylene have you? She's pretty, petite, and sweeter than the cinnamon rolls I brought this morning."

"He may have mentioned your niece, but—"

"I'm surprised he didn't fill your head full of talk about her," Fay interrupted. "He's chatted with me about her on and off for months now. I honestly think the man's smitten. Couldn't take his eyes off of her at church last week, and then when he joined us for dinner, well, let me just say, I haven't seen him smile or laugh so much in years."

Fay's words were making it clearer by the minute that Charity could never replace Jessie in Mike's heart, not that she wanted to. But there had been a moment or two when she thought she could fall in love with Mike, if she didn't have other plans.

Fay took the last sip of her coffee. "You're not after Pastor Mike like every other single woman in these parts, are you?"

Charity laughed lightly. "He's just a friend."

Fay set down her cup and clasped Charity's hands. "I'm so glad it's nothing more than that. Not that you wouldn't make a lovely wife and a nice addition to our little congregation, but, as I said before, Pastor Mike wants—and needs—someone just like Jessie."

"Of course, he does." Charity nodded, not missing the subtlety behind Fay's comment. Pretty and petite had nothing to do with what she felt Mike needed. It was the sweet part that Fay was hinting at, and everybody knew that Vegas showgirls were far from sweet.

Charity took a sip of coffee, hoping to hide the sudden pang of hurt flitting through her, when the unmistakable thud of two feet jumping out of bed and landing on the hardwood floor sounded right over her head. If that wasn't bad enough, Mike shouted, "Charity!"

"My lands." Fay's eyes widened. "Was that Pastor Mike?"

Charity wished she could say it wasn't, but that would be lying, so she merely said, "I guess he's awake now," and took a deep breath, anticipating the worst because she couldn't miss the thunder of Mike's feet running down the stairs.

Mike barreled into the kitchen. "Don't go—"

If he'd planned to say more, he chomped down on his words when he caught sight of Fay sitting at the table. Charity watched the muscles clench in his jaw. Saw his naked chest rise and fall heavily, and, unfortunately, she couldn't miss the fact that his feet were bare or that the top button of his jeans wasn't buttoned.

This did not look good.

Mike plowed his fingers through his hair and gripped the back of his neck, as if a sudden pain had jabbed him. "Good morning, Fay."

"Good morning . . . *Michael*." Fay sounded like a mom scolding her young son when she shoved up from the table and went to the counter. "Could I get you some coffee and one of my sticky buns. The ones you like so much?"

He rubbed his hand over his whiskers, then buttoned the top button of his jeans while Fay's back was to him. "Sure."

When he sat beside Charity, he rolled his eyes, and beneath the table rested his hand on her leg and squeezed.

"Did you come by just to bring the sticky buns?" Mike asked, when Fay slid a clean plate and fork and a steaming cup of strong coffee in front of him.

"There were some things I wanted to talk about, but go ahead and help yourself to a roll, then we'll chat."

Charity expected Mike to explain the situation to Fay, to tell her that nothing was going on, that their disheveled appearance was perfectly innocent. No such luck. Mike merely lifted a cinnamon roll onto his plate, cut off a wedge with his fork, and lifted it toward his mouth.

Fay cleared her throat quite loudly. "Excuse me, *Pastor,* but aren't you forgetting something?"

Mike held the fork a fraction of an inch from his lips, and his brows narrowed as he looked from Fay to Charity then back again. "I figured the two of you had met already."

"I was thinking about you saying grace. After all, it is Sunday morning."

Mike put down the fork, pulled his hand away from Charity's leg, and threaded his fingers in front of him. He bowed his head and closed his eyes. "Dear Lord. Bless our beloved Fay Atkinson for her friendship, her thoughtfulness, and for the delicious sticky buns she was so kind to bring this morning. Thank you for the uninterrupted sleep that came so easily last night, and for bringing Charity out here to the middle of nowhere. In Jesus' name, amen."

Charity's gaze drifted over her folded fingers to see Fay's closed eyes and half-frown, and more importantly, Mike's wink that flew at her from his sparkling eyes.

"That was a lovely blessing, Pastor." Fay took a sip of her coffee, but her stare continually flitted to Mike's bare chest.

"So, Fay," Mike said, finally putting the bite of cinnamon roll in his mouth, "what was it you wanted to tell me?"

"Raylene will be joining us at church this morning."

"She's been there every Sunday for the past couple of months."

"Yes, but today she's bringing her prize-winning hazelnut torte for the gathering afterward. You remember that torte, don't you? She brought it for dinner last Sunday."

"I remember."

Mike's spare hand found its way under the table and again he squeezed Charity's leg. Her heart thundered in her chest. She liked the warmth, the way his thumb circled her skin. What she didn't like was the fact that Fay's eyes continually darted toward the edge of the table, as if she knew what was going on beneath it.

Charity lifted Mike's hand from her leg and dropped it off to the side. Being the brute that he was, he put it right back, and continued his thumb swirling.

"It's a shame you won't be joining us," Fay said, leaning her folded arms on the tabletop and glaring at Charity as if she'd done something wrong. "I'm sure you'd enjoy the hazelnut torte as much as Pastor Mike. And then," Fay said, at last directing her attention on Mike, "don't forget you've promised to have Sunday dinner with us."

"I don't know if I can make it."

"Nonsense. A promise is a promise, and Raylene's spent the last week preparing a lovely menu. Peanut-crusted roast pork, baby peas, my mother's secret-ingredient scalloped potatoes."

"I don't know, Fay."

"I know how busy you get sometimes." Her eyes narrowed as she studied the portion of Mike's arm that was visible above the table. "You know we always eat at three on Sunday. If you're there, you're there. Seth Colton will be coming, too, and naturally he'll be bringing those five hooligans of his. Never known a man who needed a wife more, with the exception of you, Pastor."

Mike's jaw tightened as Fay bustled up from the table, but he didn't say a word, made no comment at all as Fay stuck out her hand to Charity. "It was lovely to see you again."

Charity stood, moving away from Mike's stilled fingers, and shook Fay's hand. "Thanks for the cinnamon rolls. They're delicious."

"Family recipe. I've already passed it down to Raylene, and she makes them once or twice a week." Fay looked at Mike and smiled. "You've tasted the ones she makes, haven't you Michael?"

Mike's chair scraped the floor as he got up. "I've tasted them, Fay, and they're every bit as good as yours."

"I'll be sure to tell Raylene that. You never know, she just might bring them by for you occasionally, rather than me making the trip."

At last Mike chuckled, breaking some of the tension Charity felt. "You do that, Fay."

A few minutes later, bundled in her coat, hat, and gloves, Fay was in her car, waving goodbye to Mike as he stood in the open doorway. When the car pulled away, he closed the door and turned, fixing his eyes on Charity. "I'm sorry about that."

"She's . . . nice."

"She's a busybody, but she means well."

"She thinks something's going on between us. Why didn't you tell her the truth?"

Mike frowned as he lifted the coffeepot and poured himself another cup. "I didn't see any need to make excuses. Nothing happened, Charity."

"That doesn't mean the minister and the show-girl won't end up being the talk of the territory."

"You won't be here to listen to it, so what does it matter?"

"I don't like being thought of in a bad light. I don't want people to think about me and say, 'Oh, she's the one that led our good pastor astray.' "

"I did the leading, Charity. If I hear any rumors, I'll squelch them."

Setting his mug on the counter, Mike crossed the room, slipped his arms around Charity's waist and pulled her against him. He felt so good, so right, yet everything between them was wrong.

"I've got to get ready for church. Are you going with me?"

Charity shook her head. It was so tempting to stay in his arms, to forget about going home, but there was nothing here for her except a man who lusted after her body but was still in love with his wife. If the paintings in the living room and Mike's constant thoughts about Jessie hadn't been enough to convince her of that, Fay's words had.

She slipped out of his arms and went to the laundry room for her clothes. Getting out of here, away from Mike's heated eyes, from his restrained desire, might not be what she wanted, but she had no other choice.

Mike leaned against the door jamb just inches away from her and watched while she pulled her jeans, sweater, and underwear from the dryer.

"Mind turning around while I get dressed," she asked, making a circle with her index finger. She half expected him to say he'd already seen her naked and seeing her again without a stitch on wouldn't bother him in the least, but he did as she asked and turned his back.

"I don't remember ever sleeping so good," he

told her as she pulled off the mostly unbuttoned flannel shirt and dropped it in the laundry basket.

"You were exhausted." She slipped her sweater over her head, tugged her still dirty but dry jeans over the borrowed boxers, and worked the zipper up. "Anyone would have slept good."

"I've gone without sleep before, more times than I can count. Sleep still didn't come easily, and when it did I'd end up waking off and on, or I'd toss and turn. Having you in my arms made sleeping easy."

"Maybe I should bottle little bits and pieces of myself. I could probably make a fortune on the sleeping-pill market."

"I'd buy every bottle."

She'd give them to him free of charge if she felt it was the right thing to do. But he wasn't thinking straight right now. He wanted Jessie, not her.

Shoving her underwear in the pockets of her jeans, she grabbed her boots and tried to walk past him, but he latched on to her waist and tugged her against his chest. "Stay," he whispered against her ear.

"Why?" She dropped her boots at her side and pressed her hands against his chest to keep some distance between them. "Because you sleep better when I'm around?"

"Because I like having you around."

"Do you say the same thing to everyone you offer a job to?" She pushed away from him and crossed to the kitchen window, where she stared out at the clear blue sky and a vast land coated with snow.

"This has nothing to do with a job, Charity."

She faced him again, leaning against the counter for support. "I know. It has to do with you and me and some strange kind of lust we feel for each other. But that's it. Lust. Desire. Nothing more."

"How can there possibly be any more if you don't give us a chance?"

"What if I did give us a chance and it didn't work out?"

"Then you could go back to Vegas knowing we tried."

"It's a crapshoot, Mike, and the odds are against us. I'm not going to gamble with what I've worked so hard to build for myself."

"What have you built? A superficial string of jobs that go nowhere? What are you going to do when you're older, when you can't dance any longer, when your body isn't young and firm?"

She glared at him, hating his words. As hard as she tried to hold it back, a tear slipped from her eyes. "I hoped you'd understand. I hoped you'd be better than all the other people who've told me my choice was crazy. But you're no better than the rest."

Slumping down in a kitchen chair, she yanked on a sock and tried to shove her foot in her boot, but Mike stilled her hands, grasping them tightly in his.

"That wasn't fair." He crouched down in front of her and reached a hand toward her face to wipe away her tear, but she pulled back. "I'm sorry," he added.

"Don't be. You haven't said anything that I haven't thought about before."

"You know it's a dead-end job."

"That's the way it appears to you, but to me it's a dream. It's the only thing I've done in my life that hasn't been forced on me, and I'm not going to give up until I make my dream come true."

The knock at the door startled both of them. Mike thrust his hand through his hair. "We need to talk, Charity."

"There's nothing to talk about," she said, shoving her other foot into her boot as Mike stood, ignoring the next series of knocks on the front door. "You've got to get ready for church, and I have to pack and catch a plane for home."

"I'll come to Vegas."

"Why? So you can see firsthand what I do on stage? So you can preach at me about what's wrong about my job?"

"You really think that's what I want to do?"

The knock was louder this time. Charity pushed out of the chair, grabbed her coat, hanger and all, from the laundry room and pushed past Mike. "That could be Jack. He said he'd come get me this morning."

Mike trailed after her as she rushed to the front door and pulled it open.

Max stood in the doorway, looking in an all-fired hurry. Behind him Charity could see Jack sitting in the truck with the engine running.

"Something wrong?" Charity asked her brother, worried that something dreadful had happened at the ranch house, or maybe Lauren was about to have her baby early.

"The airline called a little while ago. They've had to move up your flight."

"To when?" Mike asked, grasping her shoulders, pressing his chest against her back.

"A few hours from now. We've got to go or you'll miss it."

"Now?" Charity felt rushed, confused. "But I've got to pack."

"Your bags are in the truck."

"I haven't said goodbye or thanks to anyone. I—"

"Jack says there's another storm blowing in and if you don't go, there's no telling when you can get out of here."

"She'll be out in a second," Mike said.

"No. I'll go now."

Mike held her back and Max looked from one to the other. "I'll wait in the truck. Come out when you're ready."

Mike all but closed the door in Max's face. He twisted Charity around and cupped her cheeks in his hands. There were dark shadows under his eyes. He was still tired, but there was something else in his gaze, something she couldn't read.

"I'm in love with you, Charity. God help me, I didn't want it to happen, not when we've known each other such a short time. But it did happen, and it scares the hell out of me."

She found herself laughing cynically, when she really wanted to cry. "Is that heartfelt declaration supposed to make me want to stay with you?"

"I've only told one other woman that I love her—"

"And you still love her! Look at this place." Charity cast her eyes around the painting-filled room. "Jessie's everywhere you turn. Your house is full of her paintings. You keep a picture of her in your Bible. She's in your thoughts, in your dreams."

"You're wrong. You don't understand."

"You're right, I don't understand. But I don't have the time for explanations."

She pressed her hands against his chest and pushed away, flinging open the door and stepping out into the bitterly cold morning. "I've got a suggestion, though, Mike. Don't tell any other woman you love her until you're sure it wasn't a mistake, some big fluke of nature playing a trick on you. Make sure you're happy about it instead of being scared shitless. And please, until you can say it without thinking of Jessie at the same time, keep it to yourself."

With that said, she ran for the truck, for a plane that wouldn't wait, for another job in Vegas that might never lead anywhere, and she didn't look back.

Chapter 14

CHARITY LOUNGED BESIDE THE POOL, soaking up Las Vegas's springtime sun, a can of Diet Coke dangling in the fingers of one hand. She wedged a cordless phone between her shoulder and her ear. Her free hand, meanwhile, toyed with the braid slung over her shoulder as she and Sam Remington caught up on life away from the ranch and at it, just as they'd done every week for the past two months.

"So what's Logan doing now?" Sam asked, always concerned about her friend's friends, whether she knew them or not.

Charity tilted her head and looked at the *ex*-detective sitting next to her, working on a tan that didn't need much working on.

"Right now he's circling job opportunities in the want ads."

"For himself?"

"Oh, no. He hasn't quite figured out what he's going to do with himself since he quit his job, but he's determined to find something for me. Something, I might add, that he feels is a little more my style, like being secretary to a podiatrist or answering phones at a mental health clinic."

Logan shot her a grin, then double-circled what looked to be another low-paying, tedious, eight-to-five job. Sam, however, was silent at the other end of the phone. Finally she said, "What happened to the job singing backup for Elvis at the Heartbreak Hotel and Wedding Parlor?"

"It was the Viva Las Vegas Wedding Chapel and Honeymoon Haven and"—Charity let out her frustration on a long-winded sigh—"I was fired."

There was another decidedly long pause at the other end of the phone, a phenomenon that seemed to occur an awful lot lately, especially when Charity recounted a new story about being canned to any one of her family members or long-distance friends. "What did you do this time?" Sam asked.

"Why does everyone always assume it's my fault when I get fired?"

"We don't *always* assume that—only occasionally." Sam laughed lightly. "So what's the story this time?"

Charity sipped at her Diet Coke. "Are you sure you want to hear it?"

"I'll listen to anything if it'll make me laugh. After spending a week in Florida with Jack's mom, I need a pick-me-up."

"That bad, huh?"

"Miserable. Once a homeless person, always a low-life, that's the way Lady Celeste sees me. But that's not what I want to talk about right now. Tell me why you got fired. Did Elvis have anything to do with it?"

"Oh, yeah, that five-foot-two reprobate had everything to do with it, beginning with the poofy Ann-Margret wig he made me wear. Jeez, Sam, it was almost as big as he was. And then he insisted I wear fuchsia hot pants, a skin-tight angora sweater with one of those pointy bras they wore way back when, and, get this—white go-go boots."

Sam chuckled. "Please don't tell me you complained about the costume?"

"Of course not. I've worn less and I've worn worse."

"So what happened?"

"I slapped a drunk bridegroom when he asked me to accompany him and his new wife to the Blue Hawaii honeymoon suite. Seems he had a special *lei* he wanted to give both of us—at the same time—and I'm not talking about a necklace of tropical flowers."

Logan lowered his sunglasses and glared at her, but she brushed his frown aside with a wave of her hand and listened to Sam's giggles.

"The bridegroom took great exception to my refusal," Charity said, squirting sunblock on her stomach and rubbing it in. "Elvis didn't like the fact that I refused, either, so he canned me."

Logan held up the newspaper and pointed to another job he'd circled, but she swatted the paper away.

"So here I am," she went on, "without a job again, using Logan's phone because his saving's account isn't as empty as mine, using his pool because the one at my apartment complex was closed due to some kind of fungus growing on the bottom, and, well, I'm just killing time until my audition next week."

"What audition?" Sam asked.

"The second part of the audition I had to rush home for in February. I swear Duane has it out for me, making me think that first audition was all-important, stringing me along for weeks after giving me the impression I might get the job, then telling me he wants me to audition again."

"Is it worth it, Charity?"

Sometimes she wondered. And then something good would happen, a smidgen of hope would come her way, making her think she might have a chance to reach the top in this town. There was always hope. "Yes," she said softly, "it's worth it."

She could almost see Sam smiling when she said, "If it makes you happy, that's all that matters."

Through the phone, over a thousand-plus miles, Charity could hear the twins, one cooing, one crying. "Can you hold on a second, Charity?" Sam asked.

"Sure."

She pictured Sam lifting a baby to her shoulder and a part of her longed to reach out and hold one of the twins again, or Lauren and Max's brand-new baby boy. But there weren't too many chances to get away and enjoy that kind of happiness. If she wasn't working, she was fighting for a job. *That* was the life of a not-too-successful showgirl.

Through the cooing and crying she heard the screen door in the kitchen slam, she heard a familiar voice—Mike's voice—in the background asking for Jack, and heard Sam say he wouldn't be back till late.

Whatever else Mike might have said was unintelligible. But the mere sound of his deep, rich voice made her long for him. She wanted to share more conversations. Wanted to once again feel the warmth of his skin against hers. Even with a thousand miles separating them, a thousand miles and goals that didn't coincide, he still made her ache.

Again she heard the door slam and she knew Mike had gone, just as he was gone from her life. "Sorry, Charity," Sam said. "I got a bit distracted."

"Was that Mike?" Charity knew already, but she felt the need to ask.

"Yeah. He said to tell you hi."

Sam was a terrible liar. "No, he didn't."

"All right, he didn't. He just sort of shrugged when I told him I was talking to you. Said he was busy and since Jack wasn't around, he'd get going. Is that what you wanted to hear?"

"I don't expect him to ask about me." She

hoped he would but admitting that was impossible. "He's a busy man, running the ranch, preaching on Sundays, probably going out with Fay Atkinson's niece Raylene."

"Why would he go out with her? She's a teenager, for heaven's sake."

"She's what?" Charity was totally aghast. She never would have guessed that, considering the way Fay Atkinson had been trying to push the preacher and her niece together.

"She's eighteen. Nineteen at most. And she's interested in Beau, not Mike."

"But Fay said—"

"Fay's a busybody. Darling lady who'd give you the shirt off her back, but a busybody just the same."

Relief washed over her. It made no sense caring what Mike was up to, but it was hard not to be interested.

"Is he still chasing after Satan?" Charity asked, knowing she should turn the subject to something else, but she was a glutton for punishment and had to know what was going on in Mike's life.

"He caught him a couple of weeks ago."

Her good mood suddenly deflated. "That should make him happy."

"There's only one thing that would make him happy right now, and that's you coming back."

"That's not going to happen. We've got nothing in common, and—"

"He's in love with you."

"And what makes you think that?"

"Max heard him tell you so that morning he and Jack took you to the airport."

"And Max blabbed to you about it?"

"He told Lauren who told me. That juicy bit of news was a nice accompaniment to all the rumors circulating about the one and only local minister sleeping with a showgirl."

"That was an unfounded rumor, nothing more, and I'm surprised you're mentioning it months after the fact."

"I'm only mentioning it because Mike's lonely, and even though you'd never admit it, I think you're lonely, too."

Charity got up from the lounge chair and walked to the far side of the pool, away from Logan, who'd been harping at her about Mike, too.

"I don't have time to be lonely," she told her friend. "I've got Logan and my work—"

"Logan's a friend, not a lover. There's a big difference, Charity. Mike loves you. He wants you."

"He's a man who wants me to conform, a man who wants me to do what he thinks I should do." And he's still in love with his long-dead wife, she thought sadly. "He's not interested in my career, Sam. He thinks it's a loser of a job. Hell, what he wants is to put me inside a corral and tame me, because he's tame and he thinks everyone and everything should be that way. But I don't want that. I never have."

"What do you want?"

"To make my own mistakes. To have my family and friends love me no matter what I do."

Maybe she was selfish, maybe she wanted too much, but that was it in a nutshell. It seemed such a small thing to be loved—faults and all.

Mike tossed fresh hay into the corral at the back of his barn and ignored the crunch of footsteps behind him in the gravel. He wasn't in the mood for company. He hadn't been in weeks, but that hadn't kept intruders away.

"Mornin'."

He should have expected Jack to stop by to see how things had gone on the ranch during his absence. What he had to report, however, wasn't good.

"It was a hell of a winter," Jack said, hooking a boot heel over a rail.

"Yeah." Mike couldn't agree more. The last two weeks of February had been bitterly cold and March hadn't been much different. It had been one of the harshest winters on record, and the Remington ranch had lost more cows than Mike wanted to think about. They'd had large hay reserves, but there'd been too many days in a row where the snow blew so hard a man couldn't see his hand in front of his face let alone go out on the range to dump hay for the critters.

Of course, not everyone had stuck around the ranch to deal with the horrific weather.

"How was Florida?" Mike asked, keeping his eyes trained on the stallion darting back and forth in the corral.

"I'd take forty below any day. If it hadn't been for two colicky babies and a wife begging and pleading for us to be with Lauren when her baby was born, I would have stayed put right here." Jack climbed a couple of rungs on the paddock and folded his arms over the top rail, obviously wanting a better look at the mustang inside. "God, I hate Florida, especially the snobs in Palm Beach."

Mike leaned his pitchfork against the corral and joined his friend, glad to have something to talk about other than the ranch. "Did your mom show up?"

"Yeah. She wasn't about to miss the christening, so I got to spend a couple days hearing Lady Celeste tell Lauren how to take care of the baby, the house, and her business, as if she'd had a whole lot of experience. And then she started in on Sam, and you know as well as I do what my mom thinks of my wife."

Mike laughed. It was one of the few times something had struck him as funny in a couple of months.

"I heard Reece was there, too."

Jack chuckled. "You'd think they hadn't gotten a divorce twenty-some-odd years ago the way Mom turned her henpecking on Dad. Told him she was tired of hearing rumors about the latest blonde bimbo he was squiring around Santa Fe, told him he'd gained too much weight around the middle. Then dad started in on her, complaining about her stuffy friends."

It was good hearing someone else bellyache for

a change. Mike had done his own share of complaining lately, and he figured everyone in the county was tired of listening to his troubles—the ones he cared to share. Once the whispers about his scandalous affair with the Vegas showgirl had subsided, people pretty much hushed up around him. Even Crosby kept his distance. No one asked him about Charity and even if they had, he wouldn't have had any comment to make except that she'd gone home and that he hadn't heard from her since.

Didn't matter, he supposed. He had his hands full running Jack's ranch, his own fledgling operation, and preaching to a congregation where a few folks occasionally looked at him like he was a fallen man. It was their loss. He had nothing to hide. Had done nothing wrong. In his mind, holding Charity against him during the night, kissing her, coming close to making love to her, had been the best things he'd done in six years.

But she was gone now, and he'd sunk back into loneliness, which had long ago become a fact of life.

"So," Jack said, staring at the angry mustang trying his hardest to find a way out of the corral, "how'd you catch Satan?"

"Catch?" Mike shook his head. "The horse was starving and brought his herd down to the ranch to get something to eat. He hardly put up a fight when I tossed the lasso round his neck. Sure took the fun out of it."

"He doesn't look all that happy with his current lot in life, food or no food."

"Woody and I added a couple more rails to increase the height of the corral. There's no way the stallion's going to get out unless someone opens the gate, but he's far from resigned to his fate. He eats, he runs from one end of the corral to the other, and he's ready to fight anyone who gets too close to him."

"Cros tells me you've been pretty much the same way while I've been gone."

"Cros talks too much."

"Yeah, but I heard the same thing from Bill and Hank. Probably would have heard a similar story from Benny if he was a little more prone to talk."

"Losing hundreds of cows didn't settle well. That's all."

Jack never once looked at Mike, he merely stared at Satan and at the sun rising on the horizon. Mike knew the blizzard and the toll it had taken on the herd didn't settle well with Jack, either, but Mike knew there was more on his mind.

"You know I'm not big on butting in," Jack said, "but how much longer are you gonna mope over Charity?"

"What makes you think that's what I'm doing?"

" 'Cause I know you better than you know yourself. Seems to me you should be spending your energy trying to figure out how to catch a showgirl instead of standing out here trying to figure out how to tame something you already caught."

"Full of wisdom, aren't you?"

Jack laughed. "Those were Sam's words right before she sent me out here to bug the hell out of you. She says if you don't go after Charity you deserve to be miserable the rest of your life."

"I asked the woman to stay on more than one occasion. Told her I loved her."

"That's not the way I heard it."

"Yeah, what did you hear?"

"That you told her you loved her, even though you didn't want to. That's a hell of a thing to say to a woman."

"Where'd you get that information?"

"From my wife, who got it from Lauren, who got it from Max, who heard it direct from the jackass's mouth. You gonna deny it?"

"Why bother? It doesn't matter much now."

"Guess not. Charity's got a boyfriend, anyway. Logan somebody. A cop, the way I hear it. I've heard stories about him handcuffing her, too."

Mike felt his jaw tightening. He should have known she'd go back to Vegas and fall in love. Should have known she wouldn't long for him the way he longed for her. Of course, why should he have expected her to want him, when he'd let her leave thinking he was still in love with Jessie.

It wasn't the truth. She would have known that if he'd made her listen. Instead he'd let her run off to catch a plane.

Maybe he'd realized that letting her leave was easier than telling her the truth. How could he tell her that it wasn't grief or love that kept Jessie in his thoughts, that it was guilt keeping him awake all night. He couldn't bring himself to tell anyone what he'd done, that he'd let his wife die because he'd hated seeing her plugged in to the machines that kept her alive.

Why couldn't he have told Charity there was only one woman he loved? A woman who had the passion for life that he'd never had, a woman who'd made him want to live, really live.

For the first time he could remember, he turned to his friend for help. "You know, Jack, I'm supposed to be the one with all the answers. I'm supposed to be the one who knows how to deal with the problems of the world, but I don't have a clue how to solve my own."

He'd thought revealing that weakness would make him feel less of a man, unworthy of his calling. Instead it brought him back down to earth and made him realize that, as he'd told Charity once, he wasn't a god, merely a man. Nothing less. Nothing more.

"Ever thought of going after her?" Jack asked.

"Every minute of every day. Suppose it wouldn't do much good now, if she's got some guy hanging around."

"I've never known you to let obstacles get in your way when you wanted something."

"Tossing a lasso around a horse or cow isn't as tough as trying to toss one around a woman—especially a lady as wild as Charity."

"Maybe you're trying to catch her in all the wrong ways. You know she doesn't like ropes. You know she doesn't like being fenced in."

"You got any suggestions?"

"Hell, no. You're the man with the answers."

Jack slapped him on the back. "You want Charity badly enough, you'll figure something out."

Something without ropes, something without fences? But what? He was a cowboy and that's all he knew. But he wanted Charity—maybe it was time to find another way to gentle her and make her his own.

# Chapter 15

A PAIR OF SHOCKING PINK STILETTOS flew across the tiny apartment, landing in the proximity of the bedroom. "Now if only I can find my makeup bag," Charity muttered as she propped open the front door to let the warm spring breeze in through the screen, then went back to rummaging through the clutter on the living room floor.

"If you'd put stuff where it belongs, you wouldn't have this problem."

Charity shot Logan a murderous scowl. "If your feet were as tired as mine when you got home from work—*if* you worked—you'd kick your shoes off inside the front door, too."

"Yeah, well, there's no chance of my feet hurtin', cause I don't plan on working for a good long time."

Charity hated the ominous tone in Logan's voice. She knew he'd quit the job he'd once loved, knew he hadn't looked for another, and so far he'd seemed content, even relieved. But she'd known him a long time, and right now she knew something was wrong.

She stopped digging through the shopping bags, the laundry basket full of towels she had yet to hang up or even fold, and the toppled-over pile of library books on the floor, and peeked over the coffee table at Logan. "What are you talking about?"

"I finally decided to get out of Vegas."

*What?* How could he possibly up and leave when he was the only true friend she had in town? She could feel deep frown lines forming between her eyes, and knew he could see her dismay as she folded her arms atop the coffee table and tried to sound calm and completely comfortable with this cataclysmic announcement. "Do you have any plans?"

"Thought I might buy a cabin in the mountains and kick back for a year or two. Fish, play the guitar."

"You'll be bored stiff in a week."

He shrugged. "Might hire myself a pretty housekeeper to keep me company, a busty blonde—Scandinavian maybe; twenty-two, twenty-three—someone who's more interested in sex than cleaning." He took a sip of beer. "You want to apply?"

"I'm not blonde, I'm not Scandinavian, I'm twenty-five and I'm not interested in cleaning *or* sex."

"Yeah, I figured that out on our first and only date."

Charity climbed up off her knees and plopped on the couch beside Logan. She'd known for years that a steady diet of blood, guts, murder, mayhem, and vice was wearing him down, but he was so dang dedicated to being a cop that she'd never expected him to quit.

"You aren't really going to leave Vegas, are you?"

He slung his arm over her shoulder and tugged her close. Friend, confessor, and big-brother figure, she couldn't bear the thought of him leaving, and felt tears welling up behind her eyes. "I've been waiting for the right time to tell you. Maybe this is it."

"Sure. Why not?" she said half-heartedly. "I've got an audition in an hour, I'm not dressed, can't find my makeup, and I'm a bundle of nerves. Go ahead, dump your bad news on me."

"All right . . . I sold my house yesterday—"

"How could you? You didn't even tell me you were putting it on the market."

" 'Cause you would have tried talking me out of it. Because you would have gotten upset, which is exactly what you're doing now. I didn't know it would sell so fast, before the realtor could even put up a sign. But I'm glad it did. Hell, Charity, I've gotta get out of this town and if I don't do it now—"

"Fine! Go! Leave me alone and miserable."

"*That's* part of the reason I've stayed as long as I have, so you wouldn't be alone and miserable. I hoped you'd fall in love and get married, or go to Florida with your brother, or stick around Wyoming with that minister and that horse you've mentioned half a dozen times a day for the past couple of months, but you stay in this hell-hole of a town and get beaten into the ground every time you turn around."

She wiped a tear from her cheek with the back of her hand. "This town might beat me into the ground, but having you leave is gonna feel like someone dug a grave, shoved me in, then buried me alive."

The corner of his mouth quirked up. "Feeling sorry for yourself?"

"I'm losing my best friend. So, yes, Mr. Wolfe, I'm feeling *very* sorry for myself." She pulled away from his brotherly embrace and again searched for her makeup bag. "I don't know what's going on in your life," she said, yanking a crimson teddy she'd forgotten all about from a Victoria's Secret bag. Clutching it to her chest, she looked at Logan and sighed. "I don't know why you quit your job, but I know it wasn't just burnout. I've asked but you won't tell me. I've pried and you've ignored me."

"It's simply a case of too much Vegas and not enough life."

"Liar." She smiled and tossed the teddy at her friend. "So when are you leaving?"

"Soon as I find the perfect cabin, the best fishing hole, and the big-busted Scandinavian maid."

Logan shoved off the sofa and dropped down to his knees to join Charity in her search. "What exactly are we looking for?"

"A makeup bag. It's chartreuse, it's plastic, it's about nine inches by twelve inches, and it says 'Makeup' on the side. Trust me, you can't miss it."

Logan's face was only inches from hers when their eyes met. His were brown and warm and crinkled at the corners from too much sun and a lot of laughter—once upon a time. "I'll miss you, Charity."

With that, she burst into tears. They'd been threatening for months, ever since she'd run away from Mike, yet she'd managed to hold them back. Logan's abandonment was the last straw.

She threw her arms around him. "I'll miss you, too." He held her tight, his big hands soothing as they stroked her hair. God, she was going to miss him.

Even the sun seemed to mourn her impending loss, the balmy rays coming through the open door disappearing behind a . . . She frowned. It wasn't a cloud she saw when she looked through the screen, but a minister, a devilishly handsome man with a lock of blue-black hair falling over his brow.

"Seems I've come at the wrong time."

*Wrong time?* Yes. No. Maybe.

Charity scrambled up from the floor, tightening the ties on her short paisley silk robe, tugging the back hem over her derrière, and the only thing she wore beneath—an amethyst thong.

Logan seemed to be the only one composed enough to go to the door, and he opened the screen wide, as if he assumed—due, more than likely, to the sheer disbelief that had to be registering on her face—that she knew the man standing outside.

"I'm Logan Wolfe." He stuck his hand toward Mike and Charity watched the two men shake.

"Mike Flynn."

"The minister?"

"Among other things."

So much for introductions.

Charity gave the ties on her robe another tug and struggled for composure. "Want to come in?"

Mike's gaze burned a path across Logan, then blazed for a moment on Charity's bare legs and thighs. "Maybe I should come back later."

"No need," Logan said. "I was just getting ready to leave."

It had looked quite the opposite. Considering the clench she and Logan had had around each other, a casual observer might have thought Logan was going in for the score, for the big one, right there on the floor, in the middle of the clutter, and that he'd been in no hurry to leave.

But he dug into his pants pocket for the keys to his truck and stepped around Mike and onto the cement landing just outside her apartment door. "Call me after the audition," he said, then blew her a goodbye kiss and disappeared as Mike stepped inside.

The screen door slammed with a decided twang, and she could feel the floor shaking when Logan bounded down the stairs. She was shaking inside, too, now that she was alone . . . with

Mike. Alone, and running late, and . . . and she had to find her makeup bag and get ready for the audition.

"Help me, will you?" she asked beseechingly, searching through half-a-dozen Baby Gap and Kmart packages filled with baby boy things she planned to send Lauren. "I need to find my makeup bag. It's chartreuse, plastic, about nine inches by twelve inches, and it says 'Makeup' on the side. I've got an audition in . . ." She glanced at the digital clock on the VCR. "Oh, jeez, I've got to be there in half an hour, I'm not dressed, I've still got to put on my makeup, if I ever find it."

She tossed an easy-chair cushion onto the floor and was about to lose her mind when a strong arm wrapped around her waist and tugged her bottom against a familiar pair of hard, masculine hips. "Is this what you're looking for?"

Mike's other arm shot in front of her and there, in all its glory, was her makeup bag.

"Oh, thank you."

She snatched it out of his hands and raced to the bathroom, knowing full well that she was ignoring her guest, but he'd come uninvited and if truth be told, she was nervous enough without him adding to her jitters.

Pulling her once-again black hair into a ponytail, one that would dance right along with her at the audition, she tried not to look at Mike as he leaned against the doorjamb and folded his arms over his chest. But it was impossible not to notice him as she dabbed on foundation, powder, and blush and tried to put on lip liner with shaky fingers. At last, when his staring didn't cease, she turned around.

"I think Logan opened a bag of chips a while ago and there's bound to be a can or two of nuts somewhere in the kitchen. There's beer in the refrigerator and a bottle of merlot. Why don't you help yourself."

"I don't drink."

She leaned her bottom against the edge of the sink. "I guess I should have known that."

"Why should you? We might have chased a wild horse together, might have slept together, but we never shared a meal. There are a lot of things I don't know about you and a lot you don't know about me."

"Is that why you're here?" She was far snippier than she'd wanted to be, but she chalked it up to nerves. "Did you want to invite me to dinner so we can learn more about our culinary likes and dislikes?"

"Dinner's a thought. I don't have any immediate plans."

"But I do," she said, turning back to the mirror. "I've got an audition and I can't be late."

"Don't worry about me. I'm perfectly comfortable standing right here."

Unfortunately, she wasn't the least bit comfortable. His piercing green eyes watched her every move. She could see it all in the mirror, the way he focused on her bare feet, her ankles, the length of her legs, and her behind, which peeked out from under her robe every time she raised her arms.

His silence was maddening, but right now she could think of nothing to say. Besides, she had more important stuff on her mind.

Pulling a few fake lashes from her eyelash kit, she started to glue them one at a time to the outer corners of her eyelids. Mike distracted her completely when he moved to the side of the vanity and leaned against the wall. She could smell his aftershave. Was it Obsession? It smelled delightful, more sophisticated than the rugged brand he wore at the ranch.

He wasn't dressed the same, either. He had on highly polished black cowboy boots, black slacks that fit him very, very well, and a creamy white sweater. Cashmere, maybe? Something lightweight. Something that hugged the muscular contours of his chest, shoulders and arms.

His face was freshly shaved, and she longed to put her fingers against his cheek, to touch the smoothness of his skin, to see if it was warm or cool, to feel his lips against hers again.

They'd been apart more than two months, but she hadn't forgotten the taste of him, even though she'd tried.

"Are you going to be here long?" she asked, trying again to appear in control of an apprehensive moment.

"A week . . . maybe. Like I said, I don't have any plans that can't be changed."

"Do you have friends in Vegas?"

"Just you."

"So why'd you come?"

"To tell you I'd caught Satan."

"I'd heard that already."

"So why didn't you call to give me a piece of your mind?"

"What good would it have done? You're stubborn, mule-headed, and . . . and . . . oh, hell! You'd do exactly what you wanted to do no matter what—like stay in my bathroom when I wish you'd leave."

"You're awfully pretty when you're angry."

Her hand twitched and the eyelash she was trying to apply dropped on the bridge of her nose, and stuck.

"Let me get that for you."

Mike plucked the eyelash from her skin, his callused fingertips brushing lightly over her cheek. She looked into his eyes and trembled. So much for thinking she could get him out of her mind and keep him out.

"Who's Logan?" Mike asked as she attempted to put the eyelash in the appropriate place.

"A friend."

"Boyfriend?"

She grinned at him out the corner of her eyes. "Jealous?"

"Just want to know what competition I have for your attention—other than auditions."

"He's a friend. Nothing more. And besides auditions, I've got a job singing in a club every night from ten till two—"

"What club?"

"Why?"

"Curious."

She brushed her brows, making them whisk upward just a tad. "The Torch. Downtown. Not a big place but the tips are good. Other than that I've got ballet lessons on Tuesday and Thursday and voice lessons Wednesday afternoons." She pressed her hands against the sink. "That's my life, Mike."

He stepped behind her, tall, gorgeous, and powerful. They watched each other in the mirror, his eyes hot and searching, hers bemused and frantic because she was going to be late, because she had no idea what he planned to do.

He cupped his hands over her shoulders and pulled her back against his chest. His hands were warm and his fingers lightly kneaded her shoulders. She could see the jagged scar on the back of his right hand and she felt the urge to touch it, but she stood still and simply tried to breath.

"I want to know more." Mike's deep, velvety voice was almost a whisper as he lowered his head and kissed her neck, making her tense all over again in spite of the quiver of desire rippling through her. She still needed to put on her lip liner, her lipstick, and who knows what else. She could barely think. Fortunately she had enough sense to move away from a touch that had a way of making her lose all thought.

She skirted around him, saying, "I've got to get dressed," then rushed the few feet toward her bedroom, kicked her stilettos inside, and accidentally slammed the door behind her. She wished she could collapse on the bed, find a way to steel her nerves, but there wasn't time.

She tossed her robe on the bed and slipped into the shocking pink leotard that she'd bought just for this audition. There wasn't much more in the back than the thong that ran between her cheeks and the measly piece in front that barely covered all those things that should be covered for respectability's sake.

It was a stretch of the imagination to call it a leotard since—unstretched—the piece of fabric wouldn't have covered a newborn's behind, but it was exactly what she needed for her audition, just the right thing to call attention to her body and her moves.

Of course, it wasn't perfect for parading past a minister, but that's exactly what she was going to have to do since the sarong she'd bought to wear over it was still in a bag, somewhere on the living-room floor.

Somehow she sucked a deep breath over the lump in her throat, shoved her feet into her stilettos, fastened the straps at her ankles, and looked at herself in the mirror.

Pure sin. That's what she looked like.

Definitely what a man of God would want in a woman, she thought cynically.

She stretched the skimpy top trying to cover a little more of her breasts, but she immediately realized that spandex had a unique way of expanding and then popping right back into shape. Unfortunately, its shape was minuscule.

She'd strutted around half naked for the past six years and it had never bothered her. So why did it freak her out now?

*Relax. Relax.* Don't let him make you nervous. Tell him you'll have dinner with him and then send him packing, because he's taking a toll on your energy!

She took a deep breath, threw her shoulders back, and yanked open the door. Mike leaned against the arch leading into the living room, obviously waiting for this moment. His hot green eyes took in every single inch of her anatomy, scanning the 99 percent that was bare and the one percent that wasn't. Slowly. Too slowly.

That perusal was not the act of a minister. It was the scrutiny of a hot-blooded man who wanted the woman standing in front of him.

She flopped against the wall, clasped her hands somewhere in front of her pelvis—one of the places Mike's eyes kept flickering toward—and sighed. "Look, Mike, I've got to go. This audition's important, I'm already running late, and maybe you're right, maybe we should talk about why you're here and why you want to know more about me, but right now I've got to gather up my stuff, including my wits, and get out of here."

"I'll help you."

"The only way you can help is to leave. Now."

The annoying man only grinned. "I don't have anywhere to go."

"Try your hotel. See the concierge and he'll

give you a zillion recommendations. Restaurants, entertainment, shows."

"I'd like to see what an audition's like."

"That's impossible. You'd be in the way. You'd make me nervous." She frowned. "Or is that your game plan—do anything you can to make me fail?"

His jaw tightened. "My game plan's to sit in the dark somewhere and cheer you on. If you think I want to make you miserable, you're wrong. Dead wrong."

He reached into his pants pocket, pulled out a set of keys, and for some reason she couldn't explain, her stomach clenched when she thought he was going to leave.

He tossed the keys in the air and caught them again. As if the key toss wasn't brash enough, he hit her with a dimpled smile. "You're gonna be late if we don't get going. I've got a car downstairs, a full tank of gas, and I've been driving around this town for hours so I know the roads like the back of my hand. Get your stuff, Charity, and let's get going."

Her eyes narrowed skeptically. "You'll sit in the dark? At the back of the theater?"

"You won't even know I'm there."

Oh, she'd know all right. And she wasn't going to like it a bit.

## Chapter 16

THE MUSICAL SCORE FROM *A CHORUS LINE* reverberated through the auditorium, raising tension and anxiety to a feverish pitch as nearly forty women went through their individual warm-up routines while waiting for Duane to grace them with his presence.

Charity couldn't remember a time when the famed choreographer hadn't been late. It was part of his style, along with making people sweat as they waited for *the* call to come, once the audition was over. She'd waited for *the* call more times than she could count. She'd worked for the bastard, too, putting up with his torturous practice sessions, his exacting routines, his humiliating lectures. And then she'd punched him in the nose for getting too friendly.

But she'd never had an opportunity like this

one. Never had the chance to try out for the lead. Come hell or high water, she'd not put up a fuss. She'd do what she was told, then go home and scream out her frustration.

Today, *Trouble* would not be her middle name.

She'd be perfect today. The best.

She slid her fingers down her right thigh, over her calf, grabbed hold of her ankle, and pulled her leg up until the toe of her stiletto was aimed at the ceiling. She held it there, stretching, then noticed a dancer she'd seen at half a dozen other auditions move to her side.

"Who's the guy that came in with you? The one sitting in the dark so Duane won't see him?"

"Just a friend," Charity said. She didn't see the need to elaborate, not when she was concentrating on her warm-ups and psyching herself up for what was to come.

"Is he *more* than a friend, or someone you might like to introduce around—to me, maybe?"

Charity leaned toward the dancer and whispered, "He's a minister."

The girl's eyebrows nearly knit together. "Not my type. Sorry I asked."

Charity didn't think Mike was her type, either, although he did have a wonderful way with his hands. And then there were the special things he did with his lips, his tongue, not to mention those eyes. She could almost feel the heat of them now, bearing down on her, watching her bend, stretch, and pirouette.

What was he up to? Was he out to torment her by making her want him all over again? And once she succumbed, would he want to control her just the way he wanted to control Satan? Would he tell her again that dancing was a senseless, dead-end job? Would he whisper sweet nothings to her until she helplessly fell in love with him, then wave *adios,* because he still loved his wife?

The threat of all those things rested behind his green-eyed stare, a predatory gaze that lay in wait somewhere out in the dark auditorium. But she wouldn't fall for it. Not now. Not ever.

*Focus! Concentrate!* Take a deep breath, this is important, she told herself. Don't blow it by placing your energy on a man, when you need to put every ounce of effort—and passion—into your dancing.

Tryouts were tough. No one told you ahead of time what the routines would be. A showgirl had to learn fast. She could be hired one day and stuck in a show the next. Part of the tryout was to see if you were a quick study. New routines—dance steps—were thrown at you right and left, and only the best dancers, as long as they remembered the moves the first time around, survived. It wasn't a time for distraction.

The music came to a sudden halt and the stage hushed to a deathly quiet. Then the familiar staccato tap, Duane's signature dance, clicked rhythmically on the wooden floor, out of sight at first, then magically he appeared and the women around her stared at him, wide-eyed, mouths almost agape. Charity herself could barely keep down her breakfast. Average height, lean and wiry, he was dressed in black slacks, a skin-tight white T-shirt, and black tap shoes. He'd shaved his head since she'd seen him last, giving him the appearance of a dictator.

How appropriate.

"There's no time to waste," Duane barked. "Watch what I do, don't make a sound, and we'll get along just fine."

He laid out a quick routine, a little tap, a few shimmies, a lot of kicks. Charity put every ounce of her energy into memorizing the movements so she could repeat them perfectly.

Duane strutted to the corner of the stage where a spotlight shone down on him. Someone in the wings tossed him a cane and he caught it dramatically, bounced it against the floor, then used it to lean on as he studied the dancers who hung on to his every breath. "All right, girls, show me how well you can execute those steps."

The music started. Charity tapped her heart out, focusing on the cadence of the music. She twirled rapidly, kicked high, smiled brightly at Duane as she shimmied, and then did a slow, sensual, straight-postured split, stretching her leg muscles to the max as her thighs bounced against the floor.

It was impossible to miss the way Duane focused on her. The way he licked his lips, then methodically rubbed the bridge of his nose—the one she'd punched.

He strolled toward the line of women, cocky, self-assured, and announced haughtily, "I've seen better."

Duane never gave an inch. He was a bastard

with a capital *B* and he expected perfection. That's why he was in such demand. That's why producers and dancers alike put up with his difficult and odious nature. That's exactly why she was putting up with him now.

He strode through the ensemble, winding his way past the dancers like a drill sergeant inspecting his troop. He stopped in front of Charity, just as she'd expected. "*You.*" He pointed directly at the hollow between her breasts, and his cloudy gray eyes froze on her face.

Hell had begun.

"Step out here and show everyone how that routine should *not* be performed."

Her jaw tightened, but she moved to center stage.

"Shine the light on her," Duane shouted, and the heat of the bright spotlight flashed down on her. She knew she'd done the routine without a flaw the first time around, knew that Duane was being an annoying, temperamental jerk. But she also knew that doing the routine all on her own would make her stand out, and that's exactly what she wanted.

She faced the other dancers, head high, shoulders back, breasts perky, and listened for the proper beat in the music. At last, she began. *Tap.* Smile. *Twirl.* Smile. *Kick.* Smile.

Out of the corner of her eye she saw the hint of a very tall, very broad-shouldered man walking down the center aisle, the stray beams of the stage lights reflecting off his bright green eyes as he moved toward the front.

*Tap.* Smile. *Twirl.* Smile.

Mike crossed his arms over his massive chest. His face was impassive as he stared at her.

Duane's face was cold and threatening as he stared at her.

One man confused her.

One man she despised.

She wanted to scream at both of them to leave her alone, but she smiled instead, and finished the routine with the perfectly executed split.

Duane's gaze had frozen on her movements. He loathed her just as much as she loathed him, but he knew and appreciated an impeccable performance when he saw one. He wouldn't tell her it was good, and she didn't want or even expect him to. It was enough that she knew she'd done it right.

She stayed on the floor, right at center stage, and watched attentively as Duane ran through another routine. When it was time to dance again, she rose quickly, lithely, and rejoined the troupe.

They worked in the same fashion for hours on end, the number of dancers whittled down every so often when Duane singled someone out and told her to hit the road.

You couldn't survive in this business if you weren't tough and today, standing on the stage, putting up with Duane's abuse and doing the suggestive moves he'd devised, Charity felt as hard as they come, a seasoned showgirl who'd seen it all, and still hadn't walked away.

"Five minutes, everyone," the stage manager called out. Duane walked into the wings and

Charity immediately rushed to her backpack, pulled out a bottle of water and took a quick, relieving sip.

She stood in the shadows and wiped a bead of perspiration from her temple, quickly searching the auditorium for the man who'd remained invisible except for that first moment when Duane had put her through hell.

He sat halfway back, and their eyes met. She focused on the dark figure, for some odd reason feeling she needed something from him now, something to sustain her. Slowly, he smiled. It was soft. Warm. Tender.

And suddenly she felt she could survive anything.

"Time's up!" The stage manager flashed the troupe a knowing grin, rolling his eyes at Charity as he walked across the stage. They'd worked together more than once and she knew full well his feelings for Duane. But the job was good and like any Las Vegas veteran, he played the game in order to stay alive.

Duane pranced across the stage and dramatically put one hand on his butt, one on his pelvis, and did a few bumps and grinds. He grinned at Charity, swaggered a few feet further, and did another set of hip rolling, hip thrusting, sexual stunts. He worked them into every show because they were suggestive, risqué, and provocative.

When they were woven into the program they worked and worked well, and Charity pretended they were no different from any other routine. But Duane paid special attention to bumps and grinds during tryouts. They were of utmost importance to him, and he wouldn't hire someone who couldn't execute them in the most suggestive, risqué and provocative style ever seen.

An extra spotlight flashed down on the stage. The music rolled through the auditorium, and Duane went into his act, showing the girls what he wanted them to do—professionally, and in a lot of cases, personally. There was nothing sensual about what he did. The routine was as raunchy as they come. In spite of it all, Charity watched and memorized for two long minutes.

Then it was time for the troupe to perform.

Duane clapped his hands as he marched back and forth in front of them. "I want you in one straight line." The last ten women left in the audition scrambled into place. "I want to see you do that routine in a coordinated effort," he said. "I don't want any show-offs, I don't want jerky thrusts. I want it fluid. Smooth."

A trumpet sounded across the stage, mournful, almost wailing. The tempo increased, and Charity watched the dark figure in the audience move closer, closer. Mike stepped just out of sight—but she knew he was there, knew he was watching, his gaze intent.

Her heart beat out of control as she began the moves, splaying her fingers over her pelvis, almost slipping them between her thighs. Slowly, slowly, she swirled her hips, thrust them out then back then out again.

Mike came out of hiding, and his hot, green eyes flamed over her. No longer was she standing on stage doing one of Duane's nearly indecent routines. Instead she was in Mike's bedroom, in his arms, and it was Mike's fingers splayed over her belly, Mike's fingers moving lower, lower, searching for something he desperately needed, something she wanted to give him and only him.

"Stop!"

Charity jerked her head toward Duane.

"What the hell are you doing?"

She felt a trickle of perspiration glide between her breasts. She had to fight for breath. A deep one. Her eyes bored into Duane's, refusing to give him an inch. "I'm doing exactly what you showed us."

He laughed. "You've never been any good at bumps and grinds, Ms. Wilde. Come here and let me show you how they're done."

Her jaw tightened. So did her fists, but still she moved toward the choreographer who could make or break her. She stopped right in front of him and hit him with a defiant glare, mixed with a halfhearted smile. She hated the man. Hated what she knew he was about to do . . . but it was all a part of the audition, it was what she had to do if she wanted the job.

Duane circled her, his lascivious gaze slithering over her body, concentrating on her breasts, her hips. Then he disappeared behind her. He stood there for the longest time, not saying a word, not moving, and she could feel his cold-blooded stare groping her bottom, studying the way the shocking pink thong rested between her cheeks.

Stay calm, she told herself. Just relax. This is

your chance, Charity. Don't punch the lech this time.

Out of the corner of her eye she saw Mike slipping closer to the stage, saw the way his jaw had clenched, the way anger raged in his narrowed eyes.

But no one else was looking at Mike. All eyes were trained on Duane, at the way he slid his long, slender fingers over her stomach and tugged her against his hips.

Mike's fists tightened and Charity prayed like she'd never prayed before. "Get out of here, Mike. Don't watch me. Don't watch any of this." Her prayer was answered in a heartbeat, as Mike turned and quietly walked away.

If only she could breathe. If only she could relax, but the torment in Mike's eyes had settled in her throat.

But she had no time to think about Mike's departure or his torment. She had to think about the dance, the audition, her chance to be a star.

Duane pressed his cheek against hers, slid his hands down the length of her arms and pulled her hands around him, resting her palms flat against his butt. "Hold on tight, Ms. Wilde. Let me show you how this is done."

Duane again wove his fingers around her waist until they spread over her stomach. He ground his hips against her, looking for the right fit, then whispered. "How does that feel?"

*Flaccid.* She managed to smile. "Perfect. Absolutely perfect."

"Good, now follow my movements."

The music began. The double spotlights were on them as Duane forced her hips to move with his, compelled her to thrust, grind, thrust, grind.

Hate and anger welled up inside her. He was compelling her to do something she didn't want, to prove a point—that he could bend her to his will.

And she was letting him—only because the final outcome was the only thing important to her.

At last it was over. At last she moved back in line with the other women.

Duane did his drill-sergeant stroll again, but this stroll was different.

Decision time had arrived.

*"You."* Duane pointed to the woman next to Charity. "Thanks, but no thanks.

He skipped over Charity as he went down the row and narrowed the competition. Six women remained when he stopped in front of Charity and gave her the once over, a smug smirk on his face. He was determined to stretch the agony out to the very last moment.

"You. You. You. You." He pointed to four of the six women. "It shouldn't take me more than a few days to make a decision. If you don't get a call in a week—start looking for another show."

Duane was as polite and businesslike as ever!

It was down to Charity and one other woman.

Duane dismissed most of his assistants. He had all the lights dimmed. Still Charity and the other woman stood in place, until Duane graced them with his presence. He stood in front of them, a contemplative finger held against his lips.

Charity smiled, the most beguiling smile she could muster. She refused to give him the satisfaction of knowing what a miserable, low-down bag of scum she thought he was.

Duane's gaze flickered back and forth between Charity and the woman next to her. At last his grin and his pointed finger lit on the blonde. "*You.*"

Charity's shoulders slumped in utter defeat, wondering uncharacteristically why she continued to chase this dream when it had become such a nightmare.

Crushed or not, Charity smiled at the dancer beside her—the last of the five finalists—seeing the excitement in her eyes, the knowledge that she had a chance, that her own star was within reach.

Charity spun on her stilettos and headed for her backpack. Duane was through humiliating her. He was through stringing her along.

"Where the hell are you going?" Duane called after her.

"Home," she said over her shoulder, flashing Duane her best I-despise-you smile. "Unless you'd like to torture me a little more." There, she'd said it. She'd burned a far-reaching bridge in this town.

"Not so fast, Ms. Wilde."

Duane patted the other woman on the cheek. "Better luck next time, hon."

The girl's eyes narrowed, and exhaustion and a sudden reversal of fortune made her burst into tears as she ran across the stage, grabbed her bag, and disappeared into the wings.

There were only two of them on stage now, and Duane glared at her. Charity thought she'd burned a bridge. Of course, a few months back, when she'd busted Duane's nose, she was sure she'd dropped a bomb on that bridge, that it would never be rebuilt. But she was here, at Duane's bidding.

As confident as that suddenly made her feel, she knew full well that in this town confidence could be squashed in a heartbeat.

"You want this job?" Duane asked.

"More than anything."

"I haven't forgotten the broken nose."

He was looking for an apology, but she refused to give in to that. "I'll give you another one, too, if you ever touch me the way you did that night."

Duane laughed, swept his cane up from the floor, and walked toward the wings. "Don't count on getting a call," he said, not bothering to look at her. "But if you're going to get one, it'll come within the week."

He was gone, and she needed to breathe. She wanted fresh air. She wanted out of this place. And she wanted to shout out her excitement. She wanted to leap into Mike's arms and . . .

*Mike?* Oh, God, where was he?

She grabbed her bag and rushed down the stairs, reaching the rows and rows of auditorium seating. The lights were out. All was dark. Silent.

And Mike was gone.

# Chapter 17

"YOU LOOKING FOR ME?"

Mike couldn't miss the flash of relief or the moment of delight in Charity's face when she heard his voice. She spun around, her long ponytail flying about her, her mouth quirking into a joyous smile when he stepped out of the far, dark corner of the auditorium where he'd been standing. Waiting. Watching.

Suddenly she dropped her bag and ran toward him, launching herself into his arms, wrapping her long legs around his waist, her slender arms about his neck. "This is the best I've ever done, Mike. The absolute best." She squeezed him tightly, planting impulsive kisses on his nose, his eyes, his brows. "I've got a chance this time, a real chance to make it."

"So I heard."

Making it for Charity meant losing for Mike, but even though he didn't feel a hundredth of her joy, he held her close, and took advantage of any time he could have with her—good, bad, indifferent. He liked the feel of her legs wrapped about him, his hands clasped about her thighs to keep her right where she was. Her kisses weren't half bad, either, although he wished one would settle on his mouth.

Suddenly she clapped her hands to his cheeks and frowned into his eyes. "I suppose this is a bit forward of me, isn't it?"

"Not from my point of view."

She struggled, but not like she really meant it. More like she was in no hurry to leave his embrace.

"I'm awfully heavy," she said, insincerely struggling once again.

He kept his hands clasped around her thighs, immensely enjoying the feel of her warm and supple flesh in his palms. "You're just right."

She smiled coyly. "Maybe I should get down?"

"I think you should stay."

He backed her against the wall so she couldn't pull away, then slanted his mouth over hers, doing what he'd wanted to do for months. She tasted like mints. Sweet, oh so sweet, and when he traced his tongue along the edges of her lips he savored the salt of her perspiration, her passion, her drive.

"Mike?" she whispered against his mouth.

He didn't want to talk, he just wanted to kiss, so he ignored her.

"Mike?" He nearly swallowed her word, then

pulled back and looked at her lips, at her frowning eyes.

"There's someone watching us."

He twisted around, still holding Charity close.

"If you don't mind," a bearded guy with a
wide dust mop said, "I've gotta clean this friggin'
place and lock up."

Mike let a struggling Charity slip down his
body, but he didn't let go of her fingers as he
dragged her toward her backpack, swept it up in
his other hand, and beat a hasty retreat out of the
auditorium.

"Where to?" he asked, after letting Charity into
the passenger side of the car and climbing behind
the wheel.

"Home for a hot bath and a glass of wine."

He started the engine, his fingers tightening
around the key as he attempted to stifle the image
of Charity in her tub, bubbles bobbing over her
breasts, popping against the hardened tips of her
nipples.

What man wouldn't see those visions after
watching her dance for hours?

Shoving the car into drive, he pulled into traffic
and rolled down the window to suck in a breath of
fresh air, something, anything to throttle his need
to follow her into her apartment, to strip off that
speck of leotard she was wearing, not to mention
his own clothes, and climb into the tub with her.

"Is everything okay?" Charity asked.

His eyes darted toward her, toward a body, a
face, a passion that tempted and tortured him,
then concentrated on the road again. "No, why?"

"Your knuckles are white, as if you're ready to break the steering wheel in two."

He loosened his hold, even rested his left fore-arm on the window opening. "I'm not used to sit-ting all day. Guess I'm a little tense."

"Auditions are always long. I told you you'd be bored."

"I wasn't bored."

Charity reached across the car and put her hand on his thigh. His own hand clenched the steering wheel.

"Did you like the dancing?"

"Yeah." He'd liked everything about Charity's dancing, her slow, sensual moves, her sexual bumps and grinds, the splits she did, her legs spread wide, her thighs . . .

"Did it bother you when Duane—"

"I wanted to put my fist through his face. I wanted to yank you off that stage and—" He let out some of his frustration with a deep, long, pent-up sigh. "I wanted to do a lot of things, none of which were right, and all of which would have made you angry, so I moved to the back, to the dark, where you wouldn't see me." He glanced at her quickly, and worked up some sort of a smile. "Contrary to what you said earlier, I didn't want to sabotage your chances."

"Thank you."

Again he gripped the wheel with both hands. "So, what do you think your chances are?"

"Good. Bad. It all depends on what Duane's looking for. Today he might want someone with black hair, tomorrow he could want a blonde. It doesn't always come down to who's the best dancer, it comes down to who he wants or doesn't want. Sometimes it's best to forget about it, or at least shove it to the back of your mind until the call comes—or you hear through the grapevine that someone else got the job."

She seemed so matter of fact, so resigned to this life. He could never put up with the uncertainty, the wondering from day to day where life was going to take you. In his own life there was his ministry and his faith, two constants that brought him peace and fulfillment. And then there was the ranch. A snowstorm could wipe you out, or knock you on your butt for a year or two, but for the most part, you knew you'd get up in the morning and ride the range, mend fences, brand cattle, and at night fall into bed exhausted. You knew who your friends were, you knew your boss, and you stuck by each other through thick and thin.

There was none of that here, but the uncertainty, the insecurity of it all hadn't knocked Charity on her butt; it had made her strong. Determined.

"I admire your guts," he said, adding to himself that he could use her pluck back at the ranch.

"Maybe I'm foolish. Maybe I want to reach the top too much."

"You know what you want and you don't let anything"—*or anyone*—"stand in your way."

She didn't comment, she merely squeezed his leg, and silence settled between them as he headed for her apartment.

The way her hand rested on his leg, the way she'd kissed him, flung herself into his arms, made him wonder if she might—someday—let him come between her and that star she wanted.

But what would happen then? What did he want from her? What could he give her?

His nightmares hadn't gone away nor had his guilt. Charity hadn't replaced those things in his mind, not as he'd hoped. She'd simply become an all-consuming passion that he didn't know how to deal with.

It was selfish of him to pursue her when bringing her into his life could cause her pain, but he knew with certainty that he couldn't go on without her, not when he craved her the way he did.

But how could he ask her to give up something she loved? That was another question that had been with him for weeks. The only answer he could come up with was not asking her at all.

It all went back to the way she'd once told him she'd gentle the wild horses. She'd be patient. She'd give them the chance to know her without prodding. She'd take it slow and easy—not trying to break their spirit, just giving them enough freedom that they'd do anything she wanted, without having to ask.

That's what he intended to do with Charity. In the beginning her wildness nagged at him. He thought she needed taming. Now he realized he didn't want her spirit broken. It wasn't gentleness that he wanted from Charity—he'd had that before. No, he wanted her passion. He wanted her fire.

Pulling into the parking lot of her apartment complex, he climbed out and opened the door for her. She smiled, pleased, maybe shocked at the gesture.

"You're going to come in, aren't you?" she asked, leaning against the rental car.

He looked for a quick excuse, something to keep him away from her bathtub, from bubbles, from seeing her nude. "I've got a sermon to write."

"For this coming Sunday? That's just a couple of days away." She looked worried that he would be leaving soon. Another positive sign that coming here hadn't been a mistake.

"I'm faxing it to John Atkinson. He's going to fill in while I'm gone."

She reached out and brushed a speck of lint, or something equally unimportant, off of his sweater. "I never got to hear you preach."

"Maybe next time you're in Wyoming."

"Are you a hell-fire-and-brimstone kind of guy?"

He shook his head, took a step closer so she could find more lint to stroke off of his chest, and slid a hand around her back, resting his palm against warm, bare skin.

"My style's more laid-back," he said. "More do unto others as you would have them do unto you."

Her eyes flickered upward. "I think I'd like your style." She smiled softly, then tilted her face and lightly kissed his lips.

*Do unto others . . .* He wove his fingers into her hair and kept her face tilted upward, kept her mouth against his, then parted her lips gently with his tongue, tasting her again, filling her, filling himself with the sweet sensations.

She breathed deeply, her breasts rising and falling, hard nipples brushing over his sweater, against his heaving chest, burning his skin.

He was one step away from taking her to her bathtub. One step from breaking a moral code he'd always lived by.

Tearing his mouth from hers, from the sweetness he wanted to delve and devour, from temptation he needed to resist, he took a deep breath and thought about getting far away—fast. Instead he pressed his cheek against hers, because he couldn't get enough. "I liked watching you dance," he whispered against her ear. "I never knew a woman could move in so many ways."

"Years of practice," she whispered back.

"It's a God-given talent, Charity. Something you've been blessed with." And then, out of the goodness of his foolish heart, he added, "It's a talent you should never give up."

She pulled back and looked him straight in the eye. "I'll have to someday. Like you said when I left Wyoming, I won't always be young. I won't always have a sleek, hard body."

He cradled her face in his hands. "You'll always be you. That's all any man should want."

"Most men want more."

"I want more, too, but I won't take it unless it's offered."

She leaned close, feathering soft kisses over his mouth. "What do you want?"

"I want you to dance for me. Just for me."

"I've never given any man his own private dance."

He tore his mouth from the tantalizing taste of her, from her warm breath teasing his skin, and stared into the depths of hazel eyes. "Then someday, when you're ready, maybe you'll let me be the first . . . and the last."

He captured one more of her sighs against his mouth, one more taste of her wet, warm lips, and pushed away, walked to the far side of the car and opened his door. "I'll see you later."

She looked a little dazed. "When?"

"Soon."

He climbed into the car, slammed the door, and started the engine, avoiding any more questions, any more temptation except her hesitant wave, and the sweet, smoothly curved and very bare derrière that swayed as she walked away from him.

He put the car in drive and struck off for the hotel.

And an icy shower.

Charity sat atop the black baby grand, her legs crossed, belting out "The Lady Is a Tramp" for a drunk with a stinky stogie gripped between his teeth. He'd dropped a hundred-dollar bill in the oversized brandy snifter beside her. For that kind of tip, she and the piano player would give him the million-dollar version of the song, complete with coquettish winks, a shimmy or two, maybe even a glossy, red-lipped kiss on the top of his balding head.

This wasn't what she wanted to do for a living, but a good night could put food on the table, keep a roof over her head, and pay for ballet and voice lessons for a couple of weeks.

Jobs like this were a godsend when she wasn't in a show.

The Torch was extra smoky tonight, not all that great for her lungs or the freshness of her scarlet-sequined gown. She'd have to wash her hair before going to bed and air the form-fitting sheath out on the balcony because she hated the stench, but she got to sing a lot of Ella here, and the magnificent Fitzgerald had always been her favorite.

Slipping off the piano, she strolled through the crowded room, smiling at both men and women, and when she sang the last of one song, Gus the pianist played a few chords of the next, songs they'd picked out earlier. When Gus got to just the right spot, she launched into "Bewitched, Bothered and Bewildered," giving it the heart-of-Ella touch.

A young man she'd seen in the club a time or two reached out for her hand and pulled her to his table, and as she often did, she cozied up to him, sitting in his lap, walking her fingers over his shoulders, and toying with the hair at his nape. Then she sang just for him—or so he thought. He was young and cute and gullible, and the owner liked her to play up to the paying customers. But she only let it go just so far.

The kid, probably not more than twenty-one, had a five-dollar bill in his hand and she plucked it from his fingers before he could tuck it between her breasts. The Torch wasn't *that* kind of place, at least it wasn't when she performed. She stuffed the money back in his shirt pocket, knowing he couldn't afford it, and moved on, looking for another familiar face, or someone who looked clean and unthreatening.

Searching the room, her gaze lit on the man leaning against the bar—a gorgeous hunk, broad shouldered, slim-hipped, dressed in a well-cut charcoal suit. It was the man who'd set her on fire this afternoon, the man who'd walked away without tending the flames he'd stoked.

She could have murdered Mike for that. But . . . she'd liked the glow, the heat that stayed with her for hours—even though it confused her. She wanted him; yet he was a threat to all she'd ever wanted.

Sauntering toward him, she sang another chorus of "Bewitched, Bothered and Bewildered," knowing Gus would keep up with whatever she did. She stood in front of Mike, tugging on his tie, sliding it between her fingers. He'd made her burn; she was going to do the same thing in return.

Gus's segue into "I've Got You Under My Skin" couldn't have been more perfect, as if he could read her mind. She should have started singing after the first bar, but she toyed with Mike's tie instead, and Gus played along.

She drew the inside of her bare knee along the outside of Mike's leg, watching his green eyes dart to the thigh-high slit in her dress, to the scarlet stilettos that scraped over his pants. She felt like sin personified, but Mike didn't seem to mind, not when the corners of his mouth tilted, and his dimple deepened.

She smiled brazenly. "Want to dance, big boy?"

"Told you a long time ago I don't dance."

"Would you like me to teach you?"

"We gonna dance fast or slow?"

"For you, slow. Real slow. Real easy."

He shoved away from the bar, and she took his hand and led him to a small scrap of dance floor near the piano. Dancing wasn't common here; only drinking and music. Looking into Mike's sizzling gaze, a fluttery feeling came over her. What on earth was she up to?

She wasn't sin personified. For the most part she was Little Miss Innocent, the sweet virgin who danced and sang like a tramp but was still the daughter of a hell-fire-and-brimstone preacher inside.

"Getting cold feet?" Mike whispered, when he drew her right hand to his shoulder, tucked her body against his with a sweep of his hand around her back and a quick little tug.

"No." Her voice quivered.

"Then sing for me while you show me how to dance."

She'd started this. Somehow she had to cool it down. Unfortunately her fingers—as well as the rest of her body—were listening to her libido, not her common sense, and they wove into his thick, soft black hair. She took hold of his hand and stepped up close and personal, feeling the rapid beat of his heart keeping time with hers.

She pressed her cheek against his, inhaling his

aftershave, almost getting lost in memories of a night of sleeping with this man. And then Gus tickled the ivories—loudly—and she was transported back to the present. She started to dance, to hum, closing her eyes while she led Mike through a few steps.

It wasn't long before he figured the one-two-three, one-two-three out for himself, and he took the lead, his palm pressing against the small of her back, holding her tight.

At last she sang, "I've got you, under my skin . . ." There was so much truth to those words, and Mike admitted it, too, repeating the words next to her ear.

Opening her eyes, Charity saw the blur of faces in the crowd, twenty, maybe thirty people watching her and Mike, no doubt wondering what was going on. She'd tell them, but she wasn't sure herself.

Mike whirled her around the dance floor, his warm, callused fingers making slow circles at the small of her back while she sang, "I'd sacrifice anything—"

"Would you?" Mike whispered against her ear. "Would you sacrifice *anything*, Charity?"

Somehow she continued to sing, but the question haunted her. Could she sacrifice anything? A chance in the spotlight? A place at the top? For a life with Mike?

She didn't know. Sadly, she just didn't know.

It was well past two in the morning when Charity and Mike arrived back at her apartment. A cool breeze blew across the desert, rustling through the palms, stirring up the faint layer of sand that had blown over the parking lot, the steps, and her landing.

They stood arm and arm just outside her open door, and for the first time in her life she wanted a man to come inside, to spend the night in her bed—to make love to her. To love her.

But it wouldn't be right. Not without marriage, and she didn't want that. Not now.

"Why are you doing this to me?" she asked, standing as close as humanly possible, wanting him near yet wanting to push him away.

He frowned. "What is it you think I'm doing to you?"

"Making me want you."

"Is that so bad?" he asked, nibbling her ear-lobe, kissing the base of her neck, driving her crazy.

She twisted away from him, from feelings that couldn't be ignored—the physical ones as well as those in her heart.

"It is when there are a thousand miles standing between us. A thousand miles, conflicting goals, and a matching set of morals that won't let us take what we want and not ask for anything more."

"You haven't mentioned one thing that can't be worked out, Charity. But you've got to be willing to talk about what's between us, about what you want, what I want."

She pulled out of his grasp, gripped the wrought-iron railing behind her, and looked out at the city lights. "How do we work out the fact that you won't leave Wyoming and I won't leave Vegas?"

"We just need time."

"Time for me to change my mind, right? Time for me to pack my bags, give up my life."

"You'd have a new life."

"Doing what you think I should do!"

"Don't tell me you didn't enjoy the time you spent at the ranch. Don't tell me you didn't enjoy riding Satan and Jezebel and taking nose-dives off a saddle and knocking me to the ground."

"Of course I liked it. It was different and fun and challenging. But Vegas is my home and dancing is my life, and if I'm not mistaken, you told me earlier today that I had talent, that I shouldn't give it up."

"You *shouldn't* give it up, but you can dance anywhere. You can sing anywhere."

"You make it sound as if walking away from all I've worked for should be easy. But it's not, Mike."

He wove his arms around her and rested his cheek against her ear. "Nothing's easy. It's just a matter of deciding what you really want."

"I don't want to fall in love with you."

His sigh was heavy, and he laughed cynically as he pulled away from her. "Don't worry, Charity, I'm not going to force you into anything. Not going back to Wyoming with me. Not love. Not sex. Trust me, six years of being alone, six years of celibacy has left me with a hell of a lot of self-control."

And a lifetime of reaching for a star had given her self-control, too. She knew what she wanted and that couldn't be changed.

Behind her she heard the thump of Mike's boots on the concrete steps, felt the iron railing shaking beneath her fingers as he descended rapidly. She watched him walk across the parking lot, saw him yank open the car door, and couldn't miss the way he stared up at her or the anguish in his words.

"I'm in love with you, Charity. God help me, that's one thing I can't control."

## chapter 18

*SO MUCH FOR CONTROL!*

Mike smashed his fist into his pillow, plowed his head into it, and stared at the ceiling. As if the guilt and the nightmares weren't enough to keep him awake, now he had to face that he'd lost sight of what he'd been trying to do—make Charity fall in love with him without pushing, without scaring her off.

But the blasted woman was a tease. Any man would lose control considering what she'd put him through. She'd come close to seducing him more than once in the past twenty-four hours. Whether she did it consciously or subconsciously he didn't know anymore, and what did it matter anyway?

What was he thinking? Everything she did mattered. A lot.

Rolling over in bed, he stared at the clock. Five A.M. He couldn't think of a better time to call—when Charity was asleep and vulnerable.

He rummaged through his wallet for her number, grabbed the phone, and punched the buttons. It rang three times. He could hear the clanking sound of her fumbling to get the phone off the hook, heard the thump of her dropping it, then heard an annoyed but sleepy, "Hello?"

"Want some breakfast?"

"*What?*" He could pretty much picture her rubbing her eyes and staring at the phone in confusion. "Who is this?"

"Pastor Flynn."

There was a long silence. Good. She was thinking about what had happened between them a few hours ago. She was feeling remorseful. In a minute, she'd apologize.

*Clunk! Bzzzzzzz.*

Blasted woman!

He stabbed at the numbers again. *Ring. Ring.*

"Look, Mike." Charity sighed heavily into the phone. "I laid awake for hours thinking about what we talked about and my feelings haven't changed. I don't want to fall in love with you, and I don't want you doing anything more to make me want to fall in love with you. So, for once in my life I'm exercising a little self-control."

*Clunk! Bzzzzzzz.*

His own self-control was shot to hell. He punched out Charity's phone number again and listened to the ring—counting off the annoying tone eleven times before she finally picked up the phone.

"What!"

"Don't hang up on me, Charity. I want you to listen to me."

"Give me a good reason why."

"Because I'm asking you to. Did you hear that? *Asking*. This isn't an order, Charity, it's a request. Consider listening to me as partial payment for all the times I've come to your rescue."

Silence. Dead silence—but he fully expected to hear another *Clunk! Bzzzzzzz.*

Instead he heard a resigned but soft spoken, "All right, I'm listening."

"Have breakfast with me."

Another long pause. Good, she was giving his invitation some consideration. "I can't. I'm spending the day with Logan."

Logan, again. Friend or not, they sure spent a lot of time together. "Doing what?"

"Helping him pack, nothing more. He's a friend Mike, a *friend*, and since he left a message on my recorder begging for assistance I'm going to help him. Before that, I plan on sleeping since I'm currently dead on my feet."

"Are you trying to avoid me?"

Silence. "I can't avoid you, Mike. I keep trying, but . . ." He couldn't miss her painful sigh. "You're everywhere I go—the past twenty-four hours anyway—and you've been in my thoughts for months. You've been in my dreams, too, and my friends continually bring up your name. I'd avoid you if I could but . . . but . . . I'm tired and I just don't want to deal with this now."

*Bzzzzzzz.*

Mike smiled as he casually dialed Charity's phone number.

"Hello."

"But what, Charity?"

"I'm falling in love with you and it scares me."

"I know." He was scared, too, but he wasn't going to back off.

Mike heard the squeak of bedsprings and pictured Charity rolling over on the mattress, snuggling up with her pillow, holding the phone close to her ear.

"I've never been in love before," she said. "A crush or two in high school, but the guys weren't too interested in the preacher's kid."

"I told you I wanted to be your first."

"*If* I fall in love, Mike, and that's a big if. There's still the Las Vegas vs. Wyoming problem."

"Probably half a dozen other problems, too, things we already know about, things that could crop up later, when we know each other better." Some things he didn't want to think about, like guilt, and nightmares, and restless nights.

"What would you tell your parishioners if they came to you and said they might be falling in love with someone who was all wrong for them?"

"I'd tell them to pray on it. I'd ask what they loved most about the other person, find out if the love is strong enough—important enough—to make it worthwhile to work through their differences. Then we'd pray together. And then I'd probably dish out a bunch of advice straight from a psychology textbook or throw out a cliché like 'go with the flow.' "

Charity laughed, and he found himself settling into the firm and uncomfortable hotel bed, found his eyelids growing heavy...because she soothed him in a way no one ever had.

"Is that what we're going to do now?" she asked. "Just go with the flow?"

"Unless you've got any better ideas."

She was silent a moment. Thinking. "Want to spend the day helping Logan and I pack up his house?"

"Can't. I've got to meet a horse trainer this morning."

*"What?"*

He heard the bed springs again and had a pretty good idea she was wide awake and fuming. He should have known those words would rile her again. "I heard about some guy who's got a sure-fire way of taming mustangs, and I want to check out his methods."

"What does he do, use some kind of special bamboo pole for stroking horses? Does he use the clicker method or a slip rope?"

"Where'd you learn about those things?"

"I read about them in a book."

So she was interested in what was going on back at the ranch. At last, something was working in his favor. "They're good methods, Charity. They work."

"They're not the methods I'd use, but...but...oh, hell, what difference does it make. I won't be training horses in the future, I'll be dancing in the spotlight, so go spend the day with your trainer. Right now, I just want to go back to sleep."

"You could go with me and see firsthand what this trainer does with the horses."

"I told you, I'm helping Logan."

"Then what if I call you later and tell you all about it?"

"Fine." She gave him her cell phone number since she'd be with Logan all day. "Now, can I go back to sleep?"

He smiled at her frustration. If they ever got together, there'd never be a dull moment.

"Sweet dreams," he whispered, then hung up the phone and settled comfortably into bed, letting his mind wander to images of Charity riding an untamed stallion, maybe in that barely-there leotard she'd worn today. The beast bucked wildly, and Charity beamed with excitement as she held on tight and enjoyed the ride.

Life with Charity would always be one wild ride after another, Mike figured. If he had to use Satan as bait, so be it. One way or another, he was going to catch Charity Wilde—and keep her.

Another night, another round of grabby hands.

Charity wove in and out of tables, dodging one too many touchy-feely types, while she belted out a rendition of "Cry Me A River." The song was soul searing and gut wrenching, but something was missing. Something important. Something that had always been there before.

"Cry me a river . . ." Charity swept her fingers over the shoulders of a stranger, and tried not to think about love. Singing about it was bad enough.

Instead she thought about the rushed phone conversation she'd had with Mike this afternoon. The meeting with the horse trainer went great, as if she'd really wanted to hear that bit of news. In fact, Mike had said, he'd probably make the guy an offer tomorrow, he just needed a night to sleep on it. The last thing he wanted to do was make a rash judgment and end up hiring the wrong person for the job.

*Job!* Gentling horses shouldn't be a job—it should be a *passion*. Mike didn't understand. He'd never understand.

Of course, she didn't understand why her own passion had deserted her. Her rendition of "Am I Blue" ripped through the room, but it seemed forced. No one else would notice. But she certainly did.

She launched into "Stormy Weather," perching atop the baby grand in purple silk, a floor-length sheath that was slit to her thigh, had just a hint of spaghetti straps, and was cut nearly to her belly button in front. She'd twisted her hair into a chignon and truly looked as if she'd stepped out of the forties or fifties. But it was only drunks and strangers who appreciated how she looked. There was no one at home to tell her she was beautiful, no one to pull her straps down slowly, to make love to her.

Drunks and music lovers shoved tips into her oversized snifter right and left, and most of them blew smoke in her face when they did it. She couldn't help but wonder how much longer she could work in a place like this before her lungs would take a beating.

She was twenty-five, but she wouldn't be twenty-five forever.

*Snap out of it!* She had a job to do, songs to sing. It was time to stop feeling sorry for herself. This was the life she'd chosen, the life she wanted.

But her heart wasn't in the song. It was in Wyoming with a wild stallion named Satan. It was in a beautiful log cabin that sat beside a meandering stream. It was in a big four-poster with fluffy down pillows and a handmade quilt.

And with a man named Mike.

She finished her number, listened to the applause, the whistles. Was it her voice they were cheering, or her body? Did it matter? she wondered. Tips were tips, no matter how they were earned.

Stretching out across the piano, she leaned close to Gus's ear and asked him to play "In the Still of the Night." Gus's fingers tripped over the keyboard, and she felt another pair of fingers trip over her exposed thigh.

She spun around, ready to do battle. No man touched her without permission. That was a rule. But she felt the rage in her eyes soften when callused fingers moved to her waist, and bright green eyes smiled.

"Dance with me?"

Mike lifted her off of the piano and into his arms, holding her close as she sang, as he tried to distract her by whispering in her ear. "I missed you today."

She smiled, trying to focus on the words of the song, on her singing, pouring out emotions while getting caught up in the hot, spicy scent of Mike's aftershave, the smoothness of his cheek brushing over hers, the feel of his rough palm at the small of her back.

In a heartbeat, the passion had returned to her voice.

"I thought about you dancing privately for me and wondered what you'd wear," he said, his teeth tugging lightly on her ear. "Something white and silky? A little bit of lace?" He kissed the hollow beneath her ear, and she leaned into his seductive power. "Nothing?"

She flashed him a frown and pulled out of his arms. She'd get fired for sure if Mike came to the club every night, continually distracting her.

She slipped across the room toward someone safe, to the cute young guy who'd come every night since she'd started singing at the Torch. She sat in his lap, wove her hands around his neck, and looked right through him, watching Mike instead, drinking in the sight of his broad shoulders, his narrow hips, his rapid gait as he headed for the door.

Her heart lurched. Had her escape sent out signals that she wasn't interested? Had she angered him when she'd only meant to . . . tease?

Mike pushed through the door and the red neon torch outside flashed down on his face as he looked back inside, searching the smoky room. At last he found her, holding her spellbound in his gaze. When Gus played the final crescendo, when Charity belted out the climactic ending, Mike winked, the dimple beside his mouth deepening as he hit her with a smile that could have knocked her off her feet if she hadn't been sitting in a young man's lap.

And then he was gone.

Leaving her with the promise of more to come.

Gus launched into "The Way You Look Tonight" as she made her way back to the piano. She slid her hand over the ebony baby grand and her fingers bumped into a small, oblong package nearly hidden behind the overflowing snifter.

She turned her back to the crowd, pulled the clips from her hair and let it tumble down her back, giving those in the room a good show and a great song, even though they couldn't see her face or her fingers fumbling to open the gift card. At last she peeled out a piece of hotel stationary and read the words.

*Charity,*

*If you have a chance, read this and let me know your thoughts.*

*Mike*

Well, that was certainly personal!

Gus shot her a frown from his place at the keyboard. Yes, yes, she knew she'd lost her concentration, knew she had a show to put on.

She wiggled her derrière, she kicked her leg up behind her, and she flashed the crowd an over-the-shoulder smile, giving them more than their money's worth when she launched into "The Lady Is a Tramp."

Then she concentrated on the package again, quickly ripping through the paper and staring down at the pamphlet inside. "Jerry Wilson Tames the Beast: Obedience In a Week."

Her teeth would have ground together if she hadn't been warbling a song. She'd let Mike know what she thought, all right.

*Obedience in a week!*

*Hah!*

Charity marched through the lobby of the Luxor, purple silk flowing behind her and exposing one leg almost all the way to the purple silk thong she wore beneath. Curious eyes followed her as she plopped her battered leather backpack on the desk and asked for the number of Mike Flynn's room.

"I'm sorry, ma'am, it's hotel policy that I not give out that information."

"Then, would you call him, please?"

"It's nearly three A.M. I'd hate to wake him."

Charity glared at the young woman. "Tell him Charity Wilde is here to see him, tell him I'd like to come up, and ask him for permission to give me his room number."

"Maybe I should get the manager."

"Look, I'm not a hooker, I'm not a hitman, and I'm not a thief. He's a friend. A good friend."

The woman just stared at her.

Finally, Charity leaned close and whispered. "Okay, here's the truth. Mike Flynn is hot, real hot. If you saw him, trust me, you'd want his room number too. And the fact that he's so hot has made me very, very horny and I want to go up to his room and have mad, passionate, no-holds-barred sex." Charity smiled and leaned even closer. "How do you think Mr. Flynn will feel when he learns that he missed out on the best sex of his life because you refused to tell him I was here?"

The desk clerk grinned, picked up the phone, dialed Mike's room, and eventually gave Charity the number.

She headed for the elevator and punched the button for Mike's floor. A few minutes later she stood in front of his room. She felt deceitful. The last thing Mike Flynn was going to get from her was no-holds-barred sex.

She banged her knuckles on the door, it flew open on the first knock, and she plowed right in, not giving Mike a chance to utter a word. She dropped the Jerry Wilson obedience-training pamphlet on the nightstand beside his disheveled bed. "*This* is the man you're thinking about hiring?"

"Thought about it."

"How could you? Obedience in a week? Is he a sadist or something? What does he use? Cattle prods?"

Mike's brow rose. "Mind if I get dressed before you give me your honest opinion on the man's methods?"

"Does my opinion even matter?"

"It's the only opinion that matters to me—on this subject, at least."

"Okay, I'll tell you exactly what I think about your Mr. Wilson."

Mike folded his arms across his chest—his naked chest—looking quite prepared to listen. Charity paced across the room so she wouldn't have to look at him while she gave him a piece of her mind, but when she got to the big picture window she turned around and gawked at him anyway.

He was far better looking than the lights of Vegas and she was very glad she hadn't given him permission to get dressed. She liked him exactly the way he was, wearing only a pair of pajama bottoms, that hung seductively low on his hips.

Her eyes flickered up from his navel to his eyes. He was grinning at her. *Darn it!* His grin, his smile, his near naked body always threw her for a loop.

"What was it you were going to tell me?" Mike asked, raising a cocky brow.

She clenched her fists. "Mr. Wilson's methods are outdated and barbaric. If you want horses to laze around in a pasture keeping the grass short, fine, use his techniques. But don't expect intelligence or spirit because he feels the only good horse is an obedient one, one that does anything and everything you want. Period!"

Mike relaxed in a chair, crossing an ankle over his knee. "So, how would *you* train Satan?"

"You'll laugh."

"Try me."

"I'd make his corral bigger than the standard gentling corrals I've read about in all the books."

"*All* the books?"

"Okay, I ordered some off of the Internet. I got some from the library, too. There's a wealth of information out there. I even went to a wild horse and burro auction and I talked to a few people about their ways of gentling their animals."

"And what did you think?"

"That there are a lot of good ideas, but sometimes you've got to do it your own way."

"And what's your way?"

"I'd sing to them."

His blasted brow rose again. *"Sing?"*

"*Sing!* As crazy as it might sound to you, I'd plant myself in the middle of the corral and sing. Softly to start out with, then try out different styles—jazz, pop, torch—until I find just the right one, the one that will make each different horse come to me."

"And then what?"

"I haven't thought that far ahead."

"Why not?"

"Because I'm not writing a book on my untried methods, and I won't be trying them out for real, so there's no need thinking any further than the first step."

Mike shoved out of his chair, went to the honors bar, and took out a Coke. "Want one?"

"No, thanks."

He popped the cap and took a sip, acting very nonchalant when she was having a fit. "Would you like a job singing to horses?"

"Are you laughing at me?"

"I've never been more serious. I didn't like Jerry's ways, either. He was a pompous ass with a bunch of broken-down nags in the corral. That's not what I want for my place."

"What do you want?"

"You." He winked. "To work for me, that is. You'd make a hell of a trainer, Charity."

"You can't possibly know that."

"I know it, because I see the fire in your eyes when you talk about the wild horses. There's a passion in you I've never seen before, and it keeps growing stronger and stronger."

His passion was growing stronger and stronger too, and she liked it very much.

"I watched you sit Satan. I saw the way he responded to you, Charity. It's not natural. Wild horses don't get close enough to be ridden, unless they've got a rope around them. It's strange watching the two of you together, as if each of you know what the other's thinking."

"Two peas in a pod, huh?" She smiled, walked toward him, plucked the Coke from his hand, and set it on the nightstand. She swirled her fingers over the hair on his chest, tempted to go lower, but she held back. "Satan and I are just two wild creatures, aren't we? We get under your skin, too, because neither one of us wants to be tamed."

Fire blazed in his eyes. "I've got no desire to tame you, Charity." He wrapped a well-muscled arm around her waist and tugged her against his sexy chest. "I love you just the way you are."

She'd wanted to fight the love she felt for him, but she couldn't any longer. His faith in her, his willingness to put up with her no matter what, excited her, drove her wild. She had passion all right, but that passion had more to do with him than any wild stallion.

Charity threw her arms around his neck and kissed him, her passion heartfelt and tangible, burning in its intensity. This was the sign Mike had been looking for. She loved him. She'd go with him. He was sure of it.

The question he'd contemplated asking all night long was on the tip of his tongue. He knew he should wait till he could ask over candlelight, wait till he had a ring, wait till he was dressed in something more than pajama bottoms, but he couldn't hold back.

He tore his mouth away and cradled her face in his hands.

"Don't stop kissing me," she pleaded, her fingers splaying through his hair and tugging his mouth toward hers again.

"There's something I want to ask you, Charity."

"Later. Please. Just hold me. Kiss me."

Her lips were sweet, soft, and wet, and he touched them again, nearly drowning in his need for her. Soon he'd take her passion to new heights, he'd teach her things he hoped she knew nothing about, because he wanted to surprise her, wanted to see the look of wonderment in her eyes. And he knew there'd be wonder in his eyes, too, because with Charity, life would always be a surprise.

Ask her, he told himself. Ask her.

"Charity?"

Her eyes were filled with longing when she allowed him to cup her cheeks and look into her face. "Hmmm?"

A cell phone rang. He tried to ignore it. Hoped Charity wouldn't hear it. But it continued to ring and suddenly he saw a new excitement in her eyes.

"Oh, my God, Mike." She pushed back. He tried to catch her hand, but she'd already run for her backpack. "No one ever calls on my cell phone."

"It's gotta be a wrong number."

"No. It can't be a wrong number. It's got to be Duane. This is the number I gave his assistant."

"It's the middle of the night, Charity. No one makes business calls now."

"Duane would."

She pulled the phone from her backpack and lifted it to her ear. "Hello."

She bit her lip, her brow furrowing as she stared at the floor. "Uh-huh."

Did she have to torture him this way? Couldn't she give him some hint of what was going on?

"I see . . . Uh-huh . . . Yes, that sounds good . . . No, no, you didn't wake me . . ."

Mike walked to the window and looked out over the bright lights of Vegas. He was losing Charity to this world that was so different from his, a world he didn't understand, a world he didn't want to know. There'd be no more chance to go with the flow. The phone call, Charity's wide, bright eyes, and the way he heard her say,

"Thanks, Duane," told him any chance they had for happiness—together—was over.

Charity had been reaching for a star for a very long time. Unfortunately, the one she'd picked had blazed down from the sky and burned a hole right through Mike's heart.

Chapter 19

IN THE WINDOW, AMIDST THE SEA OF
colorful lights, Mike watched Charity come toward him. Alluring. Seductive. She slid warm
hands around his arms and pressed a smoldering
kiss between his shoulder blades. He wanted her
as he'd wanted nothing else in his life, but he'd
run out of ways to tempt her back to Wyoming.
She'd made the decision to stay in Vegas—with
her blasted star.

She slipped between him and the window,
teasing him with the reflection of her long, rippling hair and her sleek, want-to-touch derrière.
That vision, along with the deep, sweet, breast-
revealing cut of her purple dress, urged him to do
things he dared not do.

He fought to control his heartbeat and breathing, but she swirled an index finger through the

hair on his chest and smiled beguiling up at him before enticing him with a lingering kiss at the base of his throat. He wanted more, but he held his arms to his sides, kept his fists clenched, battling her powers—what he should have done weeks back on a dark night out on the plains.

Hot lips glided up his neck, flowed over his chin, and found their home against his mouth. Her sweet breath feathered over his skin, and he almost gave into her, almost clasped her against him, but why? It was over.

And he was being as stubborn as they come. If this seductive display was meant as an apology for hurting him, it wasn't working. A better man than him would have told her it was all right, that she'd made the right decision. But he didn't feel all that understanding right now, and he wasn't about to absolve her of any guilt.

Not even the way she traced his tight-lipped mouth with the tip of her tongue could sway him. "That was Duane," she whispered against him— words that left him cold.

He looked past her, out the window at the lights. "I know."

Pressing a palm to his cheek, she forced him to look at her, at the woman who was breaking his heart. "He offered me the lead role."

His jaw clenched. "Congratulations."

Her eyes narrowed. "You don't have to sound so happy about it!"

"I'm not the least bit happy about it. What do you want me to say? Goodbye? So long?"

"How about 'I don't want you to take the damn job, Charity?' "

"All right, I don't want you to take the damn job. And while we're at it, I want you in Wyoming—with me. I want you to gentle my horses. I want . . ." He plowed his hand through his hair, but she reached out for it, wove her fingers through his, and kissed his knuckles. Teasing. Tempting.

"That's better." She smiled up at him. "Now, wasn't there a question you wanted to ask me before the phone rang?"

"Not that I can remember?"

She stomped her foot. "Damn it, Mike. Quit holding back. Quit controlling every single one of your emotions and ask your blasted question!"

"Fine! Marry me! Is that what you want to hear? Marry me, spend the rest of your life with me, make love with me morning, noon and night, and sing your heart out to every damn horse in the territory."

He steeled himself for rejection, for the final kick in the gut. Charity teased him again, leaning forward, pressing her soft full breasts against his chest as she tilted her face up to his and kissed him.

"Okay."

He frowned. Had she just said yes? Surely he'd heard her wrong, but on the off chance he hadn't, he slid his hands around her waist and tugged her against him. "Did you say yes?"

Her smile was anything but sweet. It was the

smile of a woman who'd teased and taunted until she'd gotten exactly what she wanted. "Of course, I did." She wiggled out of his embrace while he was still trying to figure her out. She marched across the bedroom, grabbed her backpack, and headed for the door.

Sanity returned, and he was across the room in a few long paces, pulling her behind against his hips, stopping her retreat. He slid his hand over the warmth of her stomach, pressed his bristly cheek against her ear, and inhaled the spicy, exotic scent that wafted about her. "Where do you think you're going?"

Turning in his embrace, she glanced at the bedside clock and braced soft palms against his chest. "It'll take me a couple of hours to find a gown, do my hair. Why don't you pick me up at two and we'll get a license." He felt himself frowning, wondering what was going on in her head. "There shouldn't be any trouble finding a place to get married, then"—she smiled—"we can come back here and make love."

"You're talking about getting married? Now? Today?"

"Exactly."

"Isn't that rushing things?"

Her palms slid down his chest, down, down, down, until her fingers toyed with the drawstring on his pajamas. "I don't know," she said teasingly. "What do you think? Should we wait? Six months? A year or two?"

"Maybe you're right." He swallowed hard. "A few hours should be a long enough engagement."

"Then I'd better get going."

"Not yet." He curled his fingers beneath her chin, one of the only safe places he thought he could put his fingers right now. "What are we going to do about this new job of yours? If you think we're going to have a long-distance marriage, you're wrong."

"I don't want a long-distance marriage either."

"But—"

"I was *offered* the job, Mike. I didn't accept. How could I, when all I really want is"—she wrapped the drawstring around her index finger—"you?"

His brow quirked. "When did you come to that conclusion?"

"When I realized that my singing became more passionate when you walked into the room. When I realized that I've never liked strangers grabbing me, and that I was fed up with all their attempts. When I realized that smoky clubs aren't good for my lungs and that I want to be able to sing forever."

She took a deep breath and he tried to kiss her brazen lips, lips that would soon be his, all his, lips that would be in Wyoming where they belonged. But she drew back just a fraction of an inch. "There's more. Wouldn't you like to hear the rest?"

He chuckled, pressed her against the door, and balanced a hand on either side of her so she couldn't escape before he got another taste of her mouth. "All right, go on."

"I always loved the bright lights, Mike, but they've gotten dimmer with each passing year. Every once in awhile they'd glimmer, you know, when there'd be a chance at stardom, or when I'd get a great job in a chorus line. But the lights didn't glimmer at all when Duane offered me the lead role in his show. I was so positive it would be the best moment of my life, but my heart didn't flutter, I didn't get all quivery inside—not like I do when you're around. That's when I realized, once and for all, that every light in Las Vegas would go out if . . . if you walked out of my life."

It was a long piece of philosophy to get to the final result, but it ended right where he wanted it to. She loved him more than that blasted star.

At last he stole the kiss he desired, capturing Charity's honey sweet mouth, her warm and passionate heart, and her wild and bewitching soul. He loved her. He'd love her forever.

"Dearly beloved. We are gathered here today . . ."

Mike barely heard the words. How could he hear anything when he was mesmerized by the bright and tear-filled eyes of the woman he was marrying, by the gaudiness of the chapel, by Reverend Darling, who was rapidly performing his deluxe, five-minute service, that came complete with a semifresh bouquet of pale pink roses, half a dozen Polaroid snapshots, and a pint-sized wedding cake with a token plastic kissing-couple figurine on top.

As tacky and as rushed as the wedding was, Charity beamed, and that made it all seem right.

"Does anyone present know of any reason why these two should not be joined in wedlock?"

Except for Charity, there were only strangers in the chapel, and no one said a word.

But Mike's conscience toyed with the question. He loved Charity with all his heart, but did she deserve to live with his nightmares night after night? Guilt haunted him, kept him from sleeping, and could easily tear them apart. Was it fair to marry her without telling her about that night six years ago, about the wife he'd loved—and let die?

Reverend Darling cleared his throat. "*Do* you take Charity to be your lawful wedded wife?"

Charity squeezed his hand and Mike realized he must have been too caught up in his thoughts, his fears, to hear the question the first time around.

He tilted his head from the reverend to Charity. Her hazel eyes sparkled and he saw in her face all those things he'd grown to cherish—deep, strong-willed passion; commitment and drive, no matter what the odds; and love that would see them through anything.

He kissed Charity tenderly, even though they weren't yet man and wife. And then he pushed aside all that had tormented him in the past.

"I do."

He'd been given a new chance at happiness with a woman who drove him wild, and nothing, nothing, could ever drive them apart.

## Chapter 20

CHARITY CLASPED HER HANDS OVER THE butterflies fluttering around in her stomach, and stared at her surroundings. Someone had turned the white satin covers back on the king-sized bed in the suite Mike had reserved. They'd left Belgian chocolates on the silky pillows and a bottle of Dom Perignon in a bucket of ice on the nightstand. The lights had been dimmed and the drapes drawn, letting the glow of Las Vegas shine in.

Behind her she heard the sound of Mike's footsteps in the thick carpeting, heard his breathing as he stepped behind her. She waited—and wondered what would come next.

Warm lips brushed her ear and the scent of spicy aftershave wafted around her. Rough palms captured her shoulders, and slowly, gently, Mike turned her into his embrace. Green eyes smiled down at her. "Nervous?"

"This is a lot like opening night—terrifying but exciting at the same time. You can't wait to be on stage, can't wait to perform, but you're afraid you might be a flop, and you won't know how you've done until you get an ovation."

Mike chuckled. He drew one of her hands from her stomach and kissed her palm. There was something devilish in his eyes, something she couldn't quite peg. He held her hand over his heart and she felt its heavy beat, then, together, their hands slid over the ridged muscles of his stomach, to the ridged—

*Good heavens!* Charity's eyes widened in shock. Mike's hand had stilled above hers, but she moved her fingers beneath his, touching, feeling, molding. She was completely and utterly amazed at the towering masterpiece cupped within her palm.

Her eyes flitted upward to the shameless grin on Mike's face.

"That's a standing ovation, Charity. The first of many."

She laughed lightly. "You're being rather brash for a minister, aren't you?"

He slid his hands over her bottom and dragged her against him, her hand still holding him tight. "You're my wife, Charity. I'm your husband. The way I see it, as long as you're willing, as long as I'm willing, there's nothing we can't do."

Suddenly she felt just as shameless as her new-found husband and in an act that was completely unfamiliar, but incredibly nice, she slid her fin-

gers up and down the hard length of him. She felt
Mike twitch beneath her hand, heard his drawn-
out grasp for breath.

He stilled her hand, pulling it away and kissing her palm. "There's only so much a man who's
been celibate for six years can take before he ex-
plodes. So"—he drew her hand to his shoulder—
"let's slow down for a little while."

"Please don't tell me you want to watch TV or
read for a while. Not now," she teased.

"The only thing I want to watch is you."

"Does that mean you want me to dance for
you?"

"Not quite yet."

Slipping behind her, Mike kissed the spicy-
tasting skin of her shoulder, wondering anxiously
what other tastes lay in wait for him. He slid his
hands over her silky gown, his fingers splaying
over her slightly rounded belly, inching upward
until they found her breasts—and rested there,
squeezing gently to memorize the feel of them beneath fabric. Soon enough he'd know the feel of
them completely, utterly naked—against his
hand, against his tongue.

"Did you find something you like?" Charity
asked.

"I haven't found anything about you that I
don't like."

"There's a lot you don't know about me."

"I'm gonna know everything before we leave
this room three days from now."

"Well, then, since we've got plenty of time, you
just concentrate on my breasts for the moment.

What you're doing feels awfully nice. But, if you want, you could be a little . . . naughty, too."

"Is this what you had in mind?" His open mouth settled against the sensitive hollow below her ear, drawing a soft, needy moan from his wife. His fingers slipped under the bodice of her gown and discovered soft, rounded flesh and pebbled nipples. *At last.*

"You're not wearing a bra," he whispered against her cheek.

"Mmmm, no." She sighed as his middle fingers drew lazy circles around each hardened peak.

He kissed her temple, skimmed the rim of her ear with the tip of his tongue. "What about panties?"

"Just barely."

"A garter belt?"

He could feel the tilt of smiling lips against his cheek as his fingers continued to fondle, to explore. "White lace."

"What about stockings?"

She laughed lightly. "Why don't you take a peek?"

"In awhile." He pushed the silky fabric of her dress down until her breasts tumbled into his palms. "I'm content with what I'm doing now."

He pinched her nipples lightly, rolling them back and forth between his thumb and index finger, and Charity let out a soft whimper and grabbed hold of his butt.

"You like that," he asked, when her fingers dug into him.

"Mmmm. Do it some more."

"Later, maybe." He drew his hands away from her soft, sweet breasts, lifted her veil of silky hair, and feathered kisses down the curve of her spine until he reached satin and buttons. "I'm gonna take your dress off now."

"Oooh, that sounds . . . naughty."

She gathered her hair into her delicate, long-fingered hands, leaving his fingers free for other pursuits, like getting rid of everything but barely-there panties, a lacy garter belt, and secretive stockings.

With nimble fingers he caught the top button on the back of her gown and released it from the fabric loop. One down, thirty-nine to go. There were forty buttons holding the dress snugly against her body. He'd counted them as they'd stood in line waiting to get their marriage license. That meant forty long seconds or more before he could let the dress slip from her body, before he would taste her breasts, before he would have her completely.

She was a temptress. A seducer, and he wanted her desperately. He knew—even though she hadn't told him in so many words—that she'd never been with a man before. And he wanted her first time to be special. Slow—and sweet. He wanted to hear her sigh again and again. Wanted to see her wriggle beneath him, do those bumps and grinds she did so well, and he wanted to keep her begging for more.

He fought for breath, dragging in the scent of her perfume as he worked at the buttons.

Ten.

He skimmed his tongue along the ridges of her spine.

Twenty.

The bodice crumpled around her waist, and he figured he could work a button loose with one hand, and reach around her to capture at least one breast, one soft, curvy, heavenly mound of pliable flesh, in the other.

"Is there any possibility you can unbutton me faster?" she asked, her words a breathless whisper. "Of course, you could just rip it off of me."

He chuckled, and gave her nipple another light pinch, eliciting another moan from his wife. "Have patience, sweetheart. This isn't the only thing I plan to do slowly."

Thirty.

His own patience was another story. The need for her grew stronger with each button, with each swirl of his tongue over her skin, with each shudder of her body.

Thirty-seven. Thirty-eight. Thirty-nine. Forty.

At last, the gown cascaded down her body until it puddled at her feet.

Kneeling in front of her, he spun his wife around, splaying his fingers over the curves of her bottom, holding her close, taking a long, pleasurable look at the woman he'd married.

Silky black hair whispered over her shoulders, chest, and belly, parting where her breasts peeked through. He liked her hair that color. He'd liked it brown, too, but—his gaze darted quickly to the white thong she wore, to the curls hidden beneath—he liked her natural, the way God had made her.

He pulled her against him, kissing her belly, inhaling the spicy fragrances of cinnamon and cloves that reminded him of exotic lands, a belly dancer, a gyrating woman.

"Dance for me," he said, looking up into her hot hazel eyes.

"Be patient, my love."

Taking Mike's hands when they reached once more for her breasts, Charity drew him to his feet. Even through his tuxedo she could feel his heat, could feel the surging need in the tense muscles in his arms. What a blessing it was to have a man like this in her life, a man who held back, tromped on his own desire while he satisfied his lady.

It wouldn't be long and she'd dance for him. She'd give him a million-dollar show, but she wanted to see his reaction—and not just the emotion in his face.

She smiled as she nudged his jacket from his shoulders, pulled it from his body, and tossed it over the back of a chair.

In only a few heartbeats she'd removed his tie and went to work on his shirt, her fingers suddenly frustrated with the buttons, wanting, needing desperately to dance.

"Need some help?" he asked.

"I thought you'd never ask."

Mike went to work on his buttons and she dove for his belt, discretion be damned! She wanted him naked. In only an instant Mike had ripped the shirt from his chest and she slid down the zipper on his pants.

Brazen hussy that she was, she shoved his pants and his boxers down his hips and thighs and got a standing ovation from Mike that couldn't possibly be topped.

He kicked aside his clothes while she stood still, gazing in awe at his glorious bronzed body.

He took her breath away. His wasn't a dancer's body all sleek and slender and lithe. No, Mike's arms and thighs bulged from labor-intensive work, from spending dawn till dark on the open range, branding cattle, rounding up strays, and mending fences. He rode long and hard in the saddle.

She wanted him to ride long and hard in hers.

"You keep staring at me like that, Charity, and so help me, everything I've struggled to hold back is going to kick and scream and come to a rip-roaring finale, the likes of which you've never seen."

She only smiled at his angst, and let her eyes drift upward. "Mind if I touch you?"

His jaws ground together, and she stepped a little closer, slipping her fingers around him. "Mmmm, I can't quite tell if it's a velvety feel, or silk, but it is rather smooth."

"What did you expect?"

"Oh, I don't know." She went down on her knees in front of him for a closer inspection. "Duane was rather limp and—"

"I don't want to hear about anyone else."

Her eyes rolled. "I've never had sex with any-one, but you dance as close as I have with hun-dreds of men and let me tell you, you're going to feel something. You're going to see something, too, especially during costume changes, but trust me, Mike, none of them looked like you."

She tore her gaze away from his awe-inspiring penis and smiled at her husband. "Mind if I try something else."

His eyes slammed shut. She saw the muscles tighten in his hips and thighs. "What?"

"Just this." She leaned forward, sliding her tongue around the smooth, tasty ridge. "That's rather a nice sensation." She flicked her tongue over the tip.

"Stop!"

Mike yanked her up from the floor, swept her up in his arms, and carried her toward the bed. Thank God, he was going to make love to her. The time had finally come to give up her long-lived virginity, and a burning tingle rippled out of her stomach and excited every sensitive pulse point in her body.

But Mike didn't lay her down on the satiny sheets. Oh, no, he stood her in the center of the king-sized bed and walked away, not stopping until he reached the chair across the room and sat down. Then he stared at her, a slight smile touch-ing his mouth.

"Dance for me."

"Is there anything in particular you want to see?"

"Surprise me."

Closing her eyes, she dredged up an exotic tune, something from an Arabian Nights production she'd once been in, and she began to hum. Stretching her hands leisurely above her head, she pressed her palms together, and slowly, erotically swiveled her hips and belly, feeling suddenly like a cobra rising from its basket to the mesmerizing tune of a pipe.

This dance was for Mike. They'd all be for Mike. Her body was on fire. Her breasts ached for his touch. And she realized, as Mike's blazing green eyes focused on her moves, that her movements had a new kind of passion—she wasn't entertaining crowds any longer, she was pleasing the man she loved.

Mike was hot. He could barely sit still in the chair and watch as Charity's belly and hips undulated, tempted, and tormented, as her bewitching hazel eyes gazed at him. All of him. Every rocksolid expanding inch.

The song she hummed was just as seductive as her movements, and it was easy to think he'd been transported to the far-off place where her perfume came from, to one of those sheik-riding-across-the-desert-sands-with-a-woman-in-his-arms movies that Cros liked to watch. Only he was the sheik this time and there was no sand, no horse, only one exotic woman and a hypnotic tune. This movie wasn't in black and white, either, it was in living color. And it breathed. Deeply.

She stepped off the bed as if she were parading down a grand staircase, graceful, serene, her belly and hips still rotating gently, her hands still weaving high above her head, drawing her breasts up high, tight, her pale pink nipples thrust forward, pebbled, hard.

She moved closer, closer. Her fingers reached out to him and she lifted his hands from the arms of the chair. He had no idea what she planned. Heaven forbid that she should touch him again, lick him again. He wouldn't survive another erotic onslaught.

She nudged his knees apart, and smiled slyly as she looked down at the hard, stiff rod that was actively applauding all her moves. Her humming pulsed through the room, reverberated against his body, charmed him. And when she had him more fully under her exotic spell, she stepped between his legs and positioned his hands on her hips, holding them there as she swirled her belly mere inches from his face.

"You're driving me wild," Mike told her when he was able to drag enough air into his lungs to speak. "When do I get to drive you wild?"

"You already have. I don't want to be still when I'm near you. I want to move in ways I've never moved before, to do things I've never done before. Exciting you makes me wild."

He sucked in a deep breath as her belly and hips worked their hypnotic magic on him, swirling around and around, mere inches from his mouth.

He'd barely exhaled when she slowly lifted her left leg and wrapped it around his shoulders. Breathing became an impossibility as his gaze slid over the lightly tanned flesh of her incredibly long leg, studying each muscle, each curve, her inner thigh—her skimpy white panties.

"Make love to me." Her fingers whispered over his lips. "Show me that reality is better than a dream, that waiting for you was the best thing I've ever done."

Making love to Charity would be an answered prayer. She was his wife, the woman who'd make his days and nights whole again. The woman who could drive away his guilt.

Tilting his head, he kissed the inside of her knee and slowly, meticulously, caressed her silky stocking, slid his palm toward her heat. His fingers inched upward to warm, bare skin, and further still, until he reached barely-there silk, damp silk.

He watched her eyelids drop and her lashes fall against her cheek, watched a smile tilt her mouth as his thumb swirled over the patch of fabric between her thighs, gently at first, adding pressure gradually, until a sigh escaped her lips. "Mmmm, don't stop."

Stopping was the last thing he'd ever do, how could he when she lightly thrust her hips toward him, urging him on, as if he needed to be coaxed. He pressed a kiss to the soft warm skin at the edge of her panties, inhaling her scent, as he slid a finger under the silk—and found more silk, found velvet. So soft. So tender. So unbelievably breathtaking.

His finger swirled over slippery skin, then slid deep, deep inside her. She was tight and hot and her body shuddered. Her hips ceased to whirl, to thrust, and a purr sounded deep in her throat.

"Don't stop, baby," he growled. "Dance for me. Dance only for me."

She became a belly dancer, her stomach gently surging, rolling, hypnotizing. "I love the feel of you," he said, nipping the skin of her thigh, sliding a second finger inside her heat. "So hot. So wet. So ready."

Tugging the narrow strip of silk away from her soft, sweet folds, he touched her with the tip of his tongue, his gaze darting to her face to see her mouth part slightly, to see her own tongue moisten her lips. He slid his tongue over her, lost in the taste, in the downy feel of her.

Her belly rolled harder, and he slipped his hands under her bottom and imprisoned her heat against his mouth. He nibbled and sucked on her wet and blazing flesh, inhaling her tantalizing and exotic scent.

"Please, Mike, please," she begged, "make love to me."

At last, he gave in to her pleas, swept her into powerful arms and carried her to the bed. He ripped back the covers, flicked the Belgian chocolates off the pillow, and laid her down in the center of the mattress.

With big fluffy pillows propping her head, Charity watched him draw her panties inch by inch down her legs, watched his penis thrust forward, hard, magnificent, eager. He left on her garter belt, her stockings and her spiked heels, nudged her legs apart, then lay between them.

As he lowered his muscular body over her, she felt rock solid heat press against her belly and longed to feel it entering her for the first time, stretching her, filling her, loving her.

He braced his arms on the pillow at either side of her head and looked down at her, his green eyes as sizzling as his body. Sweeping a lock of hair from her forehead, he kissed her brow, and his own wayward lock of hair tumbled forward and teased her skin, just as his tongue teased her lips. "Had enough?" he whispered.

"Why? Are you tired?"

He shook his head. "I rarely get tired, and even when I do, if I want something desperately enough, I go after it until . . . until it belongs to me."

"I belong to you, Mike."

"Then wrap your legs around my waist, and dance for me some more." She did exactly what he said, crossing her ankles behind him, for once wanting to be controlled, for once, wanting to be touched.

"Move your belly, Charity. Move for me."

She throbbed inside, needing desperately to know the feel of him within her. She swiveled her hips, felt his hand slide between them, felt the probing heat of him strain against her.

"I don't want to hurt you."

She'd never seen such concern in a man's eyes, such fear and longing, and she smiled. "I'm tough, Mike."

"Not tough, Charity. Soft. Loving."

He captured her mouth in his, and she almost lost her senses to the power of his kiss. Then she felt him press into her, so hot, so big.

He wanted to rush, to thrust hard and fast into her depths, to satisfy the driving, fierce need of his body, but he held back. He would be her first lover, her only lover, her last lover. Their first time together would be a memory he'd cherish forever, and he needed it to be a long, wonderful memory—for both of them.

Charity was velvety soft. Wet and tight, and Mike sucked a deep breath through his teeth as he pushed into her, half an inch, an inch, afraid to hurt her, afraid he was too big and she was too small and that they'd never fit together.

Warm hands clasped his face. "Mike?"

His eyes popped open. "What?"

"I'm not a delicate piece of China. I promise I won't faint if you just take a deep breath and push. The only way I'm going to keel over dead is if you don't do it *now!*"

He grinned. "Always ready to oblige a lady."

He might not be a trained dancer, but he knew how to move his hips, and he thrust into the very core of her body.

A shudder ripped through her and he felt her tense. The muscles deep inside her tightened around him. He knew she wasn't doing that on purpose, knew he'd hurt her, so he held still, watching the strain on her face while—okay, he'd admit it—while he enjoyed her contractions, her throbbing, her sweet, tight heat.

At last, a slow smile touched her mouth. She wiggled beneath him, and her magical hips began to swirl, around and around, torturing him, driving him to the brink.

Hazel eyes looked up at him. "Could you withdraw—just a little," she quickly added. "Then, ummm, I'd really like you to do that lovely thrust again."

"You mean this?"

He slid out an inch or two or three. He moved back in—a little farther, a little farther, and then he repeated the process.

"That's it. A little faster, maybe." He complied readily, which brought a wider smile to her face.

Hungry hazel eyes stared up at him. "I could dance a little more, if you'd like."

"Dance, Charity. Never stop dancing."

Her sleek hips moved against him, bumping, grinding, and even though he was a better cowboy than he was a dancer, he learned her routine and taught her a few of his own, moving within her, loving her.

Each one of her moans gave him a new lease on life, each plea not to stop drove him on and on until he rolled onto his back, carrying her with him.

"Remember the way you rode Satan?" he asked on a ragged breath. "Do the same to me."

Her cloak of hair swept over him. She straddled his hips, splayed her fingers over her pelvis, and with a look of pure pleasure on her flushed face, she took the hard, hot length of him inside her.

And she danced, and rode him hard, and suddenly he knew why Satan had let her stay on him for so long. She was pure, unadulterated sin. Sexy. Bewitching. A temptress.

Thank God he'd found her.

In one fell swoop he pulled her beneath him

again and thrust deeply, sweeping his arms around her, capturing her mouth and letting her cry and moan against his lips. She writhed beneath him, and then he felt her intense throbbing as her fingers dug into his back and didn't let go.

But he did—he let go of the control that had always been a part of him, and exploded inside her.

It was the most powerful sensation he'd ever known, until Charity wrapped her arms around his neck and with tears in her eyes whispered, "I love you."

A million climaxes couldn't rival those three little words.

And a million climaxes would never be enough.

Never.

*Chapter 21*

THE NIGHTMARE CAME BACK, RIPPING Mike from sleep, from the peace he'd found in Charity's arms, a peace he thought would be his forever.

His wife's arm was draped over his waist, her body snuggled so close a casual observer might have thought there was only one person in the king-sized bed—a bed he needed to escape. He eased Charity's hand from his stomach and she stirred, her eyes opening sleepily. He kissed her palm and she smiled for half a moment before drifting back into pleasant dreams, the kind he wished he could have.

It wasn't quite five in the morning when he climbed from the bed and went to the window. Trying to go back to sleep was useless. Waking up this way, in a cold sweat with visions of Jessie's hospital room, of beeping machines, and snaking tubes, of needles in Jessie's thin, lifeless arms, and eyelids that fluttered but never opened, haunted him. They'd become a routine, as much a part of his life as preaching on Sunday and riding the prairie in rain, sleet, snow, or shine.

He pressed a fist against the wall and stared past the bright lights of Vegas, wishing he could see the heavens, wishing the horror and guilt of Jessie's death would leave him. But he might as well have been staring through the hospital-room window again, because all he could see was the woman he'd once loved.

The doctors had told him there was no hope, that she'd been without air for so long that oxygen had ceased to get to her brain. "It's highly doubtful that she'll ever function again," they'd told him. It was the words *highly doubtful* that haunted him still.

He'd been alone in making the decision. Jessie had no family but him, no one but him to stand beside the bed and watch her, only existing because she was hooked to machines. His pretty, vibrant wife could lay comatose for a very long time, or so the doctors told him. There was a slim chance she could live without the machines, too. Either way, a compassionate doctor had said, her quality of life would be negligible.

He remembered holding Jessie's hand, remembered asking her what she wanted, but she couldn't tell him. Her eyelids would flicker, her fingers would twitch, but that was all. She couldn't answer him. Couldn't kiss him. Couldn't comfort him.

He would have asked God to help him make the decision, but he'd already felt that God had abandoned them. It was the only time he could remember his faith faltering. It was the one time when he'd needed it the most.

In the end he made the decision himself. He didn't turn to God, to Jack, to his parents. He just stood at Jessie's bedside, took her soft, cold hand in his, and asked the doctors to shut off the equipment.

And then he begged Jessie to live.

But she didn't hear him, and since he'd turned his back on God—God hadn't heard him either.

A few minutes later, Jessie was gone.

His penance for losing his faith, for playing God, was the nightmares.

He thought he'd been forgiven when Charity came into his life, when Charity fell in love with him. Charity was the woman he needed, the woman he wanted desperately and loved with all his heart; but she wasn't the answer to his prayers.

A warm hand caressed his back and two loving arms stretched around his waist. He felt Charity's lips on his back, her cheek resting against his shoulder blade, felt her take away some of what haunted him.

"Something wrong?" she asked softly.

He shook his head. "Just having trouble sleeping. It's nothing new."

"Too much on your mind?"

He nodded.

"If I knew what it was, maybe I could help."

He couldn't tell her about Jessie's death. Couldn't tell her or anyone else what he'd done—that he'd killed his wife. This was a cross he had to bear on his own. "It's nothing."

He heard her sigh, long, hard, and sad. He knew what she was feeling, that she was his wife now, that he should share his burdens with her, but she didn't argue, didn't try to coax a response from him. Instead she squeezed in front of him and nestled her bare behind against his pelvis. He wrapped his arms around her and they stood together quietly, just staring out the window.

"Are you going to miss all of this?" he asked, a new fear coming to light in the wee hours of morning.

"I might, if you have trouble keeping my mind, my time, and my body occupied." Turning in his arms, she smoothed her hands over his chest, then smiled up at him. "But I find that highly unlikely."

She had an uncanny way of taking his mind off his troubles. He knew they wouldn't leave indefinitely, but he didn't want to think about them now. Instead he kissed her softly, a grin touching his mouth as he whispered, "Mind if I occupy your body right now?"

"I'm all yours, Mr. Flynn. All yours."

Chapter 22

CHARITY STRAIGHTENED THE COVERS ON the big four-poster, smoothing out wrinkles, trying to get a handle on neatness. She fluffed her pillow, then gathered Mike's into her arms and inhaled the now familiar scents of Irish Spring and Old Spice.

Two weeks they'd been married. Two weeks learning the ropes at the ranch, two weeks of meeting parishioners and trying to become a good minister's wife, something that had seemed daunting at first, but was quickly becoming one of the many joys in her life. Mike was respected and loved, and the first time she heard him preach, she was captivated by his gentleness, his humor, the way no one fidgeted as he spoke, but sat quietly and soaked in his words.

His laid-back style as a minister was completely the opposite when it came to running Jack's ranch and his own. He was respected, trusted, and for the most part, no-nonsense. Woody, one of the ranch hands, had even commented—offhandedly—that he hoped she could soften up the boss, because he'd been a hell of a taskmaster in the last few years.

She'd told Woody she'd work on it. Of course, the first thing she needed to work on was making Mike love her as much as he'd loved Jessie. Maybe then he'd be able to stay in their bed all night long. As it stood right now, he'd make love to her, hold her, then slip from under the covers when he thought she'd fallen asleep and go downstairs, where he prowled the house and caught a few moment's sleep on the couch.

More often than not he was gone when she woke, off riding the range somewhere, but he always came home for lunch—and most of the time he had an appetite for something more. She'd never deny him. Never.

She loved him and for now, she'd take anything and everything he could give her. Someday, maybe, she'd no longer have to share him with another woman.

Letting her torment out on a sigh, she fluffed Mike's pillow up against the headboard. There were far too many good things in her life to dwell on this one not-so-small problem in her marriage.

She did a few little pirouettes out of their bedroom, then skipped down the stairs. Satan was waiting for her in the corral. Another day of singing her heart out. Another day of the mustang standing at the far side of the corral staring at her as if she'd lost her mind.

When she hit the living room, she cast her eyes down on the hardwood floor and the Indian rugs, and made a beeline through a room she desperately wanted to redecorate. Jessie's paintings had a bad habit of glaring at her, taunting her, making her think she didn't belong in this house.

It was the paintings that didn't belong, but she didn't have the heart to tell Mike she wanted to get rid of them. All in good time, she told herself. She couldn't make changes so soon. Someday—hopefully—Mike would realize why she preferred the kitchen to this room. She'd tell him how the pictures haunted her, but deep inside she was afraid he'd tell her the watercolors and oils had to stay, because they kept Jessie close to him, made her seem just as real and alive as she'd been when she painted them.

Dragging her worries back to a dark place where she wouldn't think about them again today, she pushed through the door and stood outside in the cool spring air—where she could breathe again. Standing on the front porch, she looked at the meandering stream with its trickle of winter run-off. The aspens were starting to green out, and the sun would soon be turning the morning's pink sky a bright peacock blue, with only a hit-or-miss puffy white cloud floating by.

Mike had built this place himself. He'd crafted much of the furniture over the years, too. Every day she learned something new about him. Every day she loved him more.

Striking out across the yard, she watched Satan pacing the corral, his fur sleeker now that winter had faded and warmer weather was just around the corner. She grabbed the straight-back chair that had been her constant companion for nearly two weeks, opened the tall paddock gate, and secured it once she was safely inside.

Satan glared at her, then showed her who was boss by rearing up on his hind legs and batting his front hooves against the sky.

"Good morning to you, too." Charity grinned, no longer phased by Satan's antics. She set the chair down in the center of the corral, plopped her jeans-covered butt on the seat, and glared right back.

"Where should we start today, Satan? We've already covered most every Ella Fitzgerald standard. How about we give Broadway a try?"

Satan snorted and circled the perimeter of the corral, wary as ever.

"How about 'Oklahoma, where the wind comes sweeping down the plains'?"

Another snort.

"*Carousel? South Pacific?*"

Satan lowered his head and decided to munch on fresh hay. "All right, we'll start with 'Bali Hai.'"

Charity crossed her legs and launched into song. A couple of birds fluttered out of the barn, somewhere else a horse whinnied, but Satan ignored her, just as he'd done for nearly two weeks. Patience was the key, she reminded herself. A strong will, determination, and patience. If Mike wanted this horse gentled, then by God she'd gentle him—in her own way.

One hour stretched into two, then to three. She'd sung every song from *South Pacific*, tried a little bit of Doris Day's "Que Sera, Sera," but still Satan ignored her.

She refused to be daunted. After all, there was always tomorrow.

"How about something from *Beauty and the Beast*?" she asked the stubborn mustang, but got no response. "How about *The Little Mermaid*?" Satan merely turned his back on her and looked out across the prairie—the place she knew he longed to be. "That's okay, boy," she said softly. "I wouldn't want to be locked up, either. But I'm doing this for Mike."

Snort.

"All right, so you don't understand. I'd do anything for him. Anything."

Behind her she heard a dog bark. Satan's head jerked up in fright, his head whipping around, his eyes wide.

Charity spun toward the sound of crunching gravel and watched Rufus running circles around Crosby as he hobbled toward the corral.

"You think that gall-darned horse understands you?" He put his gnarled hands on a corral rail and peeked inside.

"I don't know. I'd like to think so." Charity climbed the fencing, swung her legs over the top rail, and dropped down to the ground. She pulled an apple from her jacket pocket.

"Want some?"

"Teeth ain't good enough to eat those damned things."

Charity took a healthy bite of the red delicious. "I've got some cake in the house."

"Ain't hungry."

"You're awfully chipper today."

Crosby shrugged. "I got my good days; got my bad."

Charity could relate to that. She leaned against the corral next to Crosby. "You didn't walk here all the way from your place, did you?"

"Weather's good. Knees aren't so stiff today. Figured I'd take my mornin' constitutional and come out this way for a change."

"It's almost afternoon," Charity teased.

"You get old like me and it'll take you all mornin' to walk a few miles. Besides, the gall-darned doctor told me I wasn't walkin' enough. Figure doin' this'll save me a lecture the next time I get hauled to that old fart's office."

"If you ever want company," Charity said, feeling uncomfortable with Crosby striking out across the prairie on his own, "I could meet you at your place in the morning and we could walk together."

"You got better things to do than fuss with me. Besides, I usually crawl out of bed long before dawn. Got the feelin' that husband of yours would rather have you in bed with him that time of mornin' than out roaming the prairie with me."

If only that were true, Charity thought.

"Mike's going to be home soon. I'm fixing

roast beef sandwiches for lunch. Would you like to join us?"

"Nope. Better start headin' back if I expect to get home before dark. Sure is hell gettin' old and slow."

Charity wrapped an arm around his shoulder and walked with him a ways, talking a bit about the old days, how things had changed over the years. At last they parted company, and she watched cautiously as he hobbled along a well-worn path with Rufus at his side.

A herd of pronghorn antelope had come close to the ranch to feed, and their heads popped to attention when they heard Crosby's plodding boot steps. A moment later they loped off, running away from Crosby and the barking dog. She watched their graceful departure, their swift movements as they ran up a slow rise, then quickly angled off and ran in another direction.

Something had startled them. A coyote maybe. And then she saw Mike and Buck come over the rise, heading for home. Her husband sat tall in the saddle, his black Stetson pulled low on his brow. The weather had warmed enough that he wore only a chambray shirt, and she couldn't help but think about the hard, bronzed skin beneath.

His beard was heavy, darker than normal for this time of day. That rough stubble would feel awfully nice, awfully naughty, she thought, brushing lightly over her nipples. Suddenly her breasts ached and a needy throb settled deep within her.

She sprinted toward him, breaking into an all-out run when he neared the house, swung down from Buck's saddle, and loosened the cinch. When he turned toward her, he was smiling, and she leaped into his arms, knowing he'd catch her.

Sweeping his hat from his head, he held it against her back, and let her have her way with his mouth.

"Miss me?" he asked, when she allowed him to come up for air.

"Mmmm," she whispered, kissing him softly, loving the feel of her legs straddling his waist, his hand pressing against her bottom to keep her against him, the warmth of his mouth. "I never get enough of you."

"Want more?"

Looking into his eyes, she saw a devilish glint. "Before lunch or after?" she asked, hoping it would be before.

"It's been a rough morning." He gently ran his bristled cheek over her face. "Thought I'd call it quits for the day, maybe take a long, relaxing bath. Maybe even a nap." He kissed her nose, her eyes. "You look plum tuckered out, too. You been thinking at all about a bath? A nap?"

"That's all I've thought about."

His slow easy smile made her melt against him, and she kept her arms clasped tightly about him as he carried her into the house, up the stairs, and into their bedroom.

It wasn't but a moment later that a heap of clothes lay in the middle of the floor, the claw-foot was filling with steamy water, and Mike was holding her close, kissing her, giving her a standing ovation even though she'd done nothing more than turn on the faucet and add a little something special to the water.

When the tub was three-quarters full and scented bubbles began to pop over the top, Mike lowered himself into the water and wiggled a finger at Charity to join him.

She quickly twisted her braid on top of her head and fastened it with pins, grabbed a can of shaving cream, a razor and towel, then climbed into the bath with her husband, settling down on his ready and waiting hips.

"You aren't thinking about giving me a shave, are you?" He had a slight, fear-filled frown on his face.

"Was there something else you wanted to do?"

"Quite a few things." He scratched his cheek, but his eyes darted to her breasts bobbing on top the water right along with the bubbles. "Tell you what, you give me a shave, and"—he pinched her nipples lightly and rolled them between his thumbs and forefingers—"and I'll play till you're done."

Throbbing set in, deep, delightful throbbing. She suddenly wanted to forget about the shave and get down to business, but running a razor over Mike's face had been her idea, and he was perfectly content with his bathtub toys, so she sprayed a dollop of shaving cream in her hand and swirled it slowly over his neck and face.

Suddenly Mike's hands were under her arms,

lifting her slightly. "I've got an idea, something that might make your job a little more comfortable."

She knew exactly what he meant, especially when one of his hands dove back under water and he let her down slowly, down, down, down, right onto something very hard, something very, very nice. A little purr sounded in her throat when she took him inside her, and she watched Mike lean against the back of the tub, close his eyes, and groan out a sigh of deep satisfaction.

"There," he said through nearly clenched teeth, "isn't that much more comfortable?"

"Much." She wiggled a bit to find the perfect fit. She moaned a little, Mike groaned a lot.

"All right, baby," he said, with a sigh, "I'm ready for whatever you want to do to me."

Lifting the razor to the base of his neck, she lightly touched his skin, and pulled the razor upward, sweeping away foam and black stubble, leaving behind pinkish-bronze skin, all smooth and . . . she leaned forward and kissed the spot she'd just shaved.

Mike's eyes popped open. "Might be a good idea for you not to move your lower body too much while you're shaving me. I kind of like living, and that razor's gonna do a hell of a number on my throat if I start bucking."

She smiled, and watched his eyelids close again, loving the way his long black lashes rested against his skin. Slowly, she stroked away another path of stubble, then another and another. She worked carefully at the skin under his nose, then started in on his cheeks, completely caught up in her work, until she felt something—a finger, no doubt—playing with a certain little hot button that had been resting quite contentedly in the tub, knowing it would soon get an exhilarating workout.

"That's dangerous, Mike," she said, when his eyes opened a fraction of an inch to peek at her reaction.

His finger swirled again, for just a second. She jerked, and the dimple deepened in the cheek she'd just shaved. "You almost done? I'm a patient man, but there's a point where the patience runs out."

"Are you trying to spoil my fun?"

"I want to have more fun, I just don't want that razor in your hands while we're playing."

"Oh, all right!" She giggled, and as quickly—but cautiously—as possible, finished up the shave, wiping the last of the whiskers on the hand towel, then smoothing away the last of the shaving cream.

Mike's eyes drifted open again, and one black brow rose. "Done?"

"Done."

He bucked—hard, swift, completely out of the blue—and Charity thought for sure she'd fly right out of the tub, but Mike's hands had already grasped her waist to keep her from going anywhere—and then he bucked again, giving her the ride of her life.

The next thrill came when his fingers went to work on her little hot button again, when she leaned forward and guided one of her nipples to his mouth, and he nipped it lightly with his teeth, then suckled.

It was maddening this joy she felt, having wave after wave of excitement pulse through her, driving her to want more—always more.

"Dance for me," Mike begged, and while her cowboy bucked, she swirled, around and around, then gave him a few sensual and terribly naughty bumps and grinds.

And then he held her still, thrusting higher and higher until every muscle inside her clenched, and she shouted out her joy. Mike grasped her tightly within his powerful arms and she felt him shudder inside her, felt him still, at last relaxing his soft, smooth cheek against her breast.

"I love you," she whispered, kissing the top of his head as she pressed him closer to her. She felt his fingers tighten, almost digging into her skin. He didn't say anything, only sighed, and her fears from early morning returned. Had he just thought of Jessie again? Had he just remembered all the times Jessie had said "I love you?" Remembered the way they'd made love?

At last he stirred, leaned back and cradled her face in his hands. He was frowning, looking as if he needed to tell her something but didn't know how. Then a slow, easy smile touched his lips. "What do you say we skip the nap?"

"Why?" she asked, worry overcoming her, fear that he'd gotten all he needed from her and suddenly needed to get away. "Do you need to go back to work?"

He shook his head and chuckled. "I don't plan to work any more today, but I don't want to sleep, either. I was thinking we could grab some lunch, bring it back up here and eat in bed. You know, you feed me, I feed you—and see what happens next."

"Maybe you could love me?" she asked teasingly, although in her heart she was dead serious.

"Yeah," he said, kissing her softly, "maybe I can love you."

Charity was lying on her side, her hands tucked beneath her pillow, watching Mike attempt to sleep. But he was restless, tossing and turning for the past few hours. Finally he jerked up and plowed his fingers through his hair.

He looked down at her, and even in the dark she couldn't miss the anguish on his face. "Sorry. I didn't mean to wake you."

"I wasn't asleep."

"You should be. I tried my hardest to wear you out."

Sitting up, she slipped her arms around his neck, feeling the chill of his skin, the sweat on his chest and back.

"Making love doesn't wear me out. Watching you suffer does."

"I'm not suffering. I told you before, I just don't sleep all that well."

"You rarely sleep at all. Maybe you should see the doctor. Get some sleeping pills. Something."

He laughed. "I'm not sick."

"Then what's wrong? Please, Mike"—a tear

rolled down her cheek; she brushed it away with the back off her hand—"tell me what's wrong."

"Nothing." He threw off the covers, grabbed his jeans and shirt from the floor and pulled them on.

"How can I help you if you won't talk to me?"

"There's nothing to talk about." He leaned over the bed and kissed her forehead. "Go back to sleep."

And then he left their bed and their room—again.

Charity lay on the big, empty mattress, clutching Mike's pillow against her aching heart. She tried to sleep, but instead she watched the clock, watched the minutes tick by, the hours.

At four-thirty she gave up. Mike had pushed her away and she was afraid it would happen again and again, until a wall built between them—and he'd cease to love her at all.

Slipping from bed, she tugged on jeans, heavy socks, and one of Mike's big flannel shirts, and went down the stairs.

Mike had started a fire in the living room and was sitting on the couch staring into the flames. She curled up beside him and tried to ignore the paintings that haunted her.

"You know what I wish?" she asked, weaving her fingers through his.

He squeezed them tightly. "What?"

"I wish that just once I could wake up in the morning and find you lying beside me."

"I could stay in bed if you want," he said, still staring at the flames, as if he were afraid to look at her, "but I'd toss and turn and keep you awake half the night."

"That's better than being lonely."

He frowned when he looked at her. "Missing Vegas already?"

She shook her head, and when he stared at the fire, at the painting of Satan that hung over the mantel, she sighed, knowing any conversation she tried to bring up about his troubles would go nowhere.

Instead she drew his hand to her lips and kissed the backs of his knuckles. She didn't want to fight. She just wanted him to love her as much as she loved him. She traced the long, jagged scar on the back of his knuckles with the tip of her tongue. "What happened here? An accident while you were stringing fence?"

He shook his head. "I tried putting my fist through a tree the night Jessie died." Her stomach clenched as he laughed cynically. "The tree didn't budge, but I broke four knuckles. Almost severed the nerves and tendons."

"You loved her an awful lot, didn't you?"

"She was my wife."

"Did you tell her all your troubles? Did you tell her why you couldn't sleep?"

His sigh was heavy. Distressed. "I didn't have problems sleeping back then."

"Is the reason you can't sleep because you're thinking about Jessie?"

He stole a quick, questioning glance at her, then looked back at the fire. "I told you, Charity, I don't want to talk about it."

She shoved up from the couch and stood between him and the flames. "And I don't want to be the second woman in your life."

"Damn it, Charity. You're the only woman in my life. Haven't I proved that again and again?"

"How can I believe that when you leave me every night?"

He pushed up from the sofa and put his arms around her. "Let's go back to bed and I'll show you there's no one else."

"Sure, let's go to bed." She spun out of his arms and stared at the flaming hearth. "I'll be a nice distraction for an hour or so. We'll wear each other out and you'll fall asleep for two hours if you're lucky, then you'll think of Jessie again. You'll remember how much you loved her. You'll wish she was the one in bed with you again, and you'll get up and leave me—all over again."

"Is that what you think I'm doing?"

She turned toward him slowly, knowing there were tears on her cheeks. "What else am I supposed to think when you won't talk to me?"

"We talk all the time."

"Not about this. Not about the reason why you sit down here and stare at the fire in the middle of the night."

"I don't want to fight. Look, Charity, let's just go to bed."

"You go. I'm not tired any longer."

It was almost deathly quiet in the room, only the sound of the crackling logs and her own heavy heart. Mike's eyes were tired. They narrowed, and she couldn't miss his pain, but he wouldn't talk to her, wouldn't confide in her. Instead, he walked away, and went up the stairs and to their bedroom—alone.

Like a fool she'd pushed him away, the exact same thing he'd done every night of their marriage.

Jessie's paintings glared down at her. Above her she heard Mike's pacing, and all she wanted to do was get away, to get out of a house where she felt she didn't belong.

It was cold outside. The moon was full and brightened the prairie. A herd of pronghorn scattered when they heard the door slam, and she heard the whinny of a horse, a horse trapped in a place where he didn't want to be, a place he felt he didn't belong.

Charity walked toward the corral, tired, lonely, hurt. She stood near the gate and watched Satan for the longest time. They were getting nowhere with her singing, and she just didn't feel there was any reason to go on.

Lifting the latch, she slowly opened the gate and held it wide. "Here's your chance, Satan. You want out of here—go."

Satan pawed at the ground. Hesitant, as if he thought this was some kind of trap. She yelled, "Get out," but still he stared at her.

Behind her she heard a door slam. "Shut the gate, Charity," she heard Mike yell, but she held it wide.

"Get out of here, Satan!" she shouted.

The mustang stared at the man running toward the corral, stared at the open gate, then bolted for freedom.

And then Charity heard the dog barking, heard the hobbling steps of an old man, and panic hit her. She tried to slam the gate but she was too late. Satan was halfway through

"Gall-darn—"

It happened so fast. Rufus ran toward the stallion and Satan reared, letting out a horrid cry. Charity ran for the horse, needing to protect the collie from Satan's sharp, powerful hooves, but Crosby got there first.

The mustang came down hard, then raced across the yard, nothing more than a streak of black and gray in the moonlight.

And Crosby lay on the ground. Motionless.

Charity was at his side in an instant. Blood coursed over his forehead, his temple, and suddenly she felt as if she'd been kicked by Satan, too.

Mike dropped down next to his friend, cautiously slipping his hand under Crosby's head. The old man struggled for breath as Mike put a hand on the old man's grizzled cheek.

"Got the feelin' I ain't gonna make it this time," Crosby said, his words barely a whisper.

"Don't talk like that," Mike said, his voice cracking. "I'll get you to the hospital and you'll be good as new in no time."

Crosby clutched at Mike's shirt. "Don't plug me into those damn machines."

"Quit wasting your energy with all that nonsense."

"Ain't nonsense. I don't want to go on if I can't do it on my own." Crosby's eyes closed, and what seemed like his last breath flowed through him.

Mike jerked around and glared at Charity. "Call Jack. Tell him it's an emergency. Tell him the hospital will have to send a helicopter."

She wanted to tell Mike she was sorry. Wanted to comfort him, but there wasn't time. She ran for the house, made the phone call, then ran to their bedroom and pulled quilts from the hope chest at the end of the bed.

Mike was leaning over Crosby when she returned, keeping him alive by pumping one breath after another into his lungs.

"Let me take over for a few minutes," Charity said, lightly touching Mike's shoulder. "You're exhausted.

Mike shrugged off her touch. "Just get away, Charity. You've done enough already."

Chapter 23

CHARITY RUFFLED RUFUS'S FUR AS THEY
stood near the corral, both of them lonely. Empty.

It had been a week since the accident, a week
since Crosby had been plugged into life-
supporting equipment, and too many long hours
since Mike had looked at her, since he'd held her,
since he'd done anything besides sit next to
Crosby's hospital bed and watch his friend
breathe with the help of a machine.

Satan's hooves had kicked Crosby in the chest
and glanced off his forehead, breaking a few already frail ribs, puncturing a lung, and weaken-
ing his fragile heart. Pneumonia had set in and
he'd sunk into a coma, one the doctors felt he
would never come out of.

Her foolishness had put the dear man in the
hospital and may have cost him his life. And all

she could do was stay at home and pray. It had taken her days to realize that Mike didn't want her at the hospital. She'd tried to comfort him. She'd taken him food and changes of clothing, but all he'd say is, "You can't do anything here, Charity. Why don't you just go home."

Finally she had, because she didn't want to add to his pain.

But home felt as lonely and empty as her heart.

It was nearly five on Saturday night. Fay Atkinson had called to say she'd made a special batch of brownies she'd like to bring over, and when Charity heard the vehicle coming up the muddy road she expected to see Fay's Lincoln. But it was Mike's truck she saw turning into the drive.

He stopped beside the garage and climbed out, looking tired. Beaten.

Rufus raced to the truck, hoping to greet his master. He peered into the empty cab, and even though Mike patted his head, Rufus laid down by the front tire and whimpered. He wanted Crosby, no one else.

Closing the truck's door, Mike looked toward the corral, his gaze resting on Charity for an agonizing moment, and then he headed for the house. Her heart sank, not because Mike continued to ignore her, but because she was afraid her worst fear had come to pass—that Crosby had died.

She raced toward the house and found Mike in the kitchen pouring himself a cup of coffee. "Want some?" he asked without turning around.

"No thanks."

She reached out to touch his shoulder but drew

her hand back, afraid to touch him. The last few times she'd tried he'd pulled away. It was like someone had shoved a poker through her heart. She loved him desperately, but she feared that she'd lost him.

Swallowing her hurt, her worry, she went to the refrigerator and pulled out a roasted turkey breast. "I'll make you a sandwich."

"Thanks."

Was this the way it would be between them from now on? No touching? No holding? An uncomfortable silence?

He stared out the kitchen window as he drank his coffee, standing only inches away from her as she carved the meat.

"How's Crosby?" she asked.

"Alive."

"How are you?"

"Tired." He downed another swallow of coffee, dumped the rest down the drain, and set the mug on the counter.

"I'm going up to bed. See if I can sleep for an hour or two."

"What about the sandwich?"

"I'll eat later. I can't go back to the hospital until I've put a sermon together for tomorrow."

"No one's expecting you to be there. John Atkinson said he'd lead the services."

"I was gone last Sunday. I can't shirk my duties forever."

His anguish—hell, his brooding—was driving her crazy. He could ignore her all he wanted. God knows, she deserved it. But he couldn't go on like this. It wasn't healthy.

She blocked his way when he headed for the stairs. "When did being a minister become a duty?"

"When I ceased to care about much of anything."

"Does that include me?"

At last she saw some kind of spark in his eyes. It was anger. But at least it was life. "That's what you seem to think."

"What am I supposed to think when you won't talk to me?"

"What do you want me to say?"

"That you forgive me for letting Satan go. That you forgive me for what happened to Crosby."

He gripped her shoulders. "There's nothing to forgive. Crosby was in the wrong place at the wrong time, and you wouldn't have let Satan go if you hadn't been mad."

"I was mad because you pushed me away. Damn it, Mike, you've been pushing me away since the night we got married. You've pushed me away every time you've had a nightmare, every time you've gotten out of bed to leave me."

"I don't want to have this discussion again. It's the same one we had a week ago, and the only place it'll lead is toward more anger."

"This discussion and your blasted nightmares are going to put a wall between us until you talk to me."

"I told you before. I can't sleep, that's why I get out of bed."

"That's right, you can't sleep because you dream about Jessie. Then you leave me and go downstairs so you can be surrounded by her pictures."

He shook his head and leaned against the door jamb to stare blankly across the kitchen. "I knew it was a mistake coming home. I should have stayed at the hospital."

"You've been there for a week. You plugged Crosby into those blasted machines he didn't want to be plugged into, and you pushed me away. You told me to go home, that you didn't need me around. So I came here, Mike. I've been here for days, with a lot of time to wonder if you wanted me to come *here*, to this house, or if you meant for me to go back to Vegas."

Mike's jaw tightened and when the phone rang, she watched his fists clench and his head jerk toward the living room. Then he rushed to the phone.

Fear ripped through Charity at the thought that it might be the doctor telling Mike to get back to the hospital now. Or worse, to tell him that Crosby had died.

It seemed like hours rather than seconds before he stepped into the kitchen and stared at her, the phone hanging loosely in his fingers. His eyes were rimmed with red. He was exhausted and as much as she hated to think it, he looked defeated. As if his entire world had just come to an end.

He held the phone out to her. "It's Duane. He

wants to talk to you about the lead in his show."
Mike dragged in a deep breath and exhaled
slowly. "Looks like he decided not to take your
no for an answer." He laughed, shaking his
head. "Looks like you can still have the job if
you want it."

Slowly she walked across the room and took
the phone from her husband, from the man she
loved with all her heart.

"Hello."

"The job's still yours," Duane said. "But I need
you here in two days."

Charity barely heard Duane's words. Instead
she heard her husband's boot heels on the hardwood floor and the front door closing softly behind him. She went to the window and parted the
curtains, ignoring Duane's droning voice, and
watched Mike head for his truck. A moment later,
he drove away.

Mike hadn't pushed her away this time. He'd
merely walked away, without looking back.

## Chapter 24

MIKE SAT NEXT TO CROSBY'S BED LISTEN-
ing to the hum of life-support equipment, staring
at the flecks of black in the linoleum until they began to swim together in one big mess.

His own life was a blur right now, too. A confusion of heartache, anguish, stupidity. He
shouldn't have walked out on Charity, not when
she seemed to need him as desperately as he
needed her. He should have hung up on Duane;
should have told him to go to hell. Instead he'd
handed Charity the phone and walked away because he couldn't bear to hear their discussion.

He wouldn't blame her if she took the job in
Vegas. It was the job of a lifetime, what she'd
spent her life working for. If she took it, how
could he blame her when he'd literally pushed
her away again and again?

He sighed deeply. Maybe he should go after her. Maybe he should go home and tell her again that he loved her, but how could he make her believe him? She had no faith in him now. She thought he was still in love with Jessie.

Again he stared at the heart monitor, at the breathing apparatus, at the tubes and needles that had bruised and discolored Crosby's paper-thin skin.

"I don't want to go on if I can't do it on my own." Crosby's words echoed through Mike's mind and heart, but Mike knew that his friend had been in pain, that he hadn't known what he was saying. Living, even like this, was better than dying. Crosby might not believe it, but Mike knew it for a fact.

He'd been faced with death before, and he hadn't wanted to go through it ever again. How many times could he be tested? Tortured? He couldn't let his friend die, not the way he'd let Jessie die.

He couldn't pull the plug—not again.

Behind him he heard the door open and knew it was one of the doctors, some man who had no emotional ties to Crosby, some man in white who'd again suggest that they take Crosby off of the machines. But he couldn't.

A hand slipped over his shoulder. A warm one, and then he felt a soft cheek press against his, felt gentle lips on a face that had gone unshaven for too many days.

"Mind if I stay?" Charity asked. "Mind if I hold your hand and help you through this?"

He placed his hand over hers and squeezed. He tried to fight back the tears, tears that hadn't come six years ago, tears that he swore he'd never cry, but they came easily and he didn't try to force them back.

"What about Vegas?" he asked, tilting his head up to look at his wife.

"Everything I want is here with you."

She picked up the Bible from his lap and set it on Crosby's bedside, then curled up in his lap, her hands around his neck. "I'm sorry about Satan, sorry about Crosby, sorry I've doubted your love."

Tucking her head into the crook of his neck, he pressed a kiss against her silky hair, holding her close, soaking in the comfort that having her near gave him. For over a week he'd let Crosby be his life, a man who lay still, lifeless in a hospital bed; and for six years he'd let the memory of his wife's death almost ruin his life.

As hard as it was to tell Charity the truth, he knew she was the only one he could confide in.

"The doctors want me to take Crosby off of life-support," he said.

Charity's fingers tensed at the back of his neck. "And what do you want to do?"

He shook his head. "I don't know. I went through almost the same thing with Jessie. The doctors had stabilized her heart, but there was so little brain activity that they weren't sure if she'd be able to breathe on her own. And they doubted that she'd live if we took her off support. If she did, if she came out of her coma, it was doubtful that she'd ever paint again. She might never talk or walk. If she was lucky, she'd be in a wheelchair."

He dragged in a deep breath and held Charity tightly. "The doctors told me the most realistic prognosis was that she'd spend the rest of her life in a bed, needing full-time care. Someone to feed her, to work her muscles so she wouldn't just curl up."

Mike wiped tears from his eyes. "I didn't want that for her. God, I didn't want that for me, either. She wasn't suffering while she was hooked up to life-support, and I could have kept her hooked up forever, could have waited to see if she'd come out of her coma, waited to see if the brain scans had been wrong, but I didn't wait. I told the doctors to pull the plugs."

Charity squeezed his hand, giving him the comfort he needed. She didn't condemn. She just loved him.

He put his hands on her face. "I've never told anyone about that night. I wanted to tell you, but I couldn't. That's what keeps me awake, Charity. That's what I dream about when I do go to sleep. It's not that I'm still in love with Jessie, although God knows I'll always remember her. It isn't grief that keeps me awake, it's guilt. She could have lived for years on life-support, but I made the decision to let her die. It was like putting a gun to her head."

"Don't say that, Mike. It's not true."

"But I thought some miracle would happen. I thought the doctors would shut down the equipment and her eyes would open, and she'd go on breathing. I knew it would take time for her to regain her strength, to be herself again, but I figured she'd pull through. She didn't, Charity. She didn't. It wasn't more than five minutes after they shut everything down that she stopped breathing, and I've lived those five minutes over and over again nearly every day for six years."

"You can't hold yourself responsible, Mike. You're not God."

"But I played God that night."

"No, you didn't. You took Jessie off life-support, because that's what the doctors recommended. And you let *God* make the decision whether she should breath or not. She didn't. You had no control over that."

He shook his head. "I never once asked God for help when Jessie was in the hospital. I cursed him. I turned my back on him for letting her have a heart attack, for letting me be so far away when it happened that I couldn't help her. God was nowhere around when I made the decision to let her die."

"Do you really believe that?"

"I don't know what I believe anymore. You can preach about faith and putting things in God's hands, you can counsel people about death, but it's not that easy to swallow when you're faced with it yourself. I tell myself there's a reason for all of this, but then I look at Crosby and think it's not fair. I wonder why the hell he's in a coma, why he might die."

"Because I let Satan go. Because I didn't think

the horse should be cooped up. Because I didn't think you loved me. *Those* are the reasons why Crosby's here."

"I told you before that it's not your fault. You let Satan go because I penned him in. Because I couldn't tell you or anyone else about Jessie's death—and I pushed you away when you asked. That makes me just as responsible." He cupped his hands over her cheeks. "I've never stopped loving you, Charity. Never, even when you pushed me away, even when I was angry."

Charity laughed softly. "Funny thing about love, isn't it."

"What do you mean?"

"The ones who love us the most never abandon us. It may seem like it at times, but real love's a pretty hard thing to get rid of." She kissed him softly, breathing life back into him. "I'll never leave you, Mike. No matter what. And whatever you decide to do about Crosby, I'll be here to help you through it."

They sat at Crosby's bedside for two more days, and then as a family, they made their decision.

Charity slipped her hand through Mike's when the doctor came into the room. It was quiet. Too quiet, in spite of the life-support equipment that breathed for Crosby.

Mike squeezed her hand and she could see the tightness in his jaw, the fear and sadness tearing him up inside. His Bible rested beneath Crosby's hand, and Mike pressed his own over his friend's frail fingers.

Jack stood on the other side of the bed holding Sam tightly, as he watched Crosby, watched Mike, waiting for his friend to turn to the doctor.

Mike's eyes were tilted downward in prayer, and Charity felt his fingers trembling. She heard him sigh, then open his eyes and turn toward the doctor. "We're ready."

Charity squeezed her husband's hand. Silence filled the room when the equipment shut down, and Crosby lay still, almost lifeless.

Mike's hand slipped around Charity's waist, and even though she wanted to bury her face in her husband's chest and weep, she watched the heart monitor, watched the slow, irregular rhythm of the jagged lines on the screen, then the long, straight line.

A lonely tear fell down her face.

"Oh, God." Charity looked up to see the anguish on Jack's face, the tears in his eyes, and the way Sam took him in her arms.

Mike prayed again. She wanted desperately to take him into her arms, to hold him close and tell him everything was all right, but she merely stood by him, adding her own prayer.

And then she heard *blip . . . blip . . . blip* as the heart monitor kicked into gear and the level line turned jagged again.

She held her breath watching, hoping it wouldn't flat-line again. One minute. Two. Three.

Mike reached out and touched Crosby's grizzled cheeks and his heartbeat grew stronger.

Charity's gaze flew toward the doctor. "Is he going to be okay?"

"All we can do is wait. He's old and this last bout of pneumonia wasn't good, but he's a fighter." He smiled slightly then put his stethoscope to Crosby's chest.

"I've got to get out of here for a few minutes," Jack said, and Charity couldn't miss the catch in his throat as he pulled Sam toward the door. "We'll bring some coffee back after awhile."

Mike and Charity stepped back, trying to stay out of the way while the doctor examined Crosby.

"Are you all right?" she asked, weaving her arms around Mike's neck.

He took a deep breath and smiled. "God, I don't want to go through this again."

"If you have to do it again, you will. But I'll be beside you, okay?"

He gathered her against him and kissed her softly. "I'm going to hold you to that."

Charity pushed him toward a chair in the corner of the room. He'd gone too long without sleep, too long worrying. He looked exhausted. Soon she'd take him home, take him to bed, and hold him in her arms.

He gripped her fingers as the doctor stood over Cros, and when Mike's Bible slipped from under his old friend's hand and toppled to the floor, Charity scooted in quickly to pick it up. She reached for the Polaroid, that had slipped from between the pages, Mike's reminder of Jessie. It would be one of the few images he'd keep, now that he'd asked his parishioners to come to the house and take their pick of her paintings—all but the one of Satan.

Charity flipped the snapshot over and started to slide it back into Mike's Bible. But it wasn't Jessie's photo she retrieved from the floor, it was a wedding picture of her and Mike, one snapped when they'd kissed after becoming man and wife.

Suddenly something wild and wonderful tugged at her heart. She shot a quick glance at her husband, but his mind, his concentration was focused completely on the heart monitor, on his friend. Charity tucked the picture back into Mike's Bible, then crossed the room and wove her fingers back into the hand of the man she loved.

When the room cleared and the doctor was gone, Mike pulled Charity into his arms. "Thank you," he whispered against her hair.

"For what?"

"For being here with me. For loving me."

She looked up at him and smiled. "I've spent most of my life chasing a dream. I had no idea that real life, with all its ups and downs, could be so much better than a dream—until you."

He kissed her softly, warmly, and she knew in her heart that the only light she'd ever want to be lit by would be the light in Mike's eyes when he smiled down on her.

## Epilogue

CHARITY STIRRED BENEATH THE THICK
covering of quilts, yawning as she rolled over to
snuggle against her husband's warmth. Stretching her hand toward him, she felt only a cold
emptiness in the space beside her, a place that
hadn't been empty in nearly a year.

She bolted upright, dread rippling through her
when she thought that his nightmare might have
returned, that Mike might be wandering the
house again looking for something, anything to
take his mind from his worries.

And then she saw her beloved husband by the
window, his magnificent body silhouetted
against the pink that streaked the early morning
sky. A smile touched her face as she slipped from
under the blankets and walked toward him. She
pressed soft kisses against his back, the warm

skin of his neck, the hollow below his ear. "Everything all right?"

"More than all right." He drew her naked body in front of his naked body and tucked her tightly in his embrace so she, too, could look out across the land she'd come to love almost as much as she loved her husband. Then, as Mike did so often in the wee hours of morning, his callused thumbs made slow, lazy circles over her taut and easily excited nipples.

She curled her hands over his arms and rested against him, enjoying his touch, the mere fact that they were together. "You didn't have a nightmare, did you?"

She felt him shaking his head. "I heard something outside. Crosby told me he thought he'd seen Satan this morning, and I was hoping the stallion might have decided to pay us a visit."

"It's been a good six months since we've seen him. Do you really think he's still around?"

He shrugged. "I don't know. Sometimes I want to go out and look for him, but you were right a long time ago. He needs to be free."

"Guess you can't tame every wild thing that crosses your path."

"If you think I've tamed you"—he chuckled—"you're wrong. I like you wild." His fingers inched over her belly to the insides of her thighs. "I like you hot, and soft, and—"

"Look," Charity interrupted, in spite of the delightful throbbing going on deep down inside of her. "By the barn."

Mike groaned. "Why don't I look later?"

"Later's no good. You've got to look now."

Mike tugged her hips hard against him, then leaned forward. "What am I supposed to be looking at?"

"By the barn. It's Satan."

Just as Satan had done the first time Charity had seen him, the stallion peeked his head around the barn, wary of his surroundings, yet curious, prideful, and taunting. As if he knew Mike and Charity were watching him, the mustang pranced to the center of the yard, tilted his head, and stared toward the window.

"Go after him," Charity urged, when she felt Mike's fingers tighten against the insides of her thighs.

"He'd be long gone by the time I got dressed and got downstairs. Besides, I promised you I'd leave him alone."

"But—"

Charity's words were stilled not only by Mike's breathtaking exploration of her inner thighs, but by the other horse she saw peeking around the corner of the barn.

Mike's fingers stalled. "Do you see it?"

"It's a colt."

"A yearling maybe." Mike laughed as the fearless young horse followed Satan's lead, strutting to the center of the yard and looking toward the window with defiance in his eyes.

The colt was the spitting image of Satan—with the same dappled gray coat, the same thick, shining black mane and tail that whipped in the cool night breeze.

Charity tilted her head to see the glimmer of a smile on Mike's face, then looked back toward the horses. Satan reared, his powerful forelegs battling the air around him. Charity could almost feel the floor shake beneath her feet when the splendid beast's hooves pounded down on the ground and pawed the earth a few times, as if he were issuing a new challenge to Mike, not so much to come after him, but to come after his son.

"Go after him," Charity said, turning in Mike's arms.

"Later. He's going to be around for a good long time, and you and I can go after him together. Right now, I've got far more interesting pursuits on my mind."

He swept Charity into his arms and carried her back to bed. But he didn't lay her down, didn't climb onto the soft mattress with her. Instead he left her standing in the very center, and his green eyes blazed with unconcealed desire.

"Dance for me."

Charity swirled her hips and did a naughty little bump and grind. Then she smiled at her husband. "I've got a much better idea." She beckoned him toward her with the seductive come-hither wiggle of her little finger, and in less than a heartbeat he pressed her into the tangle of quilts.

"Is this what you had in mind?" he asked, as their bodies melded together and became one.

"Mmmm, that's exactly what I had in mind— you and me dancing together. Always."